Are You There?

Vic Rizzo

Are You There?

A Cosmic Erruption

Affects the Lives of Three Children

Vic Rizzo

Plain View Press, LLC
1101 West 34th Street, Suite 404

www.plainviewpress.net
Austin, TX 78705

ISBN: 978-1-63210-023-8
Library of Congress Control Number: 2016946847

Cover design by Pam Knight
Cover art: Hubble Sees the Force Awakening in a Newborn Star
A Hubble Heritage Release http://hubblesite.org

December 17, 2015: Just about anything is possible in our remarkable universe, and it often competes with the imaginings of science fiction writers and filmmakers. Hubble's latest contribution is a striking photo of what looks like a double-bladed lightsaber straight out of the Star Wars films. In the center of the image, partially obscured by a dark, Jedi-like cloak of dust, a newborn star shoots twin jets out into space as a sort of birth announcement to the universe. Gas from a surrounding disk rains down onto the dust-obscured protostar and engorges it. The material is superheated and shoots outward from the star in opposite directions along an uncluttered escape route — the star's rotation axis. Much more energetic than a science fiction lightsaber, these narrow energetic beams are blasting across space at over 100,000 miles per hour. This celestial lightsaber does not lie in a galaxy far, far away but rather inside our home galaxy, the Milky Way.

We Find Healing In Existing Reality

Plain View Press is a 40-year-old issue-based literary publishing house. Over the years we have become a far-flung community of writers, artists, and activists whose energies bring humanitarian enlightenment and hope to individuals and communities grappling with the major issues of our time. The poems, stories, essays, non-fiction explorations are significant evidence that despite the relentless violence of our time, there is hope and there is art to show the human face of it.

*To my loving wife Linda
and my mentor Albert
without whose support and encouragement
this novel would not exist*

Prologue

"Mommie, where did Grandma go when she died?" a child asks her mother. "Can she see me?"

"Yes, Honey. She's right here with us."

"But where? I don't see her?"

"When you're older, you'll understand. There are many things that we can't see or hear, but they are near us."

❧

The twentieth century ushered in a new wonderment about "space-time" and "multi-dimensional theory"—terms that are now commonplace. Space technology opened our minds to the vastness of our universe and the possibly that ours is not the only universe.

As the atom gave up the secrets of its structure, we realized that much existed around us that we could not see, hear, or touch. We now accept the vastness of creation at the microcosmic level—phenomenon we are only beginning to understand. An understanding of this phenomenon will allow us to harness digital intelligence, to delve into the intricacies of our bodies, and to master the power of our minds.

How did we reach this point in our evolution as a specie? Divine intervention or just random probability? Do the growing list of subatomic particles play a role in shaping who we are? Might cosmic events profoundly change life here on Earth? At what point—or on what level—do the worlds of quantum physics and the mysteries of our being merge?

Consider for a moment the prospect that a hundred million light-years from Planet Earth, the orbits of two galaxies take them dangerously close to each other. Perhaps they are Galaxy NGC 2992 and NGC 2993, buried in the vast Hydra constellation. Gravity draws them together. They are doomed to collide. As they draw near, they engage in a death spiral as they merge. Their merger is not without consequences. Within NGC 2993, a white dwarf star dense beyond comprehension comes dangerously close to a red giant star within NGC 2992. The white dwarf star, with its greater mass, begins to strip matter from its approaching adversary. Bloated by the added stellar material, the dwarf star explodes, creating a hypernova—the most powerful burst of energy within the universe!

Subatomic particles, products of the enormous explosion, race toward Earth—particles destined to alter the nature of humanity. Certain children conceived during the planetary barrage acquire genetic traits previously unknown in the human genome—traits to benefit humankind or possibly traits of evil when subverted by opportunistic men.

In this story, genetics professor Doctor Mitzi Weaver recounts the extraordinary development of three children, from infancy to young adulthood—each conceived on a separate continent during such a cosmic event. When the trio abruptly vanishes under mysterious circumstances while in her care, the Sheriff of Bath County, Virginia summons her to explain the teen's disappearance. As Weaver prepares for the ordeal that lies ahead, she realizes that wary authorities are unlikely to believe her incredible story. Can she prove that she is innocent of any wrongdoing? And yet, where *did* the children go?

Chapter 1

Location: Overseer's Cottage, Carrington Farm, Bath County, Virginia
Time: September 2034

The morning sun rose over the weathered hills east of the Carrington Farm Retreat Center and illuminated the red brick cottage where Mitzi Weaver tried to rest. The events of the previous day tormented her throughout the night and disrupted her efforts to sleep.

A mechanical voice spoke, "Good morning, Doctor Weaver. Today is September 21, 2034. The time is 7:30 AM, Eastern Daylight Saving Time. If you wish to snooze, please tell me."

"Oh, go to hell! I want to sleep!" Mitzi exclaimed in a gruff voice as she buried her head under the down comforter.

The personal communications device emitted a loud chime. "I'm sorry, Doctor Weaver, that is not an appropriate reply. Please restate your preference."

"Snooze. Snooze!" Weaver shouted; a lack of suitable sleep left her irritable. She was in no mood to have a machine tell her what to do. *Why do we have these stupid things? I just want to sleep. Please, let me sleep.*

The communicator responded, "Thank you, Doctor Weaver. I will awaken you in seven minutes. Please enjoy your extra rest."

Before she could close her eyes, the Numo Beverage Bot beeped four times. *My God. Did I program that damn thing last night? What was I thinking?* As the aroma of strong coffee crept into her bedroom, the machine beeped four more times. *Why fight it. I'm not going to sleep anyway. Where's my robe?* Weaver glanced around the room. In an antique rocking chair at the foot of the four-poster bed lay a purple garment. *Dang it. What's it doing over there?* Summoning a burst of will, Weaver slipped out of bed, stepped into her shoes, and scampered toward the robe. Quickly slipping it on, she pressed the fabric against her body. *Heat up. Heat up. Hurry.* After a minute, an LED strip embedded in the garment's cuff blinked several times. *Oh, God bless the Military Industrial Complex. I love ThermaCloth. Instant warmth. Whoever invented this stuff deserves sainthood!* Comfortably warmed, she walked toward the main room of the cottage and the annoying beverage machine.

Pausing in front of the beverage maker, the unit recorded her presence and responded. "Good morning, Doctor Weaver. You requested extra strong coffee brewed from Colombian Arabica beans for this morning. Do you wish cream and sweetener in your coffee?"

"Yes, Numo. Only one cup for now—two units of sugar and two units of cream." *Why can't I do this myself? I'm a human. I have opposable thumbs.*

"Thank you, Doctor Weaver. I must caution you that two units of sugar is a total of eight grams of the product comprising 30.96 calories. Do you wish to change your choice of sweetener?"

Weaver glared at the machine. "No. Two units of sugar. Real sugar!"

"Thank you. I am processing your request." In less than a minute, a preheated china cup filled with a cream-colored mixture appeared in the service bay of the machine. "Enjoy your coffee and have a wonderful day."

Weaver smirked. *"Have a wonderful day." If only you knew Numo. What did that deputy say last night? "Be here at the Sheriff's Office by two o'clock?" That should make my day!*

Taking the cup from the machine, Weaver entered the main room of the cottage and sat down at the oak table that served as dining table and makeshift desk. A spiral bound research proposal in the middle of the table caught her eye. Mitzi turned it to her and read the title aloud, "Carrington Farm Project: An Investigation of the Decision-Making Abilities of Genetically Enhanced Individuals." *That project hasn't gone very well! What do you do when the subjects in your study up and vanish?*

As Mitzi Weaver gulped the rich coffee, a ray of sunlight found its way through a nearby window. Rising to adjust the curtains, she paused and stared into the distance. Two hundred yards from the cottage lay a large pond. *Strange how calm and peaceful the pond looks this morning. Hard to imagine that's where it happened. None of it seems real. Why? Why did the children vanish? Where did they go?*

Part I

THE INTERROGATION BEGINS

Weaver Meets Interrogators Jenkins and Cox

Chapter 2

Location: Warm Springs, County Seat of Bath County, Virginia
Time: September 2034

Lieutenant Phil Jenkins of the Virginia Bureau of Criminal Investigation halted his EcoCruiser at the top of Oakley Summit to view the narrow valley below. Encircled by weathered mountains of the Appalachian range, the valley was a patchwork of farms and forested areas. *Nothing changes in these hills. Things look pretty much like they did twenty years ago when Jonesy and I worked here.*

Driving along US Highway 220 brought back memories for Jenkins. He worked as a highway patrol officer in western Virginia for many years before moving up the ranks. A thought popped into his mind; he said aloud. "Oh, why not? Who's gonna see me anyway?"

Jenkins tapped an icon on the display screen. The police cruiser's computer announced, "Caution, manual operation mode is engaged." A quick check of the radar display indicated no other vehicles nearby. *Clear ahead and behind. 'Bout what I'd expect out here in the middle of nowhere.* An impish grin spread across his face, fed by his mischievous thought. *Let's see what's under the hood of this thing.*

With a firm grip on the steering wheel, he called out, "Pursuit mode. No alarms. Engage now." The audio command system revved the hydrogen-powered engine and the vehicle lurched forward. *Here we go, little lady!* Pushing the police cruiser to its limits, Jenkins drove through a series of double-S curves. Tires squealed as the vehicle strained to hold traction on the narrow road. He chuckled loudly, reveling in his moment of mischief. *That's enough, that's enough. Slow'er down.* "Eco-Drive. Engage now." The cruiser quickly dropped to highway speed. *Yeah, the old man still got it. Must've done that a million times with Jonesy. He was such a good partner. Can't believe that he came back to Bath County, settled down, and got elected Sheriff!*

Driving past bathhouses dating to the days of Thomas Jefferson, a patch of autumn color came into view. In an instant, Jenkins understood why his friend was happy living in this small, rural valley. *Gotta admit, this is God's country, 'specially in the Fall. Look at those maples. Just, plain, beautiful.* "Vents open," Jenkins said. Automatic vents opened and fresh air filled the vehicle, air scented with the odor of livestock and the last cutting of hay before winter set in.

For a moment, Jenkins let his mind wander as he enjoyed the pastoral scenes that flew past him before snapping back to the reason for his visit. *Didn't come here to look at the foliage. Just like Jonesy to ask me to investigate a weird case. What'd his deputy say— "How do three teenagers vanish in the middle of an open field and not leave a trace?" Oh, well. We'll find out, 'specially if Cox can make it. A little FBI help can't hurt. Be nice to work with Cox again.*

Turning off US Highway 220 on to Courthouse Road, Jenkins drove past the Municipal Courts Building into the parking lot of the Bath County Sheriff's Office. The Sheriff's Office, constructed of red brick with white trim, looked more like a two-story planation home than a public building.

Jenkins stepped out of the cruiser and paused to call his Richmond office. "Hello, Beth, it's me. How's my favorite young lady today?"

"Oh, fine." Frustration apparent in her voice, the young woman asked, "Lieutenant, when are you going to get a holographic com set like the rest of the world? They stopped making that dumb thing of yours back in 2025— maybe before that." Drawing a deep breath, she asked, "I guess you know that the video feed on that thing doesn't work? That means, I can't see you. I may as well be talking to a wall." Exhaling loudly, she continued, "I'm wasting my breath. You're not going to get rid of that stupid thing, are you? So, where are you? Did you make it to Warm Springs?"

"Not so fast young lady. First of all, I like my I-Com. It makes phone calls. That's what it's supposed to do. And, yes, I'm in Warm Springs. I hope to wrap this thing up by tomorrow afternoon. You can expect me back in the office on Monday. 'Course if you need anything, give me a holler."

"Will do. By the way, I got you a room in that place where you wanted to stay. Hope you brought a swimsuit. The woman I spoke with went on and on about their indoor springs. What's that place anyway? A spa or something? Ooops, sorry Lieutenant, I got a call coming in from the director's office. Gotta go. See you Monday. Take care now."

Closing his I-Com tablet, Jenkins shoved it into a worn leather satchel—a throwback to his early days as a detective—and walked towards the Sheriff's Office. As he opened the door, he caught the eye of young Deputy Isaac Stewart.

"Lieutenant Jenkins! Welcome. Sure glad you cud come. It's a pleasure ta see ya again. What's it been? Almost a year since you visited us?"

"Probably so, Deputy." Jenkins paused at the counter that separated the reception area from the administrative area of the office. "Mind if I come in?"

"Oh, sure, sure. Come on back." Lifting a section of the counter, Stewart motioned Jenkins through. "I know Sheriff Jones is mighty happy you cud come. He's sorry he can't be here. His mother-in-law is bad off. We don't 'spect him back 'til late next week."

Jenkins nodded. "That's what I gathered from your call last evening."

"Right, right, guess I did tell ya that. Anyway, Sheriff Jones feels this thing with them kids needed lookin' into. Said it cuden wait 'til he got back."

"I'm glad I could come. Sheriff Jones and I go way back." Looking around the office, Jenkins asked, "Has Special Agent Cox arrived yet?"

"No sir, but he called a minute ago. Said he's checkin' into tha Valley Motel. "Spect he'll be here shortly."

"Looks like you've made a few changes around here. These oak desks haven't changed since I worked out of here but that area in the back is new." Walking past the deputy to the rear of the reception area, Jenkins approached a molded glass enclosure. Inside two women sat at matching communication consoles. "Looks like Sheriff Jones upgraded your dispatch center."

"Yes sir, mighty fine lookin' wuden ya say? It's bulletproof, ya know. The Sheriff got one of them NSA grants—paid for the whole thang. There's more in the back, you wanna..."

"In a bit Deputy, but first, I'd like to go over what you have on the disappearance of the three children. I assume you asked the woman involved to come in—the one who was with the children when they disappeared?"

"Yes sir. Contacted her last night after I called ya. Told her to be here by two o'clock. Came in 'bout fifteen minutes ago. She's back in tha interrogation room."

"So, what can you tell me about what happened? You didn't say much last night—like how this woman is involved?"

"Well, she and them three kids—a boy and two girls—were staying out at Carrington Farm. Ya know tha place; it's been thar fur ever. Anyway, they all got thar about two weeks ago. Yesterd'y afternoon, they were out by the pond when them kids just up and disappeared into thin air. Anyway, that's what tha three clergy fellows said happened. They're the ones that called 911—guess that was shortly after five. It's all spelled out in tha report Deputy Lawler and me done." Stewart took a micro-tablet from his desk and handed it to Jenkins.

Taking the device, Jenkins strained to read the information displayed on the seven-inch screen. *Can't read this. Why do they make the print so damn small?* Looking at the deputy in a fatherly way, Jenkins asked, "Would it be too much trouble to get paper copies of your report? Nothing against your nifty gadget, it's just that I'm old school. I like to write notes on the actual report—so does Agent Cox."

"Oh, I'm sorry, Lieutenant. I shud'a known better. Gimme a second, I'll send it to tha printer." Steward started towards his desk. As he sat down, he glanced out of the large window at the front of the office. "Looks like Special Agent Cox made it. He's gettin' out of his car now. There's sumpin' about FBI guys, they jus' look…well, you know. Understand he's from Baltimore, right?"

"Yup," Jenkins confirmed. "He's a specialist in child abductions. Figured it wouldn't hurt to have him work with us."

"Yes sir. Child abduction is bad bid'ness. Ya can't be too cautious. That's what Sheriff Jones said. Now if ya'd 'cuse me, I'll git you them reports."

Jenkins took a seat at one of the oak desks facing the entrance. He liked Cox and looked forward to working with him again. As the agent entered the office, a strong gust of wind jerked the door from his hand. Jenkins laughed loudly. "That wind strong enough for you?"

At thirty-six years of age, Don Cox was tanned, muscular, and well groomed. His tailored suit, with its stylish lapels, did not come from a discount store as did the one Jenkins wore. Cox's speech hinted he was from Texas or Oklahoma, but his manicure and salon-styled hair pointed to an urban lifestyle. There was no doubt in Jenkins' mind that Cox was a young man with a future in law enforcement. "See you managed to get here 'fore suppertime," Jenkins jested.

Leaning on the reception counter, Cox smiled and bobbed his head. "Well, I don't like to miss supper any more than you do."

Cox considered Jenkins a colleague and something of a father figure. He knew the older man often exaggerated his southern accent to lull people into thinking he was "just a good ol' boy" and not a keen investigator. *He hasn't changed. Looks as ornery as ever.*

Standing over six feet tall, Jenkins easily carried two hundred and fifteen pounds with only a modest gut overhanging his belt. Years as a state trooper left him with a weathered face and a noticeable scar on his left cheek. His hair, the little that there was of it, was salt and pepper gray. He refused to have hair implants—so common for men with hair loss—even though covered by the 2027 National Health and Cosmetic Services Act.

Jenkins rose and motioned Cox towards the section of the counter that allowed access to the administrative area. "Come on in and take a seat."

Cox lifted the counter and headed toward Jenkins. "You know, I was hoping that you'd would have this thing wrapped-up by now. It would be nice to spend the evening sampling some local brew."

Jenkins looked at Cox and smirked.

Trying to get a rise out of Jenkins, Cox continued, "Well, old man, you didn't answer. Have you solved this thing or not? I could be drinking beer, you know."

The older man leaned back, wiped his hand across his chin, and shook his head and smiled. "Well, I would've. But I know how disappointed that would've made you. To tell the truth, I haven't even looked at the incident report. Deputy Stewart is getting us a couple of copies now. Meanwhile, our person of interest is sitting in the interrogation room. Care to take a look?"

Cox nodded. "May as well. That's why we're here."

Walking quickly, Stewart returned waving several sheets of paper, "Here's tha report. Got one for each of ya. Now, if you gentlemen will follow me, I'll show ya our new interrogation room."

With copies of the incident report in hand, Jenkins and Cox followed the deputy down a narrow hallway, "In here, gentlemen. This here's the observation room. Check out them monitors." The deputy beamed as if the new equipment was his first-born child.

Inside the small room, Jenkins and Cox were surprised to see three large monitors displaying multiple views of a mid-aged woman sitting motionless at a metal desk.

"Like I told ya, Sheriff Jones got one of them grants, that's how he got this here equipment. You can see every angle of a suspect. Zoom in if ya wanna." Stewart pointed to the console. "Jus' use that thar joy stick."

Jenkins ignored the deputy's suggestion and chose to study the images of the woman on the monitors. As she reached for a bottle of water on the desk, a slight tremor in her hand told him that she was not comfortable with her situation. *Simple but smart looking pants outfit. What you'd expect a woman to wear at a place like Carrington. Slim, almost muscular figure. Those streaks of gray in that auburn hair don't go with that figure. She must work out—probably a runner or a swimmer.* Scanning the incident report for personal data, Jenkins paused at a copy of the woman's driver's license. *Forty-three! Interesting, maybe that gray hair does belong. Not anything else here that's helpful.* "Deputy, from your report, all I know is the lady's full name is Mitzi Kay Weaver. She holds a Doctor of Philosophy degree in microbiology. Currently, she's working at Johns Hopkins Medical Center in Baltimore, where she's in-charge of a genetics lab. Doesn't say anything here about what she was doing at a luxury retreat with three teenagers? And, I don't see where you asked her what happened to the kids?"

"Well, sir, Deputy Lawler and I didn't git to interrogate her. Once the 911 call came in from that rabbi fella, me and Lawler contacted Sheriff Jones. He said to call ya, so that's what I done."

Jenkins looked at the young deputy, whose face was flushed red, "So, this is it? This is all you have?"

Stewart nodded in the affirmative, turned to Cox, and nodded a second time. "That's all we got." Eager to avoid further admonishment, he asked, "Lieutenant, if you don't need me, I'm 'sposed to be on patrol. Thar's only me working this afternoon."

"Yeah, sure, you can go. We'll call if we need you."

"Thank ya, sir. By the way, Lawler is due in shortly to cover the eve'en shift. He'd be able to answer your questions." Nodding his head, Stewart inched out of the observation room.

The senior lawmen smiled, amused by the young deputy's actions, then turned their attention to the woman in the adjoining room.

Jenkins jokingly asked, "Whatcha think Cox? Do we have ourselves a kidnapper in there or just your everyday serial killer?"

The young agent knew Jenkins liked to say something off the cuff to see the response he would get. He just smiled. "Can't tell without talking to her. I'm ready if you are?"

The two men entered the interrogation room. Standing, Jenkins introduced himself, "Good afternoon, ma'am. I'm Lieutenant Phil Jenkins of the Virginia Bureau of Investigation and this is, Special Agent Don Cox. He's with the Federal Bureau of Investigation."

"Good afternoon, I'm Doctor Mitzi Weaver, but I guess you know that?" *FBI? Virginia Bureau of Investigation? My God, someone's taking this thing seriously. Guess it is, but...*

"Yes, ma'am. We have your information here. And I assume you know why you're here?" Jenkins' voice resonated with the softness of a father figure. "Please understand this is just a preliminary investigation. Although we're recording this interview, you are not under arrest."

"Okay." Weaver responded hesitantly. *Arrest? For what? I didn't do anything.*

Cox added, "Like Lieutenant Jenkins said, our purpose is to gather facts surrounding the disappearance of the three children. I'm sure you want that as much as anyone. Am I right?"

The two law enforcement officers sat down at the table facing Weaver as she responded, "Of course." Again, a certain hesitancy was evident in her voice.

Jenkins stared at the woman for a moment, and then nodded slowly. *Somehow, her mannerism and her tone just doesn't ring true.* "Okay then, let's get started. Agent Cox and I have a few questions about the disappearance of these children. First of all, I believe their names are Ethan Lake, Chetana Kapur, and Sara Johansson."

Weaver nodded slowly and took a sip of water. *Well, it's begun. They'll never believe what happened. It's hard for me to believe!*

❦

During the next couple of hours, Jenkins and Cox took turns asking the usual background questions: "Where exactly do you work? What's your position there? How long have you been there? What do you do in a genetics lab? Where are these three children from? How long have you known them? How did you come to meet them?"

For Weaver, there seemed no end to the questions. Each question added to her growing tension and agitation. She was cooperative but not very forthcoming—she recognized that—but answering questions was not the way to tell the story of what happened to Chetana, Ethan and Sara.

A profiling specialist, Cox studied Weaver's facial expressions and body language. *Lot of tension in her expressions. She's getting tired. Perspiration showing. It's not warm in here. Hot flash? No, probably just tension. She's holding something back. But what? Need to back-off a bit. Don't want her to ask for a lawyer. Do a recap. Give her a break from answering questions.* Cox quickly summarized the facts as he saw them before stating, "You see Doctor Weaver; I don't think that you've been straight with us. Now, I know you probably think we're dense, but we're just trying to get a handle on what happened. You've offered us bits and pieces but that's about all. You alluded to some scientific research but you haven't given us any factual information."

Jenkins cleared his throat, puckered his lips and bobbed his head, "Doctor Weaver, I've got to agree with Agent Cox. I get the feeling there's something you're not telling us. Have to admit, it's making me awful suspicious about your involvement in the disappearance of these young folks. You don't want me to feel that way, now do you?"

Mitzi Weaver looked at Jenkins, her face outwardly expressing her frustration. *Look, Mister High and Mighty, I answered the questions you asked. What more do you want? The children vanished. That's it. They're gone!* She turned to face Cox and then back to Jenkins. Sitting in a straight-back chair for almost two hours left her butt numb and her body stiff. Fatigue gripped her. *I need to get out of here!*

Weaver checked the digital clock flashing on Jenkins' I-Com. The large display on the older model communicator was easy to read, even upside down. *It's coming on five. They must be as tired as I am.* She glanced about the room. *God, I can't stand this retched place. Smells like burnt coffee and body odor. And that trash can! It stinks to high heaven. Do they ever empty the damn thing?* She looked at the men and took care to form her words. In a firm but soft tone she addressed them. "Gentlemen, I'm sure that some of what I said is confusing.

In retrospect, perhaps I should have notified the Sheriff's Office last evening when the children vanished, but I was more concerned about notifying their parents. If I did notify the authorities, what was I going to say—what I have been telling you? That hasn't gotten us very far." Weaver paused to let her point soak in. "It's getting late. I'm sure you guys could use a break—I know I could. So, may we stop for now and resume in the morning—say out at Carrington? I have material there that might help you understand what happened. Forgive me. I don't mean to cast aspersions—any place is better than here."

Jenkins glanced at Cox, trying to read his sense of the situation. Cox returned the glance, and then shrugged, as if to say, "The ball's in your court, bubba."

Jenkins mulled over the facts of the case. *Don't have any real evidence at this point. What do I have to hold her on? And on what charge? If she asks for a lawyer, the whole interview is a bust.*

Mitzi waited for a response. Her impatience beginning to show, she shifted in her chair. *Damn it, Jenkins. Say something!*

"Ah, all right, already!" Jenkins capitulated. "Let's sleep on it." Fixing his gaze on Weaver, he stated firmly, "I want to remind you that everything you said here has been recorded. Tomorrow, we'll set up recorders out at Carrington. All we ask is for you to be truthful with us. Try to give it to us straight and simple, so that we can understand it. And, Doctor Weaver, please don't leave Bath County. It would give Special Agent Cox and me the wrong idea about your involvement in this case. Understand?"

Mitzi Weaver's spirit leapt. "Trust me, I understand. Tomorrow will be better. I promise. I'll see you at Carrington—say, around nine o'clock? I'm in the Overseer's Cottage. You can't miss it. It's the first place on your left after you enter the estate."

Jenkins nodded agreement and looked at Cox.

"Suits me, Lieutenant. Guess we'll see you in the morning, Doctor Weaver."

"Thank you, gentlemen. Tomorrow will be better." Standing, she started towards the door.

"Hold on ma'am. Best we walk you out," Jenkins said.

The two men led Weaver to the front door and watched as she hurried across the parking lot to a bright yellow Tesla 300 E sports car.

"Wish I could afford one of those. What do ya think they cost, Cox?"

"Not sure. But, it's a hell of a lot more than we'll make this year."

Weaver reached her car, relieved to be free of her ordeal. Neither the radiance of an autumn sunset nor the cool wind tempered her anxiety over the children's disappearance and what lay ahead. She opened the gull-wing door of the sports car and sat down. Adjusting the power mirrors, she glimpsed her face. *Doctor Mitzi Weaver, internationally recognized authority on genetic mutations— and criminal suspect! What's happening to me? This can't be real. Am I dreaming all of this?* Mitzi gently nudged the vehicle out of the parking lot and onto State Highway 42 that served as the main street of Warm Springs, Virginia. The soft purring of the two-hundred horsepower electric engine reminded her of Ethan, the only boy among the three children. At his insistence, she purchased the Tesla last year. A true boy, he loved automobiles, especially sports cars. Pushing a button on the dash, the moon roof retracted allowing cool wind to rush through the vehicle. *Ethan loved riding around on evenings like this. Why did he leave? Where did he and the girls go?*

Chapter 3

Location: Warm Springs, Bath County, Virginia
Time: September 2034

In Weaver's mind, Warm Springs was a quaint, rural village—a place that she and the children enjoyed. Mom and Pop businesses strung along State Highway 42 formed the business district. Farmers' Feed & Seed anchored one end of the village; less than a mile away, Titus Farm Implements anchored the other end. Most of the buildings dated to the early twentieth century when places like Warm Springs served the needs of rural America. The once stately bank building could not hide its original function, although now reduced to a resale shop. Several of the wood and brick storefronts sported bright colors in the off chance of catching a traveler's eye.

Driving slowly to avoid any chance of exceeding the twenty-five mile per hour speed limit, the day's events dominated Mitzi Weaver's thoughts. *It'll be better tomorrow. I'll tell them everything.* A gnawing pain in her abdomen redirected her mind. *Nothing to eat at the cottage. Better get something before I leave town. Need a pharmacy. Gotta have something for this headache. Ah, Steven's Liquor Store—scotch might be the best medicine for what ails me! Can't stop now. Gotta eat first.*

Two blocks ahead, Weaver saw a hand painted sign that announced "Mable's Family Diner, Best Home-style Cooking Anywhere." *Comfort food. That's what I need.*

Mable's was scarcely larger than a two-car garage. Located in a brick storefront, its old-fashioned café arrangement added to its charm. There were no tables for patrons, only booths along either side of the narrow dining room. Most booths were empty as Weaver entered and sat near the front.

A middle-aged woman wearing a white cook's apron approached with a glass of water and a sheet of yellow paper that served as the menu. "What'll you have, honey? Tha special's chicken fried steak and all tha trimmin's. Uhmm, delicious. 'Course, every thangs good here. I can vouch for that, seeing as how I cook most of it." The woman laughed deeply causing her large breast to bounce in rhythm with her laughter. "Tell ya what I'm gonna do. You look like you need a little liftin' up—I got some fresh baked biscuits back there. A couple of them suckers with homegrown butter will sure 'nuf do the trick. Meanwhile, you study the menu. I'll be right back with them biscuits."

Mitzi smiled—her first since last evening. Scanning the makeshift menu, she ordered chicken and southern dumplings and a side order of green beans cooked with Virginia ham. When it came, she savored every mouthful, including the finest biscuits she ever tasted. *With food this good, I could almost forget Jenkins and Cox. I know they're doing their jobs but.... Oh, hell, what happens, will happen. Right now, I'm going to enjoy these dumplings.*

After supper and stops at McDowell Pharmacy and Steven's Liquors, Weaver drove to the cottage to spend a second night without the children. There would be no laughter and intellectual conversation to brighten the place. Sadness filled her thoughts. *They were so brilliant. I miss them so. Can't imagine life without them around.*

Weaver passed through the massive brick arch bearing the name, Carrington Farm. A short distance down the cobblestone road was the four-bedroom cottage where she and the children stayed for the past two weeks.

Everett Carrington, a railroad magnate in the late nineteenth century, built the cottage for his overseer. Beyond the cottage stood the eleven-bedroom residence designed to accommodate his large family. The brick and limestone mansion now served as a boutique hotel for conference guests. The matching brick-and-limestone stables behind the mansion once housed Carrington's thoroughbred horses; they now served as meeting rooms.

Weaver came to Carrington Farms at the request of Mary Benton, the matriarch of the Benton family and Chairwoman of the Benton Trust, which owned the non-profit conference center.

As a member of the Johns Hopkins University Endowment Board, Mrs. Benton met Weaver on a tour of research facilities at the University. Intrigued by Doctor Weaver's longitudinal study to document the growth of three unique children, Benton offered her the Overseer's Cottage at Carrington Farm to conduct the final phase of the study—an observation of the three children in problem-solving situations.

Entering the cottage, Mitzi slumped into an overstuffed chair in the main sitting room. *Need to rest. Gotta to be sharp tomorrow morning. A hot bath and some of that twelve-year old scotch should do the trick.*

Hot water scented with lilac bath salt relieved most of Mitzi's back pain. A couple of ibuprofen tablets, along with a glass of scotch-on-the-rocks, took care of the rest of her aches and pains. *Good booze and a soft bed. What more could a woman want?* Relaxing a moment, she sheepishly answered her question. *Ooh, a good man with a hot body would be nice! What am I saying? That's how it all happened. If Emily, Kumari and Christina did not become pregnant fifteen years ago, there would never have been any children. None of this would have happened!*

In spite of the stress that lingered, Mitzi's eyes grew heavy. As slumber approached, she struggled with what she should tell Jenkins and Cox. *Where do I start? Should I tell them how each child came to be? So much to tell. So much has happened!*

Part II

CONCEPTION

The Story of Ethan, Chetana and Sara

Chapter 4

Location: Health Sciences Center, University of Colorado at Denver
Time: June 2018

Emily Lake was living her dream as a senior resident in Pediatric Medicine and Surgery at the University of Colorado Hospital. Since winning her high school science fair, Emily yearned to become a physician. Yet today, her dream was less about medicine and more about having some time away from the job.

At five and a half feet tall, with smooth skin, large brown eyes, and long brunette hair, she appeared as "the girl next door." A youthful face belied her thirty years.

"Doctor Lake, Doctor Lake."

"What is it Jamie?" Lake's expression communicated her impatience. "I'm trying to get out of here. I've been on the floor since six fifteen this morning."

As a rule, Doctor Lake was the most approachable of the residents, but this morning she was in a hurry to leave the hospital. She glanced at the white-gold Rolex on her wrist. *Wow, 9:45 AM. Gotta go!*

Jamie Wharton, Head Nurse of the Pediatric Intensive Care Unit insisted, "Doctor Lake, Baby Romero is having trouble breathing. Someone needs to see her."

"Isn't she Belo's patient? Am I the only pediatrician on the floor?"

Nurse Wharton paused for a second, watching as Doctor Lake feverishly scribbled a note to renew a standing order. "Yes, she's Doctor Belo's patient, but he hasn't come up this morning. He's still in surgery. I checked Baby Romero a minute ago. Her lungs don't sound good. I think she needs a ventilator."

"Okay, okay," Emily said. She finished her notes and handed the chart to the charge nurse. "Come on Jamie, let's see Belo's patient, then I really must go."

The two women started at a quick pace down the hallway leading to the Intensive Care Unit. The young physician began rummaging through her lab coat pockets for her phone. "I must call my husband. He's going to be pissed!" Scrolling down the contact list, she clicked on *Kevin.* "Hi, honey—yeah, yeah, don't start—I promise I'll leave in ten minutes. Do you have everything packed? Yeah, I gave you everything. If I forgot something, there's a store up there. I have to go. Love ya!" Emily shoved the phone into the back pocket of her well-worn Levis. Jeans were not her usual attire, but like any true Texan, she loved soft jeans, and today she was supposed to be on vacation.

Entering the intensive care unit, Doctor Lake ordered, "Jamie, get me Romero's chart." Inserting the earpieces of her stethoscope, she listened to the premature infant's tiny lungs.

"I see what you mean, Jamie. She doesn't sound very good. Get her on a ventilator then call Doctor Jared. She's great with pulmonary problems. I'm sure Doctor Belo will want her to see Baby Romero. I'll note the order for the ventilator, but tell Belo as soon as he gets out of surgery what we've done."

With the crisis defused, Emily raced past the nursing station shouting, "Listen up everybody, I'm off to Cascade, Colorado and the Mountain Music & Flowers Festival. Don't look for me—don't try to call! Doctor Belo is covering my patients."

Without breaking stride, Emily stripped off her lab coat printed with nursery rhyme characters and tossed it into the laundry cart. A quick shoulder butt and the heavy metal door securing the pediatric care floor swung open. Arriving at the elevator, she punched the *down* button. *Hurry, hurry. I gotta get downstairs.* The elevator doors opened. Moments later, she reached the doctors' entrance in time to see Kevin park the Cadillac Escalade near the doorway. *Right on time, ya sweet thing.*

Kevin was Emily's best friend and her only lover since they met at the University of Texas in their senior year. At six feet three inches tall, he immediately caught Emily's attention when they first met, but his smile and personality captivated her heart. Kevin was a business major when they met but baseball was what really mattered to him. Although he received a full scholarship, a serious shoulder injury in his senior year shattered any dreams of playing major league baseball. A decade later, the muscular young ballplayer was thirty pounds heavier—his once strong jaw line now softened by the addition of a double chin. Changes in his physical appearance did not lessen her love for him. Nine years of marriage and one child later, she still loved him madly.

Chapter 5

Location: Interstate Highway 25, south of Denver, Colorado
Time: June 2018

Emily Lake dozed in the front seat of the SUV aided by the rocking motion of the heavy vehicle. On any other day, she would study every facet of the majestic Rocky Mountains that bordered Interstate 25 from Denver to Colorado Springs, but not today. She was tired. The hour and half drive gave her time to relax. Half-asleep, a blast of *The Eyes of Texas* awakened her. She knew the source. "That's your phone. It had better be damn important! We said 'no calls'—remember that?"

With a sheepish grin and shrug, Kevin Lake sought forgiveness before picking up his cellphone. "Hello. Oh, hi, Bill. Yeah, we're on our way right now—just at Colorado Springs." Following a long pause, Kevin apologized, "Sorry Bill can't help you—ask Rodrigo, he'll know what to do. Sure, sure, he can do it. He's been working with me on your IPO from the beginning. Trust me; Rodrigo has been in the securities game almost as long as I have. He can handle it." Kevin nodded his head as his client spoke, as some Texans do, as if the other party on the call could see them. "Okay, but remember, I will be off-the-grid for the next ten days." Following a short pause, he stated emphatically, "Like hell, you better not send a helicopter for me. Emily will cut my nuts off. She's a surgeon, you know! Take care. See you when I get back. Don't worry! Your stock issue will go off without a hitch."

Showing his phone to Emily, Kevin pressed the off button before placing it in the vehicle's console.

Emily smiled at Kevin, "That better be your last call—we promised—no phones. And you're right—I'd cut off your nuts and make a coin purse out of your scrotum!" The two laughed and the mood changed instantly.

"You mentioned Melissa before you dozed off. Are you sure your mother can handle her? Ten days is a long time."

"Mom will be fine. She'll love every minute with Melissa. Our problem is she's going to spoil the hell out of her."

Kevin nodded agreement. "That's what grandmothers do, but not for much longer. Melissa is growing so fast. What's the saying, 'today kindergarten, tomorrow college'. She'll be grown before we know it."

"Oh, Kevin, don't say that. I miss having a baby." Emily reflected on the fact that her biological clock was ticking louder and louder. She really wanted to give Kevin a son. *Maybe this will be our time. I would love to have a son.*

✺

Emily Lake knew that besides death and taxes, one other thing was certain—Kevin could not drive to their mountain cabin without a short detour through Colorado Springs to eat at Big Tex BBQ. The restaurant was a cavernous place that smelled of hickory smoke. Along the walls were heads of trophy elk, deer and black bear. Rustic wooden tables filled the room, each set with a roll of paper towels, condiments and plastic bottles of barbeque sauce.

Kevin led Emily to the rear of the restaurant and selected a table near one of the large television screens. As they sat down, a server dressed in a denim skirt, red shirt and matching red boots approached. The young woman was a caricature of Texan culture with a matching accent.

"Howdy! Welcome to Big Tex. This y'alls first time here?"

"I'm afraid not, we've been here several times. Thanks to my hubby. He can't live without barbeque."

"Okay, then. Ya'll wanna minit, or ya ready to order?"

Emily nodded in the affirmative. "Oh, I think we know what we want." Without looking at the menu posted at the end of the table, she ordered. "I would like the small chopped beef sandwich with a tall iced tea. Make that sweet tea, please."

"And, I'll have a luncheon rib plate with ranch beans—and some sweet tea," Kevin said, while trying to avoid the look of disapproval on Emily's face. He knew what it meant: he promised to pay more attention to what he ate.

"I'm Gloria. Ya'll make yourself at home. I'll get your drinks and be right back. Hey, look, thar's a bulletin on TV." She called to the bartender, "Shorty! Hey, Shorty, turn up tha volume. Thar's 'sumptin' important on tha TV."

Kevin and Emily positioned themselves for a better view of one of the three television monitors as did the other men and women seated near the bar.

As the volume increased, an off-screen, feminine voice spoke. "We're going to Bill Harding who is in Silver Spring, Maryland. He is standing by at the main office of the National Environmental Satellite, Data, and Information Service, a department within the National Oceanic and Atmospheric Administration. Bill, are you there?"

A reporter dressed in a dark suit appeared on screen. "Thank you Nelda. We're here at NESDIS headquarters. We've been told that a senior administrator will be making an important announcement—hang on, let's go to the podium."

The screen image changed quickly to a middle-aged man standing behind a wooden podium mopping perspiration from his baldhead and gasping to catch his breath. A hush fell over the two dozen reporters and videographers positioned in front of the spokesperson.

"Thank you for coming today, I am Jonathan Burton, Director for Deep Space Satellite Research. Late last evening, one of our probes detected an unusual phenomenon. The data received thus far suggest that a major cosmic event occurred—the collision of two galaxies identified as NGC2992 and NGC2993. The merging of these two galaxies has been the subject of study for some time but no one expected the release of such a significant amount of energy this early in the process. We anticipate the bombardment of our atmosphere with a broad spectrum of infrared rays, x-rays, and subatomic particles much like that from solar flares, with which you are all familiar. This event should commence seventy-two hours from now and continue for up to four days. We are alerting everyone to prepare for possible disruptions in satellite communication systems around the world. Although this is a potentially troubling situation, we do not anticipate any serious debris will strike the Earth. Although we recommend caution, there is no need for anyone to panic. That concludes my statement. I will now take your questions."

Emily turned to Kevin, a puzzled look on her face, "What do you think, Kevin? Are we in any danger? I'd hate to cancel our plans."

"I doubt there's much to worry about. If it were something critical, they would have activated the national alert system or something. Betcha the stock market is going to bounce around but it'll settle down quickly enough. Besides, for ten days, we'll be in the mountains. We wouldn't have phone service anyway!"

After eating, the two continued their trip to the mountains, forgetting the news bulletin. It was, after all, their first vacation in over two years.

Chapter 6

Location: Pike's Peak Highway, west of Cascade, Colorado
Time: June 2018

The magnificence of the Rockies in late spring never ceased to amaze Emily. Each time she traveled through the high country of central Colorado, she experienced the same sense of awe. *How can anyone grow tired of such beauty?* Even Kevin's persistent burps—the byproduct of a second helping of beans—could not dampen her spirit. She watched as he maneuvered the outsized vehicle along the winding road leading to the cabin. Every turn of the road brought a mesmerizing view. On the right, a steep drop-off into a rushing stream below. Ahead, a dramatic view of snowcapped mountains in the distance. To the left, a vertical cliff towering three hundred feet hugged the road. As each mile marker sneaked past, the elevation increased and the air grew thinner.

In less than an hour's drive from Big Tex BBQ, they reached the top of the mountain range and their cabin retreat. Emily found the four-room log cabin the first summer she and Kevin moved to Denver. Overlooking an expansive valley, the modest log cabin boasted a million dollar view of the surrounding mountains. Nestled in a grove of tall spruce and fir trees, the cabin sat on a small knoll cleared of trees to build the cabin. Not a hundred feet below the knoll ran a clear mountain stream on its way into the valley below.

Pulling into the driveway, Kevin sang out, "Home again, home again; the pigs are in their pen."

Emily never understood Kevin's need to sing his little jingle each time they arrived at a destination. "Yes, dear. We are here. Good to know the pigs didn't get out."

Kevin laughed. "Well, that's one less thing we need to do. I hate rounding up pigs and putting them away. What's more important is whether Hank made it. Hope he got the lights and water going."

Hank Purdy was a permanent resident on the mountain. For a small fee, he agreed to start the electrical generator, turn on the propane for the hot water heater, and prime the water pump—all necessary tasks to make the cabin livable. Living off the grid was a challenge, but one that the couple accepted as part of the cabin's charm.

"Well, let me see. Hand me the keys and I'll check." Door keys in hand, Emily jumped from the SUV and hurried into the cabin. *Now for the moment of truth. Hit the lights.* With a touch of the switch inside the front door, the lights shone brightly. Elated, she called out to Kevin, "Hank's been here! I love that old man."

The couple worked quickly to get everything out of the SUV and into cabin. There was much to do: beer to refrigerate, meat and fish in the freezer, canned and dry food stored, and clothes hung. With the work completed, Emily and Kevin sat down in the large Adirondack chairs on the front porch to enjoy a well-earned rest and the natural beauty around them.

"Isn't this wonderful," Emily said, grasping Kevin's hand. "Look at all the flowers this year. So many colors. Unless you've seen them, it's hard to believe they would grow way up here."

"Yeah, you're right. Hank calls the flowers 'God's palette.' Gotta agree with him."

The two sat quietly for almost an hour before Kevin asked, "You getting hungry?"

"Yeah, I could eat something. What do you have planned?"

"Well, my lady, tonight's menu consists of Chef Kevin's world renowned Louisiana Po'Boy" sandwich and all the trimmings. What more could man or woman want?" Kevin loved to cook for his wife. He knew Emily loved his Po' Boy sandwiches, a delight she rarely allowed herself—but then, this was a special occasion.

It wasn't long before tantalizing aromas of frying seafood and French fries filled the cabin. Emily inched up behind her husband leaning her head on his shoulder. "How much longer? I'm hungry."

"Jus' about ready. Why don't you get us a couple of beers? I'll be right there." Kevin skillfully turned shrimp and catfish fillets sizzling in a large, iron skillet. Fried to perfection, the delicacies would adorn a classic French baguette along with crisp lettuce, juicy tomatoes, pickled yellow peppers and Kevin's special sauce.

"A feast for the gods," praised Emily as the pair sat down at the hand-hewn wooden table that came with the cabin. As they gorged themselves on the mammoth sandwiches, washing down large bites with beer, Kevin provided his usual witty discourse. His golfing buddies kept him supplied with jokes for every occasion—some funny, others downright vulgar. To each joke, he added exaggerated expressions and voices. Emily laughed aloud at his antics.

She could not help herself; he was a natural comedian. Of course, the beer helped make everything seem all the more humorous.

As the couple finished eating, Kevin stood, a bit tipsy from the beer he consumed. "Tell ya what I gonna do, little lady," he propositioned in his best Texas drawl. "I'll clear this mess. In the meantime, you take a nice hot bath." Then with an exaggerated wink of his eye he said, "I'll see ya in bed when I'm done."

Chuckling at Kevin's corny impersonation of a matinee villain, Emily headed towards the bedroom. Pausing at the door, she assumed the role of a damsel in distress, "Oh, you evil man! What perverse things lay in my future?" Turning in a theatrical motion, she disappeared through the doorway.

Kevin cleaned the kitchen in short order, showered and slipped naked into the now warm bed. Even in summertime, the nights are chilly in high mountain country. His head scarcely touched the pillow before he felt Emily's hand grasp his penis. All he could think was, *O' momma, it's gonna be one of those nights!*

Kevin was right—that night Emily conceived Ethan. She would have the son she wanted—a very special son.

Chapter 7

Location: Pahalgam, Northern India
Time: June 2018

"Welcome to the Mansion Hotel. How may I be of service?" the desk clerk asked as the Indian gentleman and woman approached. The clerk epitomized what years of training in British hotels could do. Meticulously dressed in a gray suit, he nonetheless wore a bright red turban and sported a well-groomed beard.

The guest introduced himself. "I am Ram Kapur from New Delhi. This is my wife, Kumari. We have reservations." Ram used his very best English accent, as he often did when trying to impress someone, even a hotel clerk.

Six feet tall and almost two hundred pounds, Ram was larger than the average Indian man. His size, weight and European skin tone allowed him to compete in English rugby clubs while attending Cambridge University several years earlier.

The clerk scanned the reservation monitor. "Yes sir, I have your reservation. You are with the banking conference, I see. The meetings will be on the second floor, starting at nine in the morning. One moment please." The clerk perused the registration materials, just long enough to ensure his customer's respect for his thoroughness. "Ah, yes, I have a very pleasant suite for you on the top floor. It overlooks the valley to the south. There's a small balcony on the east side that provides an excellent view of Nanga Parbat, our most magnificent mountain. It is over twenty-one thousand feet high, so lovely. Atu, our bellman, will show you to your suite. Your baggage will be up shortly, not to worry." Turning to the bellman's stations, he called, "Atu, forward, please." Nodding his head respectfully, the clerk bid them a most pleasant stay. "If you need anything, do not hesitate to call on us. We are here to serve."

Ram and Kumari were accustomed to receiving the courtesies accorded their caste. Ram's family was *Brahmin*, the most honored caste, consisting of scholars, teachers and priests. Kumari's family was *Kshatriya*, the second highest caste, consisting of administrators, law enforcers and warriors.

With the bellman Atu leading the way, the couple walked through the well-appointed lobby. Kumari soaked in the exquisite blending of Indian and English furnishings. Red velvet sofas and matching overstuffed chairs added an air of sophistication to the grand lobby. Nineteenth-century European, crystal chandeliers dotted the ceiling of the two-story room. Hand-woven rugs in vibrant yellows, maroons, and blues covered the dark hardwood floors. On every wall were vivid murals depicting epic Indian sagas and Hindu deities.

Kumari exclaimed, "Oh Ram isn't it lovely! I told you. It is as I remember it from when I came here as a child. The carpets are as beautiful as...." Realizing that she was speaking in the presence of a lower caste person, she paused and did not say more until the bellman unlocked their room, opened the silk drapes covering the entry to the balcony, and departed.

After Atu left, Ram locked the room door. When he turned around, he saw Kumari standing at the balcony. Gazing through the open doors, she appeared enchanted by the view. A cool breeze gushed past her and gently tossed her long black hair in rhythmic harmony with the fabric of her full-length *sari*. Lengths of green and gold silk fabric wound tightly around her hips emphasized her slim figure. A snug fitting blouse of white Egyptian cotton outlined her firm breasts and accentuated her narrow waist. *So beautiful! Such soft, creamy skin. Shall I ever grow tired of seeing her?* The sweet fragrance of Kumari's perfume began to arouse him when she interrupted his thoughts.

"Oh, Ram, it's like a second honeymoon. Isn't that what your American friends call it—a honeymoon? Do you realize that we'll be married a full year, next Thursday?" Unlike many Hindu women, Kumari did not have an arranged marriage. When Kumari first saw the ruggedly handsome Ram Kapur, she knew they would spend their lives together. Moving nearer her husband, she appealed, "Can't we stay a short while after the conference? There are so many shrines and temples to see up here."

Stepping back from his wife, Ram scolded, "Kumari, you and your temples. America has automobiles, France has wine, and India—what does India have—countless deities and temples!" She touched a sore nerve with Ram; he was not the devout Hindu she was.

"Quiet, Ram, you will offend," Kumari cautioned. "Just because you attended Harvard and Cambridge, you're not so smart. Living in America has made you forget who you are. Yes, we are blessed with more gods than the French and the Americans. That only means that the gods like us more!"

The tone of her voice and the frown on her face told Ram that it was time to change the subject. He quickly considered, *"A short vacation would be nice. And there are several great golf courses nearby. A little time to enjoy the pleasures of married life would also be nice!"* "Okay, that's enough," he said, "Let me see what can be arranged; perhaps a couple of days of shrine walking won't kill me. But now, let's have our tea. We must not take too long. Mr. Bhatt and I are going to visit with the Indian Finance Minister in the hotel bar before dinner. I'm told he appreciates a quality scotch whiskey. Can you imagine that?" Ram liked single malt whiskey: he could not miss taking a jab at Kumari's Hindu faith, which avoided alcohol. But seeing the disgust in her eyes, Ram softly caressed her cheek and in a low voice added, "And good scotch is not the only thing I discovered in England. I found you there!"

A large smile began replacing the frown on Kumari's almond-shaped face, "Your western friends would call it 'fate' that my father should be in London on business when you were there. And 'fate' that the Indian Ambassador should have a reception at the Embassy so we might meet." Assuming a coquettish pose and voice, she admitted, "And I was ill-prepared for such a rakish devil as yourself. But Parvati, Goddess of Love, must have wanted me to suffer, and forced me under your spell!" As she finished speaking, she feigned fainting and fell onto the bed in front of Ram.

Amused by her theatrics, Ram gave in. "Okay, enough with the gods and goddesses. If you must, please ask your god of good fortune to watch over my meeting tonight. This will be a good chance to impress Mr. Bhatt. As Senior Manager for Federal Bank, Bhatt is the boss of my boss, you know." Grabbing his jacket and taking his wallet from the dresser, Ram said, "Now, let's have our tea, please!"

Kumari looked at Ram as he moved away from the bed. The bulge in the front of his pants spoke volumes; she made her point. Somehow, he would find a way for them to take a short holiday.

๛

The following morning Ram felt very confident about his contribution to the meeting with the Finance Minister. During the meeting, Bhatt arranged dinner with the Minister and invited Ram and Kumari to join them.

"Good morning Mister Bhatt," Ram said, greeting his higher-ranking colleague with the respect due him. "I hope that you are well this morning."

"Yes, Ram, I am very well, in large part due to the successful visit with the Minister. I was quite pleased when he agreed to dine with us. That was quite an honor, you know. And, I must say, having your lovely wife sit with us certainly contributed to the success of the evening."

"Thank you, Mister Bhatt. I, too, felt that the evening went well." Ram spoke in his best English accent.

"Ram, last night, your wife mentioned that you will be celebrating the first anniversary of your marriage. I would like to recognize your contributions last evening with a small gesture. On several occasions, you have mentioned how devout Kumari is. I have a brother who is also committed to his faith. In fact, he resides in a monastery north of here. It is a beautiful place—high in the mountains, very ancient, very holy. There are several bungalows there for travelers. The bungalows have all the amenities of a good hotel with a great deal more privacy. Let me contact my brother and arrange for you to stay there part of next week. Not to worry, I will see your duties are covered. What do you say?"

Pure delight swelled within Ram; not only was his boss impressed, Kumari could have her wish. With a pinch of reserve that barely masked his jubilance, Ram accepted, "What may I say? It is so kind of you. Moreover, I know Kumari will be very pleased. Thank you so very much."

Bhatt tapped Ram on the shoulder and smiled. "Then it is done. I will let you know the details tomorrow before I leave for New Delhi." Noticing a well-dressed figure entering the conference room, Bhatt continued, "Oh, there is Sir Walton. He is our guest speaker this morning. Come now. We must greet him."

Ram followed Bhatt into the conference room. After meeting Sir Walton, the two found seats near the front of the room. As Walton rambled on about geo-political factors affecting investments in India, Ram kept returning to the same thought: *A week in the mountains. Kumari is right. We are blessed!*

Chapter 8

Location: An Ancient Hindu Monastery, Near the Village of Chandanwari,
The Himalayan Mountains of Northern India
Time: June 2018

"Kumari, please hurry," Ram pleaded. "The desk called while you were in the bath. The driver from the monastery is waiting in the lobby." Taking a deep breath, he sighed, "I would like to get there before afternoon tea." The hint of sarcasm in his tone did not sit well with his young wife. He quickly added, "Let me help you. What may I do?"

With several personal items in hand, the couple hurried downstairs. As they entered the lobby, Ram noticed a young Hindu monk dressed in a saffron colored robe near the main entry doors and approached him.

Before Ram could speak, the monk bowed with his hands clasped in front of his face. "Good morning, sir. You are Mister Kapur."

"Yes, and this is my wife."

"Oh, such a pleasure to meet you. My name is Emeth. It is my honor to serve you this glorious morning. The vehicle is waiting just outside. Please follow. I will take you there."

Parked in front of the elegant hotel was a much used and not-so-well maintained van. It was not what Ram expected. *When Mr. Bhatt said the monastery would send transportation, I assumed it would be a car. Hope no one sees me getting into this dilapidated heap. This thing must be twenty years old. Looks Russian made. Very utilitarian. What's that smell? Goat urine?* Ram struggled to roll down the window next to his seat. *At least it's cool enough to leave the windows down. Anything to kill that odor.*

The odors and condition inside the van gave unmistakable evidence that its primary role was to carry provisions to the monastery. Every surface of the interior showed signs of the van's heavy use. The seats, draped with an assortment of blanket remnants, did little to hide the gashes in the brown vinyl seat covers. *Not what one would call elegant! What do they call it in the States..."early American thrash" motif?* Ram chuckled under his breath at his weak attempt at humor. *Bloody miserable vehicle. At least Kumari looks happy.*

None of the unpleasantness troubling Ram seemed to bother Kumari, who was delighted with the scenery around her. "Oh, Ram, it's so beautiful. The view is beyond description! Look at the peaks. I love the glaciers. Aren't they wonderful?" Kumari could not contain her pleasure, "You are such a good husband. I do so love you."

The trip to the monastery took most of the morning, although covering only forty-five kilometers. The loose gravel road twisted back and forward up the mountain making progress slow and tiresome. Ram was pleased when they reached the mountain village of Amarnath, which means "Immortal God, Lord Shiva"—a fitting name for a place that exists to serve religious pilgrims. Located twelve thousand feet above sea level in the Himalayan Mountains, the small village provides accommodations to travelers making a *yatra* or journey to the holy shrine of Lord Shiva. Pilgrims believe they see the image of the deity formed by ice stalagmites within a nearby cave.

Just outside of Amarnath lay the couple's destination. As they entered the monastery, Ram and Kumari gazed in amazement at its size. A wall of natural stone enclosed two acres. Within the enclosure, guest quarters, dormitories, and work sheds buttressed the wall leaving a wide plaza in the center. At the far end of the cobblestone plaza stood an ornately carved Hindu temple. Constructed of gray granite, the façade displayed images of deities and stylized columns carved into the stone.

The van stopped at a guest bungalow just inside the gate. A monk and several young novices, all dressed in bright yellow garments, came from within the small structure and stood before the van. Two novices assisted Ram and Kumari from the van while the remaining novices attended to the luggage.

His palms joined in front of his chest and bowing, the monk greeted the couple. "Namaste. We are pleased you are able to stay with us. I'm Ankur Bhatt."

Out of courtesy, Ram returned the traditional Hindu greeting, "Namaste." The greeting acknowledges the presence of divinity in all human beings conveying the meaning, *"with all my physical strength* (represented by clasped hands) and *my intellect* (represented by the bowed head), *I pay respect to the Atma* (soul) *within you."* He watched as Kumari reverently copied his movements. Her glance and smile affirmed her pleasure with his greeting.

When all was in order, Bhatt's brother directed the novices to leave as he turned to the couple. "The midday meal will be served within the hour. One of the novices will come for you. Do not worry, he will guide you, but you will soon learn your way around."

Alone for the first time since early morning, Kumari surveyed the small garden in the front of the bungalow—a profusion of brightly colored flowers surrounded beds of white foxtail lilies and blue Himalayan poppies. *This is the perfect place to celebrate our anniversary. Perhaps, the blessed Goddess of Fertility, Kali, will grant me a child in this holy place!*

The brisk walk to the communal dining room left the couple with a good appetite. They enjoyed the meal of brown rice, vegetable curries, a variety of chutneys, honey sweetened yogurt, fresh fruit, and unleavened breads. When finished, they strolled back to the bungalow. The pace of the meal, and life within the monastery, calmed the two of them. Unhurried, they paused to view the mountains, the workmanship in one of the stone structures, and the many flowerbeds.

Inside the bungalow, they relaxed side-by-side on the comfortable feather bed. The plainness of the room did not diminish the warmth each felt for the other.

"Ram, do you think that we can make a *yatra* to the shrine tomorrow?" Kumari asked in a sweet voice. "I know that it's a long walk, but a holy journey should include some sacrifice."

Although Ram was athletic, still participating in a rugby league in New Delhi, the prospect of taking a five-kilometer hike up a mountain just to see an ice flow did not interest him. He was about to make an excuse to avoid the ordeal when he made the mistake of looking at Kumari. Her soft smile, like that of a child begging for a treat, stopped him cold. Ram capitulated. "If you think that you are up to it, then, yes, we may go."

Kumari leaned over, placed her arms around Ram's neck and kissed him sensually. The remainder of the afternoon they exchanged expressions of love and playful sexuality. Kumari's two older sisters instructed her in the art of pleasing a husband—Kumari was an excellent student. That night, the Goddess of Fertility, granted Kumari's wish for a child. A girl she would name, Chetana: a child with the gift of touch.

Chapter 9

Location: CERN Particle Accelerator, Geneva, Switzerland
Time: June 2018

As the flight from Stockholm, Sweden approached Aéroport International de Genève, Christina Johansson exclaimed, "Oh, Oskar. Switzerland is lovely. Look there—the lake is so blue! That must be Lake Geneva. Are those the Alps?"

Switzerland is nestled between Germany on the northeast, Italy on the south, and France encircling its western border. Only a tenth the size of the state of California or twice as large as Massachusetts, it is a land of mountains and alpine lakes.

This was Christina's first visit to Switzerland, but it was not the first visit for her husband, Oskar Johansson. Christina was a stereotypical Swedish woman: golden blonde hair, powder blue eyes, and a pleasing figure. At twenty-eight years old, she looked like a fashion model. Oskar was equally Nordic in appearance. With a lean, muscular body—the product of competitive downhill skiing since childhood—he could easily be mistaken for a professional athlete. At thirty-two, his appearance gave no clue that he was a respected nuclear physicist.

As the aircraft made its final approach, Oskar called out, "Look to your right—see that large round building? That's CERN. The labs are located in those factory-looking buildings behind it." The two strained to view the ground below. "Actually, CERN is the old French name for the nuclear research facility started in 1954. The correct name today is the European Organization for Nuclear Research, but everyone still calls it CERN."

"So which building houses the famous Large Hadron Collider that you are interested in?"

Oskar smiled, amused by his wife's question. "The collider is not in a building; it is in an underground tunnel that stretches twenty-seven kilometers. Actually, only part of it is in Switzerland, most of it is in France. Anyway, we are not here to see the collider; we're here so you can see Geneva! It's lovely this time of year—before the humidity rises in July and August."

Nearby Lake Geneva moderates the temperature of the city in early spring, but by midsummer contributes to its uncomfortably high humidity. Oskar Johansson and Christina would have to wait to enjoy their lake holiday planned for the weekend. Today, important business awaited Oskar at CERN. He was seeking access to the most powerful particle collider in the world. He dreamed of having an opportunity to utilize the collider's power to test his theory regarding the properties of gravitons. His love for the lowly graviton lay in its ability to travel within multidimensional space and time.

"So when did you intern here?" Christina asked.

"About a year before we married—almost nine years ago. Hard to believe that it has been that long. Ah, those were heady days. The internship started after I completed my doctorate. It was only for two months, but still quite an honor. Every time I see pictures of the 'Globe'—that round building in front of the laboratory complex—so many memories come back. Speaking of memories—what do you say; want to take a tour of my old hangouts?"

"That sounds like fun. Do you think any of your old girlfriends are still around? They better not be!"

The heavy Scandinavian Airlines Airbus landed without incident. Oskar and Christina deplaned and gathered their luggage before heading to customs areas of the airport. Thanks to Sweden having joined the European Community in 1995, they quickly cleared airport security and traveled the short distance to CERN by taxi. Arriving at the laboratory complex, they passed through several security checkpoints before reaching the physics research complex.

Waiting at the last checkpoint to greet them was a pleasant looking woman in her early thirties dressed in a blue lab coat. "Good morning, Doctor Johansson! It is so nice to meet you. I am Doctor Mueller's research assistant, Celia Foxe. And, I assume that you are Christina or should I say Doctor Johansson?"

As a linguist, Christina was in the habit of geographically locating individuals based on their speech pattern. *She sounds American. Midwest probably. Cute. Somewhat geekish. Lovely smile.*

"Christina is fine with me. And shouldn't I address you as Doctor Foxe?"

"Yeah, but everyone calls me Celia. I understand that you are with Swedish military intelligence?"

Oskar, knowing how his wife disliked talking about herself, especially her job, quickly interjected, "Actually, Christina is a senior cryptographer. Her language skills are quite an asset in breaking code. Not to mention that she's my personal math consultant. She could teach theoretical math if she wished.

With a quizzical look, he added, "I am impressed with your knowledge of my wife's professional career."

"Oh! I should explain," Foxe responded. "One of my assignments is to review the preliminary background checks on people coming to the lab. It's part of the process for anyone being considered for projects here. Actually, our security staff does most of the work. I just review the final reports for Doctor Mueller."

Somewhat relieved, Oskar sought to clarify, "You said 'preliminary.' Will there be more inquiries? You must know that Christina has a top secret clearance with NATO."

Celia Foxe contorted her face into a frown, "I am afraid so, Doctor Johansson, but Doctor Mueller will tell you more about that when your experiment is approved. From what I have heard, getting your experiment approved is pretty much a formality. Doctor Mueller and several of the senior research fellows are quite interested in gravitons and multidimensional theories." Pausing for a moment, she asked, "So, you hope to prove there are alternate worlds?"

"Not really," Oskar replied, amused by the simplistic manner in which Foxe summarized his research proposal. "I just want to chip away at the problem. Actually, I hope that Doctor Mueller and his staff will help me with the final experimental protocols." As an afterthought, he added, "And, why don't you call me Oskar."

"Oskar it is!" Foxe's voice made it clear she did not like using courtesy titles. "I am sure that you will find everyone very helpful. Anyway, that's for later, for now, Doctor Mueller asked me to give you the grand tour. It won't take very long." Pausing to check her personal communications device, "Oh, there's a luncheon scheduled at 12:30. Everyone wants to meet you—and get a free lunch!"

Oskar studied his surroundings as the three walked down the hallway. There were some changes in this older section of the laboratory but much of it was the same as he remembered. *Nice of Mueller to arrange a tour for Christina. Besides, it's been nine years since I was here. I'm sure that a lot has changed—certainly around the collider!*

❧❧

"Well, here we are! Doctor Mueller's office. That concludes our little tour. Good morning, Helen, this is Doctor Oskar Johansson and his wife, Doctor Christina Johansson. Would you let Doctor Mueller know that they are here?" Directing her comments to Oskar and Christina, Celia advised,

"Helen is actually the brains of the operation. She keeps all of us on-schedule and in-line."

Helen Jeffers was Swiss, middle-aged, and conservatively dressed in a dark blue jacket and matching skirt. Her desk communicated that she was a stickler for organization. "Welcome, Doctor Johansson. Would you like anything while you are waiting—coffee, water?"

"No, no thank you, I'm fine. Christina, would you like something?" Christina nodded in the negative.

Turning her attention to Celia, Jeffers inquired, "Will both you and Doctor Johansson's wife be joining us for lunch? Doctor Mueller did not mention that you would be attending."

"Oh, no, Helen. I'm taking Christina to lunch." Turning to Oskar, Celia said with a prankish grin, "Don't worry. I'll take good care of her. Doctor Mueller said he would deliver you to the hotel after your meeting." Reacting to the opening of the door behind her, "Ah! Speak of the devil, here's our Doctor Mueller."

Mueller was a robust man around fifty with a perpetual smile partially hidden by grayish whiskers. As he walked into the office, he spotted the couple and moved to greet them. Starting first in German, "Willkommen mein freund," he quickly changed to English. "Oskar! Welcome back to CERN. Did Celia give you a good tour of the place?"

"Yes, she did—very informative."

Mueller turned, "And you must be Christina. Good to meet you. I'm so pleased that you were able to come." Taking Christina's hand in his, and softening his voice, he said, "You know, Oskar may be here for a while, if his experiment proves to be fruitful. It looks very promising."

Caught off guard by his touch, Christina felt that Mueller was genuinely concerned for her family situation. Although asked by him to accompany Oskar, she viewed such requests as little more than orchestrated opportunities to "check out the wife." However, today was different; it was important for Oskar, and Mueller was not like some of the other men she had met. Recovering, "Yes, Oskar and I've discussed it. That's the problem with 'two career' families, but our daughter is almost four years old now. We'll manage."

"Excellent!" Mueller seemed pleased with Christina's response. "Then, let me steal Oskar for a couple of hours. I promise to deliver him to you when we are finished. Trust me, it's summertime. Everybody here plays golf. We'll be finished before five!"

Chapter 10

Location: Maxine's Bistro, Geneva, Switzerland
Time: June 2018

On the trip from the laboratory to the bistro, Celia and Christina engaged in the usual chattiness that occurs between women of the same age and the same intellect. Both were aware that a bond of friendship was quickly developing between them.

As Celia pulled into a curbside parking space a short distance from the bistro, Christina noticed the distinct French flavor of the area. *Such an ideal spot for a bistro, especially in the summertime. Look at those gorgeous sycamore trees. I love the wrought iron fencing everywhere. Gives a quaint look to the area!*

The bistro provided seating on the sidewalk, with several tables enclosed by an ornamental fence. Covered with white linen cloths, the tables stood in stark contrast to the black fence surrounding them and the forest-green awning that partially covered the dining area. Tall sycamore trees lining the street shaded the tables not covered by the awning.

Celia directed Christina to a table located in a corner of the sidewalk area, her regular spot. As the two seated themselves, a stunning woman wearing a white blouse and short black skirt approached with tableware rolled in napkins and menus for the couple. Before the waitress could speak, Celia greeted her. "Hi, Kelli. This is Christina; she's visiting CERN with her husband. Kelli's a transplanted American."

Christina realized that the two women were more to each other than waitress and regular customer.

Kelli placed the napkins and menus on the table as she greeted Christina, "Welcome to Geneva. Is this your first visit?"

"Yes, it is, but hopefully, not my last." Christina gave Kelli a once over. *Such pretty green eyes and wavy red hair. Very nice tits! C, maybe D, cups? She sure knows how to show them.* Noticing Kelli was ready with her order pad, Christina said, "Celia told me you have a true American burger here, but I must watch what I eat these days. What do you suggest with a few less calories?"

Falling immediately into her role, Kelli responded, "Actually, we have a lovely onion soup with a melted Swiss cheese topping. Comes with a nice basket of breads. We have a superb baker!"

"Sounds lovely." Pleased with the suggestion, Christina scanned the menu for beverages. "And I would like some hot tea with lemon, as well?"

"Very nice." Changing her voice to mimic an American, Boston accent, Kelli asked, "And, what'll you 'ave, Celia? Tha usual with a mayo side?"

"That'll do nicely," Celia smiled at Kelli's effort to criticize her fondness for burgers and the fact she did her graduate studies in New England. "And I'll have hot tea. With milk, no lemon, please."

Kelli gathered up the menus. "Okay, then, I'll be right back." With the precision of a military honor guard, she pivoted on her heel and toe and returned to the bistro's entrance.

Christina's eyes followed Kelli's departure, before returning to Celia, "So, how long have you known Kelli? She's really nice looking. Isn't that what you say in America?

"Yeah, she's a complete package. I've known Kelli for a couple of years. Met her right after I arrived in Geneva. Actually, I have Kelli to thank for introducing me to Claude, my finance'. She took me to Paris a couple of months after we met, thought I needed to see the Musée du Louvre. My French was pretty poor back then, so it was nice to have someone to act as guide and interpreter." Celia paused to take a sip of water. Collecting her thoughts, she continued, "Anyway, on the train coming back from Paris, I met Claude. He was more interested in Kelli when we first met, you know, Frenchmen and large bosoms!"

Christina gave an understanding nod. "Yes, men will be men—French or not."

Celia confided, "Fortunately for me, Claude's traveling companion was an Italian artist. That's all it took. Kelli and Luigi hit it off. She's working on a Master's degree in Art History. Thirteenth century painters or something like that. Anyway, with Kelli occupied, I had Claude all to myself. We found that we have a lot in common. I think my PhD in particle physics turns him on, and his ass certainly turns me on!"

"Celia!" Christina could not control her shock and amusement at Celia's comment. Regaining her composure, "So, is there a wedding in the near future?"

"Nah, we're both too busy. But, we have some great weekends together." Without hesitation, she offered, "I know that this is sudden, but tomorrow is Friday and we don't have anything hot in the lab next week. I plan to meet Claude at his grandfather's chalet for a long weekend. Would you and Oskar like to visit Mont Blanc in the French Alps?" Celia could see that her offer evoked a look of delight from Christina. "I'm sure that Claude would be happy to have the company. He loves cooking for people. He'll whip-up a gourmet meal for us. What do you say?"

Caught by the suddenness of Celia's offer, Christina answered, "I don't think that we should impose. The two of you must have so little time together with your busy schedules."

Celia responded in an inviting voice, "No problem. Trust me. It's a large place with four bedrooms. Promise, you'll not hear us in bed, if that's bothering you."

My, nothing shy about her! Christina managed a hesitant reply, "I don't know what to say. Oskar loves the mountains. Actually, we don't have anything definite planned for the weekend—just seeing some of Lake Geneva. After a thoughtful pause, Christina agreed, "Okay! For now, I'll say yes."

Christina's joy was undeniable. Pleased, Celia said, "Sounds awesome. I'll give you my cell number—call should Oskar have any questions." Pointing towards the cafe door, she added, "But now it's time to eat. Kelli's headed this way!"

With her nose raised and wrinkled, as if she smelled a foul odor, Kelli placed Celia's order in front of her, "Here we are madam, one greasy burger." Turning to Christina, "And a marvelous onion soup for you. I added a house salad to your order, *gratis*. Give me a sec and I'll get you a basket of bread. Anything else you girls want?"

"Nope, looks good to me, Kelli," Celia said. "As we say in America, 'jump in'. We may be able to get in a little shopping on our way to the hotel if we hurry."

Chapter 11

Location: CERN Laboratory, Geneva, Switzerland
Time: June 2018

Oskar rose early the following morning and took a taxi to CERN to meet with the collider engineering staff, an important step in having his research project approved. Christina did not accompany him, choosing to stay in bed. Although she hoped to see more of the collider, the trip from Sweden and last night's tavern hopping took their toll. She was exhausted.

As Oskar entered the laboratory security area, Celia's now familiar voice sang out, "*God morgon*, Oskar. How was last night? Did Christina enjoy your evening out?"

Oskar smiled at Celia's attempt to greet him in Swedish. "Yes, it was a very nice evening. Thank you for asking." As he ambled down the long hallway, he recalled last night's happenings. *Christina really enjoyed visiting my old hangouts. We don't spend enough time together. Need to change that. Being here while she's back home is going to be hard.*

Celia asked, "So what do you think about the news from Noah?"

Showing confusion, Oskar said, "I'm sorry, I don't think I met Noah yesterday?"

"Oops! My fault. Americans love to speak in acronyms. I should say, the National Oceanic and Atmospheric Administration in the States. That's N-O-A-A. We say it as 'Noah'."

"Oh, I see. Yet, I'm still at a disadvantage." Seeking clarification, "Was there some announcement?"

"Seems we're going to be bombarded by cosmic particle emissions for most of next week. Evidently, a galactic collision released an unusual amount of electromagnetic radiation."

"Will you be involved in analyzing the event?" Oskar asked.

"I wish!" Celia answered with a frown. "Looks like the Cosmology folks are going to do most of the fun stuff, but I can still hope. Should know more next week when the data starts flowing in."

"Is our trip to the Alps still on or do you need to cancel?"

Celia shook her head. "Oh, this thing is not going to stop us. Can't see how a little increased the background radiation would interfere. They said it's not going to be much more than a good solar flare, anyway." Gesturing to her guest, she invited him to follow her. "Come on. I'll escort you to the office then I have to run. Lot's to do today."

As Oskar said goodbye to Celia, he entered Mueller's office area. Helen was not at her desk; she and Mueller were inside his private office talking in German. Taking a seat, Oskar thought about what Celia said about the cosmic disruption. *I'd love to work on a project like that. Bet they find some rare forms of electromagnetic radiation. Could be very interesting work. Certainly worthy of publication!* There was only a moment to reflect before Helen returned to her desk and advised Mueller that Oskar was waiting.

"Good morning, Oskar. I hope you slept well." Mueller was his jovial self. "There is much to do today. We need to hear what the engineering staff thinks about your project. You know, analyzing the transmutation of gravitons is not going to be easy." Taking two hardhats from a shelf near his office door, he advised Helen, "We're going now. Don't expect us back for at least two hours. If Doctor Johansson's wife calls, tell her I'll deliver him back to the hotel before noon. I understand that Celia has something planned for the two of them—a weekend trip to Mont Blanc. Well, Oskar, let's go. You're not going to believe what we have done down in the hole."

Chapter 12

Location: Holiday Inn, near Geneva Airport
Time: June 2018

"Good morning. Did you have a good night," Celia asked as she met Christina and Oskar in the hotel lobby.

"We slept well, thank you." Christina replied. "And you?"

"Oh, fine. I'm a heavy sleeper." Celia turned toward the entrance. "If you're ready to go, I'm parked out front."

The three walked to Celia's BMW parked near the hotel entryway. A hotel bellman was standing nearby and opened the passenger side door.

"Why don't you sit up front with me, Christina? Oskar can have the whole backseat to himself. We can put your bags in the trunk."

Dressed in a white wool pantsuit, Christina slipped into the front seat as directed. *Celia looks comfortable in those American jeans. I wish I had brought more leisure outfits. Doesn't matter. We're only going for a couple of days.*

Celia entered the driver's seat. "I called Claude last night. He'll meet us at the chalet. Did I tell you that it's in the Mont Blanc region?"

"Yes," Oskar replied. "You told Christina at the bistro. After I checked my e-mail last evening, I searched Mont Blanc. It's a really high mountain—over fifteen thousand feet. Wish I had my skis with me."

The two women shared a lively banter along the way with Oskar content to listen most of the time. After leaving the congestion of the city, Celia powered the BMW over the winding roads from Geneva to the chalet in record time, much to Oskar's delight. Arriving at the chalet, she pointed out Mont Blanc for him. It was an impressive sight, as was the chalet. Its traditional A-frame design rested on a gentle slope. Partially built into the mountain, the first floor was constructed of large stone blocks while the top floor consisted of natural logs chinked with white mortar. A narrow balcony with an ornate balustrade divided the first and second floors. The chalet's prominent feature was its steep roof of rough-cut fir shingles. The roof ran from the ground to its two-story pinnacle.

"Oh, it's beautiful here!" Christina exclaimed. "All the summits are still covered with snow." Her eyes swept the terrain. "Look over there. All those flowers—like the ones we saw along the road." Flushed with joy, the text of a forgotten scripture resonated in her head. *Surely, the Lord has made this place!*

A handsome figure with a full crop of black hair appeared on the balcony above them. Clean-shaven, muscular and wearing a knit shirt and leather trousers, Christina understood what Celia meant: Claude's ass was a real turn-on.

Calling out in French to Celia, Claude greeted her, "*Ma Cherie! Viens bien m' embrasse'.*" Addressing Oskar and Christina, he continued, "*Et ces amis avec toi. Bienvenu.*"

Aware that her guests did not speak French, Celia responded in English, "And I love you too!" Turning to Christina, "Claude bids you 'welcome.' Claude, this is Christina and Oskar Johansson. Now the introductions are out of the way—what's for dinner? I'm starved."

"*Ah, Mon amour,*" Claude declared in his native tongue before continuing in English, "All the time you are thinking about the stomach—never the heart!" With a beaming smile and an eagerness to hold his finance', he scurried down the outside stairs to the driveway below. With a wave of his hand, he signaled. "Come. Celia will show you where to put your things. We are all on the ground floor. We have four bedrooms. Plenty of space for sleeping."

Entering on the first floor, Claude dashed up the metal spiral staircase located just inside the entry doors. Stopping halfway up, he called, "*Mon amour.* Please place them across from us so they will be near the facilities."

"Yes, my love." Celia replied. "Claude wants you to be near the bathroom. I stress the word '*the,*' as in '*the only,*' if you get my point." Pointing to the rear, she started in that direction. As she did, she described the layout of the rooms. "Like Claude said, there is plenty of room for sleeping. There are four bedrooms down here—two on either side of the hallway." Celia stopped at an opened door. "Claude wanted you here. Put your bags anywhere." Oskar tossed their bags on the bed. "Come, I'll show you *the* bathroom." At the bathroom door, she said, "We have to share, but it is nice. There are two showers and two toilets, 'no waiting' as we say back home. When they built this place, they didn't have indoor plumbing. Originally, this floor was a stable. The family cow and any other animals were kept down here." Pointing to the staircase, "Enough history! Let's go upstairs. I'll bet you are as hungry as I am."

Claude was busy preparing dinner when his finance' and guests appeared. The second floor was a large open space that served as the living room, dining room, and kitchen. In the center of the room was a circular fire pit with a metal covering that vented through the vaulted ceiling. "*Vous venez*—come in, come in. Make yourselves comfortable. Celia, pour our guests some wine. There are *hors d'oeuvres.* Enjoy. I will not be long."

Claude was indeed an exceptional chef and his efforts soon filled the chalet with the pleasing aromas of regional dishes prepared from local ingredients: red chard, spring lamb and heavy cream. Most of the dishes were new to Oskar and Christina. Every mouthful was a delight. The repast concluded with a delectable *Montefalco Rosso* from Umbria, Italy, and a tasty triple *crème brie*.

The evening could not have been more pleasant. Claude and Celia were a "dynamic duo." They seemed to feed off each other, keeping Oskar and Christina laughing, while Claude made sure that their glasses were never empty.

With the early summer sun setting, Celia declared, "Folks, it's been a long day—and knowing Claude, it should be a long night!"

Claude cast her an embarrassed, sheepish grin. Unprepared for Celia's straightforwardness, he lamented, "*Mon amour!* You are so unkind to me."

"Oh, Claude, I only say what is true." Looking to their guests, "Since we have to share the bathroom, why don't you two go first. I'll help Claude put everything away."

"Are you sure?" Christina asked. "We can help."

"No, Celia is right," Claude replied. "Go, go. Besides, I want to lay out a few things for our breakfast."

The altitude, the thin air, and the fine food left Christina in a very relaxed mood. She was ready for bed. As Oskar and Christina bid "goodnight" to their hosts, Christina took her husband by the hand. Walking toward the staircase, she thought, *Come along, lover. I think tonight is going to be your night!*

That night proved to be very special. For on that night Christina conceived Sara—a child who could hear what others could not hear.

Part III

THE ENLIGHTENED ONES

The Search Begins

Chapter 13

Location: Office of the CEO, UrComputec, Mumbai, India
Time: June 2018

Sudhir scurried about his luxuriously appointed office on the outskirts of Mumbai, his eyes fixed on the monitor that dominated one wall. A sleepy face appeared on the screen. "Rishi! Wake up. Wake up. Did you hear? Are you watching the news? It's going to happen!"

Still in his bedclothes, Rishi moved closer to the video communication console in his bedroom. "Sudhir, slowdown. What are you saying?"

"I'm telling you, a few hours ago, the Americans announced that a major cosmic event happened. Check your bloody monitor! Go to BBC North America."

"Okay. Give me a minute." A second later he returned with a tablet in his lap. "Ah, yes, yes, there it is. Be quiet so I can listen." A long pause followed as Rishi listened to the Anglo-European reporters discuss the National Oceanic and Atmospheric Administration report that deep space probes detected a significant release of energy. The reporters explained how everyone should prepare for the bombardment of the atmosphere with infrared rays and subatomic particles. The event, anticipated in seventy-two hours, would disrupt communication systems around the world.

"So Rishi, what should we do? Is this just a coincidence or is Manish right?"

Sudhir barely finished his questions before Rishi responded. "You call Bijay, Hari and Abhay. I'll call the others. We're scheduled to meet at the end of the week anyway, we'll talk then. I will get Harshal to bring Manish to the Cricket Club. As much money as Harshal has given that bloody holy man, he should be able to get him there on short notice. Make your calls. Go! I'll see you in Delhi."

Sudhir slumped back in his custom fitted executive chair, his fingers caressing the padded armrests covered in delicate kangaroo skin. Around him were the accoutrements of wealth: a hand carved mahogany desk inlaid with ivory, a personal computer and communications center with three wafer-thin monitors, and two large couches upholstered in raw silk fabric. An educated person, he tried to comprehend what might be happening. *How in the bloody hell did Manish do it! Is it just coincidence? What did he say? Yes, yes, I remember, "The heavens will be disturbed and the Enlightened Ones will appear. The great god of creation, Brahma, will bring forth children of great power and intellect." What's the probability that he could predict a cosmic disruption?*

The successful executive was not a fan of the young guru who called himself, Manish—a Hindi name derived from *"man"* meaning *"mind"* and *"ish"* meaning *"god"*–the name literally meant *"mind of god."* Sudhir felt that this contrivance of the holy man's name was no accident, only a smart marketing move by Manish to influence his clientele. *I don't care if he calls himself "an elephant's ass." I just want to know what comes next! And, who are these Enlightened Ones?*

Chapter 14

Location: The Executive Lounge, Empire Cricket Club, Delhi, India
Time: June 2018

The end of the Twentieth Century ushered in India as a major provider of on-line software and technical support services, employing over 350,000 individuals in call center operations. A reservoir of educated men and women, willing to work for half the salary of their North American and British counterparts, gave India a competitive advantage in the new market place. Young techno-entrepreneurs formed companies to provide the needed support services, reaping large financial rewards in the process.

A bond developed among a handful of these young entrepreneurs. Rich and intellectually gifted, they sought comradeship and business connections with others like themselves. Informally, they called themselves, the Bombay Gentlemen. Having access to personal aircraft, the men met regularly at different locations throughout India and at Indian Ocean resorts catering to the rich. Each meeting, hosted by one of the group, provided a stimulating intellectual exchange for members.

A year ago, Harshal introduced Manish to the group. As Harshal suspected, the young seer and guru intrigued the members of the group. It was not that Harshal believed in the occult nor that the other men believed that Manish could really predict future events, what fascinated them was how Manish repeatedly defied the laws of mathematical probability. How could Manish be right in his predictions so often? It was both uncanny and captivating—an intellectual carnival act played out before their eyes. Amusement for rich intellectuals.

Over the course of several months, members of the Gentlemen's group listened to Manish predict major stock market shifts in Indian markets and in London. On two occasions, he predicted severe weather events that affected satellite communications—communications critical to the operations of call centers lying thousands of miles away from their service markets.

On the day of the group's meeting at the Cricket Club, Harshal arranged for the young guru to attend as Rishi asked. He was pleased that Manish's predictions captivated his colleagues. Holding a doctorate in mathematics from Cambridge University, Harshal originally found Manish's ability to exceed the laws of probability intriguing. If Manish was only making educated guesses, he should not be right time after time. Although Harshal's intellect told him one thing, his Hindu upbringing told him something else: Manish was truly a holy man!

As Harshal entered the plush conference center of the Empire Cricket Club, Abhay greeted him. "Welcome to my club, old boy. The others are in the executive dining room. They've been waiting for you. Follow me. It seems our agenda for today has changed—such a shame—I hoped that you could meet my top players. Perhaps another time."

Abhay lived up to his Hindi name as the "brave and fearless" one of the group. Dashingly handsome and athletically built, he could trace his family tree to a medieval *maharaja*. He was the only unmarried member of the group—a playboy, time permitting—and the proud co-owner of the Empire Cricket Club.

As the pair entered the dining room, Rishi called out, "So, Harshal, where is the bloody monk? I thought you were bringing him?"

"I'm afraid our holy man doesn't travel well—airsick you know—upchucked a bit onto his robe. Not to worry. He'll be along shortly. My pilot took him to Cavendish's for a change of clothing. He'll look much better in a nice English suit—far better than that terrible saffron robe of his!"

Everyone smiled and gave a "hear, hear" in support of Harshal. The monk frequently had an odor about him—a blend of strong cooking spices and nervous perspiration.

When Harshal took his seat, Abhay addressed the assembled group. Feigning an English accent and an aristocratic manner, he assured his friends. "Well, then, I see no reason to delay having a spot of tea." With a nod of his head, two attendants dressed in starched white cotton tunics and black pantaloons scurried to do his bidding.

As the men rested in ornate leather chairs placed around an oblong mahogany table, Abhay continued, "So our holy man has a hot prediction. What does it mean for us?"

Rishi, the youngest of the group, spoke up. "I am not sure of the correct course of action," his voice and demeanor showing a bit of false modesty. Although the youngest, he knew exactly what course of action the group should take. After all, he did possess the highest intelligence and excellent business sense. Smallish in physical statue, through of average height for an Indian male, he attended the best preparatory schools in India before completing advanced degrees in mathematics and theoretical computing at the

Massachusetts Institute of Technology in Cambridge, Massachusetts. Jokingly, he would say, "I attended university in Cambridge," leaving his listener to think that he meant Cambridge, England.

"Okay, Rishi. Tell us what you really think," Sudhir cajoled. At forty-six, he was the elder statesman of the group.

"Well now," started Rishi as he leaned back in his chair, his hands forming a temple below his chin. "If our holy man has it right, somewhere out there are some very special individuals. I pose this question to you, 'What is the economic value of possessing a cadre of Enlightened Ones?' If these gifted individuals wish nothing more than to sit like Buddha under the Bodhi Tree and tell us how to find inner peace, they may have little value. If, by 'enlightened,' Manish means they possess special talents, like a savant in math or music, then there is a potential for great profit."

A rumble of affirmation rolled through the group of entrepreneurs. Hari, a software specialist, visualized powerful programs that his company could develop with a gifted person. Bijay, envisioned engineering geniuses capable of designing the next generation of computers, machines unimagined by his engineering staff. Abhay, whose call center provided customer service assistance to the credit card industry, envisioned something more: if these Enlightened Ones possess extraordinary physical strength and speed, the Empire Cricket Club would dominate the Cricket World Cup matches!

As the wait staff returned and began laying out a sterling silver tea service, Bijay addressed the group. "Gentlemen, let's review this situation pragmatically." His words reflected his status in the group as the most incisive decision maker. "What systems must be put in place to find these special individuals? We don't know if they are here in India or scattered around the world. Bloody hell, we don't know much of anything about them! Are they male, female, both? What characteristics do they possess? We could be searching for the proverbial needle in a haystack. And, at what cost?"

Each member looked at Bijay, studying the dark features of his round face in hope of finding clues to what he was going to suggest. Bijay, "the victorious one," was the richest of the men, riches gained by aggressively acting when opportunities presented themselves. If he did not see the venture as profitable, then none of the others would.

A momentary silence befell the men, amplifying the noise of attendants placing cups, saucers, and delicately engraved spoons on the table. One of the servers adroitly placed a large tray of scones, sweet rolls, and local pastries in the center of the table. A gentle nod from Abhay to the headwaiter conveyed that it was time to pour the tea, releasing the Gentlemen from their self-imposed stillness.

"Look here," Rishi declared in a strong voice but one partially blocked by a mouth filled with puff pastry, "If we have the technology and the mathematics to fling an object into the heavens and strike a moon of Jupiter some six hundred million kilometers away, I think we can formulate an algorithm to search for exceptional human events. Let us review what we know. First, the individuals will be born within a year. If over two millennia ago three bloody wise men crossed a desert and found a single baby lying in a manger, we damn well have the resources to find that proverbial needle!" Although Rishi was not very religious, his mother was Christian. As a child, she read bible stories to him—stories he never forgot.

Rousing grunts and murmurs affirmed the group's acceptance of Rishi's proposal. This small group did have the resources to undertake the challenge. The search would be a pleasant diversion even if no financial gain materialized.

The situation called for a well-developed plan of action. Sanjay was the group's recognized strategist. He would bring a plan to the group's next scheduled meeting. In the interim, he would confer with each member as needed. As the men concluded their discussion, a member of the club's security staff appeared with a bearded man next to him.

"Well, look who has graced us with his presence," Abhay jested. "It is his eminence, Sir Manish!"

Everyone turned to see the holy man dressed in a cream colored, three-piece suit of the finest New Zealand tropical wool. A very black, bushy beard obscured most of the shirt he wore. His portly frame, usually rapped in layers of flowing cloth, stood exposed for inspection by all. Without question, the guru and seer was out of his sartorial element.

Harshal, stood and held out an inviting hand. "Come, Manish. Sit here by me."

A waiter moved quickly to place a saucer, cup, spoon, and raw silk napkin before the holy man. A second waiter fetched a pot from its warming stand and filled the cup with aromatic tea. Manish devoured a double portion of *anarsa*—a Hindu pastry made with cane sugar, rice, poppy seed, and butter. The men sat quietly for a moment, allowing their guest to finish his tea before encouraging him to broaden his prophecy.

"Manish, my dear friend and most honored guest," Harshal said as he touched the holy man's shoulder. "As you know, your prophecy of a great cosmic disruption is upon us. You have truly opened the eyes of each of us here today. Might you tell us more about these, Enlightened Ones? We wonder if they will be male or female. Are they to bless only the Hindu faithful here or shall they appear in every land?"

Emboldened by the cosmic events announced earlier, the seer was eager to satisfy his wealthy and attentive audience. "The Enlightened Ones will be male and female; of that, I am sure. There will be but a few, and they will be broadcast as grain across the Earth." The holy man offered little more, although the men asked several probing questions. In the weeks that followed, fate would intervene and the group would lose the holy man's guidance.

The Gentlemen's group learned no more from the young sage after their meeting at the Cricket Club. Engrossed in his thoughts while crossing a busy street in his village, he failed to see an ancient pick-up truck barreling down the road. Struck, he died instantly of his injuries. Harshal summed it up best. "Manish was so bloody busy looking into the future that he forgot to look for trucks in the present! Damn fool."

After that day, none of the men spoke about the guru. Undaunted, the Gentlemen agreed to continue the arduous task that lay ahead—to find and to possess the Enlightened Ones.

Chapter 15

Location: Beach Estate of Sanjay, Colombo, Sri Lanka
Date: August 2018

Sanjay rushed about his palatial home checking last minute details with his culinary staff and housekeepers. This was the first time the Bombay Gentlemen would meet at his new private retreat. The food must be impeccable—a delight in every mouthful. Each guest bedroom must be spotlessly clean and furnished with new bed and bath linen. The hospitality must be unsurpassed.

A Sri Lankan boy walked quickly towards Sanjay. "Sahib, Sahib, your guests are here. They passed through the gatehouse but a moment ago."

"Very good. Go to the front door and assist with the baggage. Place each man's baggage in his room. Don't make any mistakes. Do you understand?"

"Yes, Sahib." The young servant bowed, and then dashed away.

Sanjay looked into a large mirror near where he stood. Memories of his childhood in a lower middleclass household left him self-conscious about his appearance. *A raw silk shirt and fine linen trousers. Very nice combination. What the bloody hell, these are my friends!* Self-assured, he moved to greet his guests at the entry to the mansion. As he arrived at the entry doors, two young female attendants, dressed in saris of thin red silk trimmed in gold fabric, entered. Behind them walked Rishi, enthralled with the lusciousness of his young guides.

"Well, there you are," Rishi called out, as Sanjay approached. "Not bad old man!"

Sanjay gave a gentle bow of appreciation for the kind words. "Come; let's go to the pool area. It is most comfortable there."

In the center of the sprawling mansion was a large oval pool, open to the sky. Its azure water—encased in white marble—sparkled in the bright light of the tropical sun.

Impressed by the opulence of the pool and surrounding area, Rishi stood quietly for a moment. "This is lovely, Sanjay. You have out done us all."

"Thank you, my friend. Now let's find the others."

As each guest arrived, they settled into their usual conversation: how they were prospering; the difficulty of doing business in India's arcane bureaucratic system; the rising cost of competent labor; and the price of aviation fuel.

For the reminder of the day, no one broached the topic that each came to discuss. The men understood that following breakfast the next morning, Sanjay would give his report. They could wait. Pleasure first, business second.

❧

Sanjay moved about the mansion checking on the morning's activities. Although the culinary staff did stellar work preparing and serving dinner, Sanjay planned a very special breakfast for his guests. There would be no traditional English breakfast of fried eggs, greasy sausages, and dry toast with bitter marmalade—not in this tropical climate. Local fruit, sweetened creams and custards, flaky pastries, and exotic juices would adorn a well-appointed buffet table on the grand veranda.

As instructed, the Gentlemen met in the main room of the mansion prior to breakfast. When all were present, Sanjay led his colleagues outside. "Come, my friends, our breakfast awaits. I do hope it pleases you."

Sanjay spared no expense in the construction of the veranda. Designed to impress, it was ten meters wide and fifteen meters long, and covered with polished stone. An intricately carved white stone railing enclosed the space. A dozen meters below the railing lay the clear waters of the Indian Ocean.

At one end of the veranda stood the buffet table; at the other end was a second table. Each table, covered with a red silk cloth and set with brass tableware, stood in stark contrast to the white stone of the floor and railing. Flowering hibiscus plants in ceramic containers added a tropical ambience to the breakfast setting.

As the men stepped onto the veranda, Bijay called out, "My word, Sanjay. This is spectacular!" The others quickly added their adulations greatly pleasing their host.

Walking towards the buffet table, Sanjay invited his guests to breakfast. "Gentlemen, please select whatever pleases you. One of my young ladies will assist you." Near the buffet table stood several young women dressed in brightly colored Ceylonese costumes. As each man selected items from the buffet, one of the women carried his choices to the table.

The breakfast was a success. The men enjoyed their food and the service provided by the young women. After everyone finished eating, the time for business arrived.

Sanjay guided everyone back to the main room, now set with a large conference table and chairs. After the men took their seats, their host spoke.

"My friends, I apologize for the slight delay in formulating the plan to find the Enlightened Ones. Although it has taken some time to get things in order, we have made very nice progress. My thanks to each of you for your generous contributions. Here's what I suggest we do."

The plan called for each man to use his special talents and resources. Hari and Rishi would develop software to search files worldwide for clues to the existence of children with special skills or physical attributes, the Enlightened Ones. Abhay's would gather the necessary data using the software and his company's access to credit card networks. Creating the computing capacity to analyze the data fell to Bijay. He would create a supercomputer using a network of microcomputers, modeling the machine after the one first created by the Los Alamos Nuclear Research Center in New Mexico, but on a larger scale. Harshal would provide access to the needed microcomputers. His firm provided call center services for two of the world's largest antivirus software companies. He would insert a "backdoor" into the antivirus software to access the needed computers worldwide. Sanjay and Sudhir would analyze the data and coordinate future actions using their in-house staffs.

The men knew the task was daunting and expected three or four years to pass before any hard evidence would appear. The investment of a little time and a few resources could return a handsome profit. They could wait.

Part IV

SIGNS OF THINGS TO COME

Early Childhood Events

Chapter 16

Location: Overseer's Cottage, Carrington Farm, Bath County, Virginia
Time: September 2034

The Overseer's Cottage sat half the distance between the entrance to Carrington Farm and the mansion that served as a conference center. The historical registry marker near the front door of the cottage stated that it was built in the late nineteenth century, a decade before the main house. The furnishings were true to that period, although the rooms included modern conveniences and electronics.

On any other night, Mitzi Weaver would have no difficulty falling asleep in the cottage's overstuffed bed with its down-filled comforters, but tonight was different. Her mind replayed the events of the previous day at the Bath County Sheriff's Office. Each time she closed her eyes, threatening visions of Jenkins and Cox appeared. Thoughts of what they might ask about the disappearance of Chetana, Sara, and Ethan increased her anxiety and hindered sleep. An upset stomach added to her overall discomfort and caused her to awaken. *This indigestion is killing me. Best take something.* Not fully awake, she sat up in the bed, her head in her hands. Sitting upright brought new problems: nausea overwhelmed her. *I'm going to throw up. Get to the toilet. Hurry. Hurry!* Summing all her strength, she reached the toilet before she heaved. *Oh God, that was nasty. Terrible taste. Yuk!* Her ordeal partly over, she slumped on the bathroom floor and cursed last night's foolishness. *Damn it. I know better. Shouldn't have mixed scotch and ibuprofen. And Mable's food! Can't believe I ate all of those rich dumplings.* Several deep breaths and a sip of tap water did little to settle Mitzi's gastric distress or to vanquish the foul taste in her mouth. Returning to her bed, she tried to rest for a moment with little success. *This is hopeless. I can't sleep. Maybe a cup of tea? Chamomile? Yeah, that's what I need.*

It did not take long to prepare the tea, even in the dark. A few words to the automatic beverage maker completed the task. With the cup of warm tea in hand, Mitzi Weaver sat in one of the overstuffed chairs in the living room. She grabbed a throw blanket from the back of the chair and covered her shoulders and lap. *This is nice. If only the kids were here. I miss them so.*

In the quiet of the night, Weaver drifted back in time to when the children were very young, before she met Ethan, Sara, and Chetana. A time when their parents experienced the first inklings of how special their children were. Moments that their parents cherished and shared with Mitzi years later—Ethan's love of balls; Chetana's terrifying encounter in the garden; and the strange voices heard by Sara.

Half awake and half asleep, Mitzi Weaver went over each story in her mind. *I wonder if Jenkins and Cox should hear these stories. Probably not. Wonder what they'll ask me in the morning.*

At that moment, the grandfather clock by the fireplace struck one o'clock. *Damn, morning is already here! Gotta sleep.* She closed her eyes and rested as best she could.

Chapter 17

Location: University of Colorado at Denver, Health Sciences Center
Date: April 2020

The Health Sciences Center conducted its Well Baby Clinic every Tuesday morning. This morning Ethan Lake was to see Dr. Henry Belo, Emily's colleague at the university hospital. Mothers and their babies filled the waiting room when Emily Lake entered with her son. The room looked more like a children's playroom than a medical clinic. The walls were brightly colored. Life size murals of storybook characters on the walls seemed to be playing a game of chase.

"Good morning, Doctor Lake," greeted Connie Gonzalez, the receptionist at the check-in desk. "And, this must be Ethan? Isn't he the cutest little devil. Go ahead and take a sit. Doctor Belo is running a little behind but he should be with you shortly."

Today, Doctor Emily Lake was not in her role as Senior Pediatric Resident. This morning she was just another mother bringing her child for a twelve-month checkup. While she could appreciate the medical society's position on treating one's family members, Emily felt that she was best qualified to assess Ethan's health, but a second opinion could not hurt.

"Ethan Lake. Ethan Lake, please," an anonymous voice called over the public address system in the waiting room.

Emily rose, threw the strap of the diaper bag over her shoulder, adjusted her clothing, and walked toward Nurse Saylor who was waiting at the entrance to the examination area.

"Let's use Exam Room A," the nurse said as she led Emily towards one of the examining rooms. "Doctor Belo is on his way."

After the nurse closed the examination room door, Emily scanned the small space. Although she used this room last week, she observed that its character was quite different from the perspective of a patient. The room was cold and the patient chair was uncomfortable. Emily made herself as comfortable as possible with Ethan on her lap. She knew the routine all too well; she would wait here for at least ten minutes before Belo would arrive.

To pass the time, she brushed her baby's light brown hair and considered what she needed to tell her colleague during the examination. *Ethan hasn't had any significant health issues. Amazingly, not even the sniffles. Besides, that's not what Belo should check. The twelve-month checkup is to check whether a child is progressing normally. Normally? What's normal? Belo is in for a shock. Ethan isn't exactly a normal kid!*

As she wiped animal cookie crumbs from Ethan's mouth, she reminisced. *I can't believe how fast the time has passed. It seems only a few months ago that Kevin and I engaged in our little "mountain adventure" and made this little fellow. How'd I misjudged my menstrual cycle? Who's kidding who?* Hugging Ethan, and then kissing him on the forehead, she said, "You know I wanted a young man like you—don't you? And, you are a 'handsome little devil' like Connie said!"

A firm knock on the door gave notice that Doctor Belo was there. *Not bad. Only a ten minute wait. Belo is almost on schedule this morning.*

Emily worked with Henry Belo for the past several years. She respected him as a physician, but considered him more a surgeon than a clinician. She doubted that he was ready for what he was about to see.

"So, this is Ethan," Belo said as a greeting to Emily when he entered. After washing his hands, he reviewed the printed notes entered by Nurse Saylor. "I see that all of his shots are up to date. No visits to the clinic except for his checkups." He took a stethoscope from his lab coat pocket and moved toward the child. "Let's check his heart and lungs."

Emily lifted Ethan onto the examination table and placed her hands around his bottom to steady him.

Belo inserted the earpieces of the stethoscope into his ears and moved toward the examination table. As the physician came near, Ethan straightened his back and pushed his chest forward; his mother taught him what to do when she examined him. When Belo placed the instrument on Ethan's bare chest, the child cried out, "Oh, that thing cold."

Puzzlement marked the pediatrician's face. *Did he just say a complete sentence? That's not supposed to happen at his age. Very interesting.*

Emily smiled. She knew what was going on in her colleague's head and sought to confirm his observation. "Thought I'd let you see that for yourself. I think he's functioning at around 24 to 28 months of development. Go on, ask him something."

Formulating a test for a child two years old, Belo asked, "What's your name?"

"My name, Ethan," the child replied, using phraseology expected of a two year old.

"Where's your ear?"

Ethan quickly placed a hand on each ear and reported, "Here my ears!"

Before Belo could continue his assessment, Ethan reversed roles in this game he played with his mother many times before, "Where you tongue?" he asked, making a slight error in grammar.

Amazed, Belo stared at Ethan for a moment. "I think you have a very bright young man here, Emily. What have you been doing, teaching him with some of that 'kid genius' software?"

Emily chuckled, "Nope. He goes to the childcare center on campus each morning along with thirty or forty other kids."

"How's his coordination? He's walking I assume?"

"Yes, he started walking around ten months. He's getting into everything these days. As for his coordination, Kevin taught him to catch a nerf ball. You know—those soft foam balls. I think he'll surprise you. Try him. Throw something."

Under usual circumstances, Belo would not have been inclined to participate in such an exercise. A child of twelve months may toss a toy a short distance, but lacks the eye-hand coordination to catch a ball. Nevertheless, since a colleague asked for a demonstration, why not? Ripping two paper towels from the dispenser, he crushed them into a ball. "Okay, Ethan, get ready." Belo backed a few feet from the child and tossed the paper wad toward the boy.

Belo's throw was not the best—high and to the right of its target—but it did not matter. Ethan extended his right hand and snared the paper ball with ease.

"Holy crap," blurted the physician. "Ooops, excuse me. Must admit, your little guy is good. I didn't expect him to catch the thing."

"I told you," Emily said, exhibiting her motherly pride. "I don't know how my husband did it but there's no question that Ethan is rather advanced at catching things. Unfortunately, Kevin doesn't seem to be able to get him to throw any better than a normal kid his age. It's frustrating the hell out of his daddy."

The two physicians continued a clinical discussion of how Ethan was progressing. At the close of the visit, Belo typed a short note in Ethan's computerized medical record.

Well baby check, 12 mos., healthy weight, no reported problems. Child demonstrates above average language skills and the ability to catch thrown objects, consistent with a 3 or 4 yr. old.

Chapter 18

Location: Home of Ram Kapur, New Delhi, India
Time: August 2020

As he walked across the teakwood deck that traversed the rear of his home, Ram Kapur called to his wife, "It's so nice to have a few days away from the office. I hope you want some coffee. I've asked Neela to bring us some." As he sat down in a hunter green wrought iron chair next to his wife, he shuffled through a stack of magazines on the table in front of him. Stretching and yawing, he said, "I thought that EuroBanc project would never end." A chuckle crept into his voice. "I don't think I've never seen such picky managers. I swear; we checked every economic indicator imaginable. I thought they were going to ask us to count the number of condoms used by street prostitutes in Belgravia!"

"You foolish man." Kumari scolded her husband but could not help but laugh.

The two sat silently for a few moments and watched as their daughter, Chetana, examined the manicured flowerbeds and ornamental shrubbery within the walled garden. They were fortunate to have such a nice garden— thanks to Mr. Singh and his family who maintained the grounds. It would not be proper for Ram to do menial labor like gardening.

"The monsoon left everything so lush and green," Ram observed. "I see that our little girl is enjoying every flower and bush. I tell you; she's going to be a biologist one day."

Kumari smiled, "I don't think that I mentioned it, but last week she brought me a shew."

"A shrew? Was it dead?" Ram's face showed his amazement.

"To the contrary! It was alive and appeared quite happy to be resting in our daughter's hands."

Neela, a young woman who did light cooking and cared for Chetana, approached. "I have your coffee Mr. Kapur." She placed the coffee service of fine china on the glass table and turned to Kumari. "M'am, it's almost ten. Should I give Chetana her morning snack?"

"Yes; that would be nice."

Ram and Kumari watched as Neela walked towards Chetana, who sat next to a jasmine bush covered with fragrant white flowers. The child seemed captivated by the plant or by something near it. As the servant neared the child, she stopped and called out in a frightened voice, "Come. Come quickly. There's a snake. Help us, please!"

Ram shot up from his chair, anxiously searching for something to kill the reptile. Desperate, he grabbed a chair, leapt off the deck, and ran toward Neela and his child. Next to Chetana stood a king cobra posed to strike, its hood spread and its mouth opened. The black serpent rhythmically waved its head as Ram approached. *Careful. Careful. He's only inches from Chetana. Don't frighten him.*

As Ram prepared to strike the deadly snake, Chetana called out. "No, Daddy. No. Leave him alone. He won't hurt us." As the words left her mouth, she reached out and touched the snake's head. The reptile quickly lay down. Slithering past the child, it disappeared into the undergrowth.

"Thanks and praise to all the holy ones," Neela cried, overcome with joy. "The child is blessed. With her touch, she commands serpents." A devout Hindu, the servant girl fell to her knees and bowed to Chetana.

Ram took his daughter into his arms and reached down to the young woman. "Enough of that, Neela. We are all lucky the creature fled. There are no gods at work here."

Kumari remained frozen with fear as the drama unfolded. Seeing her child safely in her husband's arms, she begged, "Bring her, Ram. Bring her to me."

Neither Ram nor Kumari spoke of the events of that morning for several days, although both replayed Neela's actions and words in their minds. Surely, their child could not command creatures to do her bidding—but, then, there was that incident with the shrew!

Chapter 19

Location: Children's Center, Swedish Intelligence Building,
Stockholm, Sweden
Time: September 2021

Christina Johansson arrived at the Children's Center with Sara as she did each workday morning. As a linguist in the cryptology section of Swedish Intelligence, Christina often worked extended hours and left Sara in the childcare facility. Located in the building where she worked and funded by Swedish Intelligence, the facility enabled Christina to visit Sara for meals and to be available if the need arose.

Over the past two and a half years, Christina and Greta Gesner, the Director of the Early Childhood Program, developed a close personal relationship built around caring for Sara. When Sara's special talent for learning language first appeared, Gesner provided guidance to the child and exposed her to learning materials specially designed for intellectually gifted children. Not three years old, little Sara's vocabulary was that of an older child. To the delight of her parents and Greta, she could speak Swedish and English equally well.

As Christina and Sara entered the childcare center, Gesner greeted them. "Good morning, Doctor Johansson. And, good morning to you, Sara."

Sara nodded without speaking as her mother replied, "Good morning Greta. How are things with your son? Still have that bad chest cold?"

"Oh, he's much better." Changing the subject, Gesner asked, "Do you have a moment? There's something I would like to discuss with you regarding Sara."

"Sure, I've nothing pressing at my desk."

"Fine. Let's take Sara to the breakfast room then go to my office."

༉ळֆ

Gesner's office was no larger than a closet, into which was crammed a desk, a bookcase, and two straight back office chairs.

As the pair entered the office, Gesner asked, "Have you noticed anything strange about Sara's behavior recently?" The women sat down in the two office chairs, their knees almost touching in the small room.

Christina reflected for a moment. "No, not really." After a pause, she smiled. "Oh, do you mean her little friends?"

"Yes, I do. I guess that's what you could call them."

Christina looked inquiringly at Gesner. "Isn't it common for little girls her age to develop imaginary friends?"

"Yes, that's true. Over sixty-five percent of children will have imaginary friends between three and five; but I think Sara's case is different. She told me she hears people."

"She hears people? I don't understand. How's that different from having imaginary friends?"

Greta Gesner reached out and touched the back of Christina's hand. "Let me explain. Last week I was working with Sara on the computer when she asked if I heard someone ask a question. As we were alone working on her language software, I told her 'no' and asked what she heard. She told me 'Someone asked a question—didn't you hear it'?" Christina, you know I'm not a psychiatrist but I think she needs to be evaluated. This is not how little girls interact with imaginary friends."

"Just because she said she heard an imaginary question? I can't place much credence in that, Greta."

"I know. At first, I didn't think much of it either. Then I realized that she didn't know who was asking the question, that's what concerned me. Children with imaginary friends know who is speaking. It's as if the 'friend' is right there with them. That's what troubles me. When children hear voices and don't know who is speaking, it could be a sign of childhood schizophrenia. Although rare, I encourage you to get a consultation. If Sara has a problem, early intervention can make a significant difference."

"Greta, if it was anyone other than you, I would tell them to go to hell! But if you think we should consider it, I'll ask Oskar. If he agrees—and I'm not saying he will—who do you suggest we see?"

Gesner could see that Christina was distraught. "I have worked with Doctor Erica Schulman on several occasions. She's really good with young children. I have her phone number. I'll give it to you this afternoon when you come for Sara."

"Okay," Christina said as she stood. "I'll let you know what Oskar and I decide."

Chapter 20

Location: The Office of Erica Schulman, MD, Stockholm, Sweden
Time: October 2021

Oskar and Christina sat patiently with Sara in an interview area that resembled a nursery, complete with tables and chairs designed for small children. An assortment of toys were scattered about the brightly lit space. Little Sara entertained herself organizing wooden blocks in one of the activity centers.

A casually dressed woman, fortyish in appearance, her hair in a short ponytail, entered the room and introduced herself to Sara, ignoring Oskar and Christina. "Good morning, I'm Doctor Schulman. What is your name?"

Sara looked up at the woman. "My name is Sara Johansson. This is my mother and my father."

Schulman looked toward the two adults, smiled, and then sat in an adolescent chair in front of Sara. *Exceptional verbal skills for a three year old. Quite impressive. Seems to play well by herself.* "What are you doing?"

"Nothing. Just playing."

"Do you like to play with toys?" Schulman asked.

"Yes, I guess so, but I like to work on the computer better—especially when I'm learning new words."

Schulman paused to watch as Sara continued to work on the puzzle. *Good cognitive and motor skills.* "So you like learning words—talking with other people can be fun. Do you like to talk to your friends?"

"Yes, but mostly we just play."

"Why don't you tell me about your friends?"

Sara stopped stacking the wooden blocks and looked at Schulman. "You want to know about the voices. That's why I'm here, isn't it?"

The middle-aged woman sat up as straight as she could in the small chair. *Very perceptive child. Must have a high IQ.* With a broad smile, she answered, "Yes, Sara, tell me about the voices you hear."

"They ask me questions."

"They? Who are they?"

"I don't know. I can't see them."

"Do you answer their questions?"

"Kind of—I guess. Sometimes they ask silly things."

"Silly things? What kind of things?" Schulman shifted position again unable to find a comfortable position in the small chair.

"Oh, just stuff. Stuff like who I am and where I am—things like that. Once they asked what I was. That's silly. I told them I was a little girl. They asked me 'what's a little girl'—I thought everyone knew that!"

"I see. I guess your friends never met a little girl. Maybe they're all grown-ups." Schulman smiled as she considered the child's answer. *Striking imagination. Seems to create her own dream world and special friends.* "Do you speak out loud to them?"

"I did at first. Once when I was alone at home—I thought someone was hiding in the room—so I answered aloud. I even said something in English. It didn't seem to matter to them which language I used."

Schulman reflected for a moment on the child's responses. *Strange that she doesn't speak aloud. Most children talk to their imaginary friends. Interesting. She speaks two languages fluently.* "You said they ask you questions. Which language do they use most, Swedish or English?"

"It's not like that," the child said, her face contorted to convey that the adult did not understand. Laboring to explain herself, she continued, "It's like they just put a thought in my head—I understand what they want to know—I really don't hear words."

The expression of the psychiatrist indicated her concern with Sara's response. At that moment, a chime sounded. Schulman rose from the small chair. "Ah, that's all the time we have for today. We'll start here next week." She looked toward Christina. "I assume that next Wednesday is good for you. Same time?"

"Yes, that should be fine," Christina answered hesitantly.

As Doctor Schulman left the interview area, she made a mental note. *Could be schizophrenia but she's so young. Need to watch her a while longer. Too early for a diagnosis.*

Oskar and Christina returned Sara to visit Schulman three more times. The psychiatrist admitted Sara's behavior was troublesome. After some deliberation, she settled on a diagnosis of "hyperactive childhood imagination," and advised Oskar and Christina to monitor Sara's behavior.

If her behavior changed or if specific signs of schizophrenia developed, they should return.

Sara continued to hear voices as she grew. They did not go away. Years would past before anyone solved the mystery behind the voices.

Part V

MEETING THE CHILDREN

Weaver Meets Ethan, Sara, and Chetana

Chapter 21

Location: Overseer's Cottage, Carrington Farm, Bath County, Virginia
Time: September 2034

A glint of sunlight worked its way through the heavy curtains covering the bedroom windows. As the light grew more intense, Mitzi Weaver tossed her head left and right to escape the annoyance.

During the night, a cold front reached into the hills of western Virginia causing the temperature to drop. A chill filled the stone cottage. Mitzi grabbed the down comforter at her feet, dragging it up to her chin. *That's better. So cold.* Snuggling under the cover, the sun blocked from her eyes, she tried to rest for a moment. As she dozed, the cottage telephone rang. Struggling to reach the outmoded landline, she answered, "This is Doctor Weaver."

"Good morning, ma'am. This is Harold, the security officer at the main gate. I have two gentlemen here. They say they have an appointment with you. Should I send them up?"

Oh my God! They're here. It must be late. Adrenaline coursed through her body, now fully awake, she responded, "Yes, Harold. I am expecting them. And, could you do me a big favor?"

"Yes, ma'am. I'll try."

"Call the hotel kitchen and ask them to send me an urn of coffee and a tray of their breakfast rolls. I am running behind this morning. Wasn't expecting my guests quite so early."

"Certainly, Doctor Weaver. Glad to help."

Hurrying to get dressed and make herself presentable, Weaver tried to focus her mind on how to tell the children's story. *Where do I begin? Can't tell them everything at once! There is so much that Jenkins and Cox need to understand. They need to know who Chetana, Sara, and Ethan really were and what happened here. Which stories do I tell them?*

❧❧

Gourmet coffee and pastries from the Carrington House kitchen served their purpose; Mitzi Weaver made Lieutenant Jenkins and Special Agent Cox feel at ease in the Overseer's Cottage. Each man had a large cup of coffee and ate two croissants with black currant jam. The three engaged in the kind of light banter that people do over coffee. Cox remarked about the unusually warm fall weather and the arrival of this morning's cold front. Jenkins mentioned how September once meant the start of the baseball World Series. Both men reminisced about the death of major league baseball, a victim of exorbitant player contracts and owner greed. They could not remember when the last major league game was played. Jenkins thought it was the 2025 World Series; Cox claimed it was during the early part of the 2026 season, before contract negotiations broke down.

Jenkins took a sip of coffee, rubbed the side of his face, confirming that he failed to shave. "Well, folks, I guess we better get started. Cox, would you please check our lapel cameras. And make sure we have good audio going to the voice analyzer. You know how picky the lawyers get if the analyzer isn't set right."

"Be happy to do it," Cox replied. He tapped a button on the recording device in front of him causing a holographic screen to appear. "Let's see what we have."

Jenkins positioned himself to view the image from his lapel camera as shown on the holographic screen. "Gotta admit, Cox, it's a damn sight easier interrogating a suspect using a voice analyzer. In the past, we relied on experience and intuition to tell whether a butthead was lying—oh, my apology Doctor Weaver—no offense meant."

"None taken, Lieutenant. I don't consider myself a suspect...nor a butthead!"

Jenkins nodded, uncomfortable with his lack of professionalism. "How's it going, Cox? Are we about ready?"

"Need to check the audio input one last time. Doctor Weaver, say something for me."

"Hi, I'm Mitzi Weaver. Will that do?"

Cox adjusted two of the virtual dials displayed on the holographic screen. Nodding towards Jenkins, "Looks like everything's working. I've verified the date and location info and copied over the voice signatures from yesterday's taping. Think we're ready to go, Lieutenant."

Comfortable that the equipment was operating, Jenkins began, "Okay, let's get on with it." Taking a spiral notepad from his pocket, he scanned one page and then a second. "So, Doctor Weaver, I reviewed the video from yesterday's session. We really didn't get very far. You admitted as much last evening when we discussed relocating our interview to this location. Cox and I think it best if you start at the beginning. Why don't you just tell us—in your own words—how you came to be involved with these three children in the first place."

Mitzi paused, evaluating the question, "Do you mean how I initially met each of them?"

"Actually, before that." Jenkins consulted his spiral notebook. "You mentioned something yesterday about a cosmic blast and a study you did. Why don't you start there?"

Taking a deep breath as if in preparation for one of her many marathon races, Mitzi started. "Well, as I said yesterday, this all began some sixteen years ago. I was a post-doctoral student at Johns Hopkins back then, doing basic research in microbiology and genetics. A couple of days after the Ross-Katsura Disruption, my supervising professor suggested that I investigate its impact on human reproduction. He was interested in the genetic complications that might be linked to the event."

Jenkins raised his hand towards Weaver and shook his head. "Whoa, whoa. What's this "Cats Sury" thing?"

"Haru Katsura, the Japanese astronomer. He and the American astrophysicist, Earl Ross, discovered the cosmic disturbance that resulted in the fallout that struck the Earth—the Ross-Katsura Disruption. The disruption is critical to understanding what happened to the children."

Jenkins nodded his head as he wrote in the spiral notebook. "Ah'right. Got it. Now you were saying about this disruption having an impact on human reproduction. You mean birth defects and stillborn babies—that kinda stuff. Right?"

"Yes, that's right. It wasn't a very complicated study. Gathering the data was the major problem."

"How'd you get your data?" Cox asked.

Weaver was not sure why Cox was interested in her study methods. "It was simple enough. The techs working with me gathered information on normal births, deformities and deaths from the World Health Organization. At the time, they were the only organization gathering such data."

"Okay, go on," prompted Jenkins. "You said the study took a while. How long?"

"Let's see. We gathered data for about two years, starting from the date of the event. We reasoned that any problems not evident during pregnancy or at birth should be noticed within a year after the final cohort of children was born."

Jenkins looked puzzled. "Let me get this straight. I believe that a 'cohort' is just a fancy name for a group of folks—in this case, the babies. You reasoned that the last affected child would be born within nine months after this cosmic event, and you waited a year to see if any birth defects would pop-up. Is that about it?"

The previous day's interview made Weaver aware that Jenkins frequently asked questions that might make him appear a little slow on the uptake, but she knew better than to underestimate him. "Yes, that's right."

"So, what'd you learn from your study?" Jenkins asked.

"The results were quite interesting. We found that there was a statistically significant increase in fetal deaths and birth defects following Ross-Katsura." Mitzi sat up and proudly smiled. "This was my first major study. We couldn't get it published in the *Journal of Pediatrics* for almost a year. That's how Emily, Ethan's mother, came to see the article. Like I said yesterday, she's a pediatrician."

Jenkins smirked and waved his hand aimlessly. "Yeah, I recall. I believe you said that you knew her from your undergraduate days at the University of Texas. I think you said that she called you after reading the study. That right?"

"Yes, to both of your statements. We were lab assistants our senior year at UT in Austin. She was pre-med and I was a biology major. We developed a close friendship that year, but lost touch when we graduated and she moved to Colorado for med school."

Cox leaned forward wanting to move the interrogation forward. "Okay. So, back to when Emily called you. What happened?"

Mitzi Weaver slipped back to that day at Johns Hopkins when Emily Lake called with an intriguing question—a question that would change Mitzi's professional and personal life.

Chapter 22

Location: McKusick-Nathans Institute of Genetic Medicine,
Johns Hopkins University
Time: October 2022

Mitzi Weaver worked feverishly to clear correspondence from her desk. Everyone wanted more information on the genetic problems associated with the Ross-Katsura Disruption. She was in no mood for another interruption when the phone rang. "Hello, this is Doctor Weaver."

"Hi, Mitzi. This is Emily Lake. I was Emily Sopko. Remember me?"

The voice on the telephone sounded familiar. "Emily? Is that you?" In rapid succession, Mitzi went on. "I got your graduation announcement when you received your MD. Are you still in Colorado?"

"Yeah, still in Colorado at the University Hospital in Denver. I'm a Senior Resident in Pediatric Medicine. And you! I see that you're in microbiology at Johns Hopkins. I knew you would get to the top in a hurry." Emily paused, uncertain whether to ask the question that prompted her call.

"So why are calling today—not that I'm not pleased to hear from you!"

"I read your article in the *Journal of Pediatrics*, Mitzi. It was very interesting, but I have a question. I know that you looked for fetal deaths, deformities and other 'pre' and 'postnatal' complications, but did you consider if there may have been positive outcomes?"

"Positive outcomes?" Mitzi repeated, her voice clearly indicating her uncertainty regarding the question.

"Yes. Instead of negative conditions, like birth defects and deformities, did you consider that there may have been an increase in the number of gifted children?"

"No. We didn't. The World Health Organization's disease and morbidity reports only cover medical and surgical conditions that fall within the International Classification of Diseases. As a physician, you know that. Why the question?"

"Oh, it's a personal thing. You see, I have a son—."

Mitzi squealed, interrupting Emily in mid-sentence. "Congratulations! You have two children now—don't you?"

"Yes, Melissa and Ethan. It's because of Ethan that I'm calling. He is...well, he's very special. He's three and a half now and has the vocabulary of a child almost twice his age. He loves anything to do with numbers. Can you believe that he's doing simple addition and subtraction problems? I know it's hard to believe that a three year old is doing math, but he's a very special little guy."

Weaver was pleased to hear that her friend's child was doing so well, but was still uncertain where Emily was going with her inquiry. "And, what does this have to do with my research?"

"Here's the whole thing in a nutshell." Emily took an audible breath. "Ethan was conceived on the day that thing happened—what did you call it in the article—the Ross-Katsura Disruption. Could his genetic make-up have been altered, like the children with deformities, but in a positive way?"

Mitzi paused mulling over Emily's question. With some uncertainty in her voice, she answered. "I...I guess so. We didn't explore that possibility."

❧❧

Over the next few weeks, Emily and Mitzi exchanged several telephone calls and e-mail messages. Emily described in clinical language Ethan's development: how he began forming sentences when only ten-months old, a full year ahead of other children; and, how when he was two years old, he possessed a vocabulary of a three or four year old child. Moreover, there was his math aptitude and his interest in the world around him—all skills associated with much older children. Another trait Ethan liked to demonstrate was his ability to catch and hit a ball—skills that pleased his father. Emily explained how Kevin told her repeatedly, "The boy's a natural—a chip off the old block." Emily did not know what a *natural* was until Kevin explained. "It's a person born to play baseball—a natural player. He just knows where the ball's going be and is on it quicker than a frog on a fly!" Kevin liked using southern sayings.

Weaver was too busy to visit Ethan in Colorado when Emily called. Besides, first things, first. Her interest as a microbiologist and geneticist piqued, Mitzi needed to explore how she might answer Emily's question: "Did Ross-Katsura have positive effects on *in utero* genetics?"

Chapter 23

Location: Penthouse, Grand Hyatt Dubai, United Arab Emirates
Time: January 2023

"I love this place!" Abhay walked across the terrace of the penthouse suite of the Grand Hyatt Hotel. Below lay the exquisite and extravagant architecture for which Dubai is known. "Don't you just love what money can do?"

The magnificent buildings of Dubai, each an effort to demonstrate wealth and innovation, cast a fairy-tale like spell over Abhay. Not even the well-heeled members of the Bombay Gentlemen were immune to the intoxicating aroma of power and opulence that filled the air.

Sanjay called to Abhay and the other men standing on the terrace. "Gentlemen, gentlemen, please. We must get started." As the men found places on the leather couches that filled the grand room of the penthouse, he continued, "We must decide what is to be done about this new information."

"So what did your man find in Bhutan," Sudhir asked. "Did he find the boy?"

"Yes, my man found where the child lived, but he was too late." Sanjay waited for everyone to find a seat before continuing. "It so bloody disappointing. As I understand it, my man found that a local tribesman killed the boy the night before he arrived. Such luck!"

"What?" Hari's voice and manner conveyed his indignation. "Someone murdered a child? Why?" Hari, the father of five children, was a devoted family man. Admittedly, he possessed a darker side, having participated in the honor killing of his youngest sister when she refused to consummate a marriage arranged by their parents.

Sanjay turned to Hari and answered his question. "Yes. I'm afraid someone did kill an Enlightened One. As our reports indicate, the child possessed the power to 'see into a man's soul'—according to the locals. We have good evidence of his power. Faithful Buddhist believers visited the young boy. The child's touch could impart a sense of wellbeing. Some said he could open a gateway to nirvana. However, there was a catch: the believer must be free of wrongdoing! When first the child touched a supplicant, it was as if he could read the person's mind. If he saw evil, he told the person to go and correct the wrongdoing."

"You mean the little bastard was a mind reader?" Abhay blurted. "Damn, imagine how useful that would have been."

"To continue." Sanjay disliked interruptions and gave Abhay a disapproving glance. "The day the child died, he met with a tribesman. Seems the fellow slept with his brother's wife, so the boy told him to go and make amends to his brother. Well, that public statement so offended the man that he returned later that evening and torched the child's house."

"The child burned to death!" Rishi exclaimed. "Bloody terrible way to die!"

Sanjay gave Rishi the same glance of disapproval that Abhay received. "Now to continue. That is not the end of the story. While the child and his family burned within the house, the tribesman stood in front of the small dwelling. Suddenly, he began screaming, as if consumed by the fire himself. Many of the locals told my man the boy reached out to the tribesman with his mind and transferred the pain he was experiencing to his tormentor."

"Sanjay! My good man." Sudhir stood and shook his head to show his disbelief of what he heard. "Are you saying the boy was a telepath?"

Not wishing to confront the elder member of the group, Sanjay lowered his head and drew his shoulders together. "I'm not sure. Perhaps, just perhaps, he was."

Harshal raised his arms high and called out, "Maybe there is some upside potential to our investment after all. While I grieve the loss of the boy, I'm encouraged by this report. I was beginning to lose faith in the tales that Manish told us."

"But we have identified only one candidate," Hari offered. "And he is now dead!"

A wide smile began to form on Sanjay's face as he shook his finger at Hari. "Not so my friend. Yes, this boy died but several other candidates surfaced this month—one in Napal, another here in India, two in Europe, and two in the United States."

"Marvelous!" Hari said enthusiastically. "I see profit at our doorstep."

Satisfied that their venture was moving in the right direction, the consortium of business executives evaluated alternative plans for tracking the progress of the children described by Sanjay. The key to success was finding and gaining control of the children with the greatest intellectual potential.

Bijay suggested, "Let's not be wimps here, my friends. We must be prepared to take decisive action when the time comes. I'm prepared to do whatever is necessary to achieve a profitable outcome in this endeavor!"

Chapter 24

Location: McKusick-Nathans Institute of Genetic Medicine,
            Johns Hopkins University
Time: February 2023

A year ago, Mitzi Weaver received a call from her friend, Emily Lake who asked if Ross-Katsura could have caused certain children to develop special skills and talents. Her son, conceived during the cosmic particle shower, showed signs of exceptional development. Intrigued by her friend's question, Weaver consulted her colleagues about the proposed research. With the help of the University Research Projects office, she received preliminary funding for the study. The first step was to learn more about the composition of the Ross-Katsura. A visit to the Physics Department on campus pointed her to the Fermi National Laboratory located near Chicago, Illinois.

"Santini."

Weaver was not sure what she heard. *Did he say "Santini"? Is that any way to answer a damn phone?* Biting her tongue, she politely asked, "Is this Doctor Benjamin Santini at the Fermi National Lab?"

"You got him," the young male voice replied. Santini was twenty-six years old, an age when physicists start to peak intellectually. An Irish mother and a Sicilian father gave him sandy blond hair, light olive skin, and "Sandy" as a nickname. His IQ and his egocentric personality made him appear aloof to most people, and to some, downright rude.

"This is Doctor Mitzi Weaver with Johns Hopkins. Peter Cantu, in the Physics Department here, gave me your name. He said that you co-authored a report on the Ross-Katsura Disruption."

"That's right, me and eight other guys—four here and four in Europe. So you read the initial report or did you read the proceedings from the conference in Chicago?"

Weaver felt somewhat embarrassed. "Actually, I read the synopsis you distributed during your presentation in Chicago. Pete attended and gave me his copy. Even the synopsis is a little over my head. I'm in microbiology and genetics. Cosmology and subatomic particles are, well, they're out of my field."

"So why are you calling," Santini asked in a demanding tone. He did not like interruptions when he was working.

Mitzi took a deep breath and exhaled before responding. She did not like "academic assholes"—her preferred term for colleagues like Santini—but she needed his help. "Here's the deal. I published a paper on prenatal complications linked to Ross-Katsura. We demonstrated a statistical link between the event and certain complications of pregnancies like genetic deformities, premature deliveries and stillborn births. What we are investigating now is whether there are links to less salient conditions—physical strength, growth rates, and intelligence. To do so, we think it is important to understand the nature and composition of the fallout. I was told that you might be able to help us."

Santini was an unbound intellect in constant search of new problems to solve. Weaver's problem struck his fancy. "This isn't my usual type of research. I lean toward theoretical problems, not applied research. Although, I do find your problem intriguing."

"I wish you would consider working with us," Weaver said in a gentle voice. Her thoughts were not as kind. *You arrogant asshole. Yeah, imagine that, physics applied to real people! What's the world coming to?*

"Before I agree to anything, Doctor Weaver, I need to hear more about what might be involved in this project. Just what are you looking for in the fallout material?"

The two spent the next half hour discussing research problems related to identifying which particles, rays, and electromagnetic pulses associated with the disruption could affect embryonic development. Weaver tolerated Santini's initial arrogance and naivety about her field of study. At the end of the phone call, Santini recalled that someone at the CERN Laboratory in Switzerland was doing a comprehensive study on the particle composition of Ross-Katsura. He offered to contact the person, Doctor Celia Foxe.

Chapter 25

Location: The Overseer's Cottage, Carrington Farm, Bath County, Virginia
Time: September 2034

Lieutenant Phil Jenkins stood and stretched to relieve the tension in his back. He listened as Doctor Mitzi Weaver recounted how she came to know the three children who disappeared two days ago. He recalled something from the previous day's interrogation. "Now this Foxe woman, wasn't she the one that worked with Doctor Johnson in Switzerland?"

"That's Johansson—Oskar Johansson. Yes, he worked with her, although at the time, I hadn't met either of them. I was working with Sandy—Doctor Santini. He introduced me to Doctor Foxe via a Skype video connection. Skype was like our video communicators today, but it used InstaDat, or the Internet, as it was called back then."

"Okay, get on with it." Jenkins' gruffness reflected his need to relieve himself of his morning coffee.

Mitzi Weaver explained that when she contacted Celia Foxe, she learned Foxe was completing an investigation of the atomic and subatomic particles delivered by the cosmic wave. To her surprise, Celia knew of the Johns Hopkins study. In fact, the World Health Organization was a co-sponsor of Foxe's study. The Organization was concerned that a pandemic might occur because of exposure to the cosmic barrage—cancer or diseases similar to those experienced by Japanese exposed to radiation in World War II. When Mitzi explained that she was studying the potential positive genetic effects of the event, Foxe offered an interesting bit of information. The daughter of a visiting physicist, an Oskar Johansson and his wife, Christina, had an exceptionally gifted child who was born nine months after the event. Could this be just a coincidence or something more?

Weaver was elated to learn of another gifted child, like Ethan Lake, Emily's son. She arranged to visit the Johansson family in Stockholm to meet Sara and her family.

Chapter 26

Location: Johansson Family Home, Stockholm, Sweden
Time: March 2023

The Volvo taxi jerked to a stop, then accelerated quickly only to come to an abrupt stop. Traffic leaving Stockholm-Arlanda Airport crept along at a snail's pace. Cars and transit buses competed for every inch of roadway. Horns blared. Engines belched noxious diesel fumes.

Mitzi Weaver was not a road warrior. She found no pleasure in international travel. Sixteen hours earlier, she boarded a Maryland Area Regional Commuter train at a station near her apartment, in route to Baltimore-Washington International Airport. There she caught a flight to Chicago O'Hare International. After a three-hour layover in Chicago, Mitzi boarded a Scandinavian Airlines flight. Nine hours later, the aircraft landed in Sweden. As the aircraft pulled into the jet way, a cabin attendant announced that local time was 7:46 AM. Weaver did not sleep on the plane. Sleep deprived and feeling the effects of jet lag, she struggled to concentrate as she negotiated her way through customs and the congested airport terminal. What she needed was a relaxing bath and several hours of sleep, but she was eager to reach her destination—those personal indulgences would have to wait.

The traffic began to clear as the taxi found its way onto the highway leading to the main campus of the University of Stockholm, some forty kilometers south of the airport. Committed to making up lost time, the driver stomped the accelerator, leaving his passenger fearful for her life as he weaved in and out of traffic.

An hour after departing the airport, Weaver reached her destination. She paid the taxi driver and stood for a moment on the sidewalk in front of the Johansson home. *Damn jetlag is killing me! Breathe. Breathe. Get your act together, Mitzi! You're here. You have to talk to this little girl.* Cold morning wind buffeted her face and helped to clear her head. Partly revived, Mitzi studied the house and yard before her. *Steps! Why did there have to be steps? I'm so tired. My God, they are steep!*

The Johansson house was an ultramodern structure built into a small knoll to increase its energy efficiency—a wise choice for a northern clime. Several inches of snow covered the yard. A dozen steps led from the street to the front door. On either side of the glass entryway were oversized windows that provided passive solar heating.

As Weaver summed the strength to tackle the steps that led to the house, the front door abruptly opened, startling her.

A woman around thirty, with flaxen hair and blue eyes, stood in the doorway. Standing next to her was a small child, with the same color hair and eyes, undeniably the woman's daughter.

"Hi, come in," the woman called out in English, flavored with a Swedish accent. "I'm Christina and this is Sara."

Mitzi gathered the jogging bag that contained everything she would need for a three-day visit and started up the steps. Halfway to the door, she said, "Thank you for allowing me to come. You have a lovely home." Mitzi felt no need to introduce herself farther. Christina was expecting her.

The interior of the house looked like a display at the Ikea Store back in Baltimore. White pine covered the floor of the large entry room. A flat screen television, recessed into the wall, dominated one side of the room. In front of the television sat a three-piece, sectional couch that separated the kitchen and dining area from the entertainment center. The couch, covered with a coarsely woven white fabric, matched the chairs around the table.

"Hi, I'm Celia. Do I look different in person?" a voice behind Mitzi asked.

Turning to see who spoke, Weaver recognized Celia Foxe from their video conferences. "I didn't expect to see you here. It's so nice to meet you face-to-face." Mitzi started to extend her hand in greeting when Celia engulfed her in a bear hug. *Wow. She sure is friendly. My kind of person.*

As the three women visited, Christina prepared a pot of tea and a tray of *smörgas*, a traditional Swedish, open-faced breakfast sandwich topped with butter, cheese and cold cuts. Mitzi did not realize how hungry she was; the food and friendly hospitality energized her. While the women sat at the dining table and chatted, Mitzi observed that Sara did not speak but kept a watchful eye on them from across the room.

Christina called to Sara in Swedish. Sara rose and started towards the women. As she approached, she said in English, "Mother, you should use English. I don't think that Doctor Weaver speaks Swedish." As if to explain her mother's actions, she continued, "Momma asked me to come to the table so you could talk with me."

Mitzi could not believe her ears. Her mind raced. *Did this child just say what I heard? She can't be more than four. My niece is her age and doesn't speak that fluently, much less in a second language!* All Mitzi could manage was, "Thank you, I'm afraid the only language I speak is English." As if in defense of her lack of language skills, she added, "I do read a little Spanish."

Sara smiled, amused by Mitzi. "I know. Not everyone likes languages." Standing only three feet tall and weighing thirty-five pounds, she wore a green turtleneck shirt, a short black skirt, and black leggings that accentuated her thin frame. The dark green shirt made her champagne hair appear almost platinum. Her mother's genes were evident in Sara's hair color and in her full lips; lips that appeared a bit too large for her cherubic face.

"Do you know how many languages I can speak?" Sara asked, and not waiting for a reply, continued. "I speak five languages—Swedish, French, German and Arabic—and of course, English. Momma taught me Arabic. It's hard. The letters are not like English. Daddy taught me German. Momma and Daddy both speak English. I taught myself French. Celia helped me. You know, Daddy works in Geneva sometimes. They speak German and French there."

Mitzi sat quietly, mesmerized by the child's fluency and almost adult behavior. *This can't be! How can a child her age have learned five languages?*

Sara looked at Mitzi, quizzically, unable to interpret the woman's silence. She was, after all, a child, with only a child's understanding of interpersonal communication. Not sure how to cope with the silence, Sara asked, "You want to see my room?"

Mitz and Sara spent the next two days getting to know each other better. Mitzi recorded every word Sara spoke, including conversations with Celia in French and with her mother in Swedish and Arabic. The evening before Mitzi was to leave, Oskar and Sara spoke in German; he would point to an item and Sara would call out its name. Captivated with the game, Sara began saying the name of every item in each of the five languages she knew.

On the flight home, Mitzi listened to the recordings she made of Sara. The child's skill fascinated her, although she could not understand anything the child said. Of this Mitzi was certain; little Sara, was exceptionally gifted. *I must visit Emily and meet her son, Ethan. Could he be as amazing as little Sara?*

Chapter 27

Location: Mountain Retreat of Hari,
　　　　　　Near the City of Imphal, Northeast India
Time: April 2023

Hari chose to host the meeting of the Gentlemen's group at his three-story chalet in the mountains of northern India. The structure rested on the rim of an emerald green valley. From the chalet's balcony, one could see several ornate Buddhist and Hindu temples in the valley. The location had a sense of remoteness while being only a half-hour drive from the airport at Imphal, the capital of the northeastern state of Manipur.

Sanjay announced to the gathered men, "Our investment is about to bear fruit. The potential gain that lies ahead is as vast as the glorious valley that is at our doorstep."

Rishi whispered to Bijay, "Sanjay reads too much poetry. He sounds like a Shakespearian actor."

Bijay chuckled causing him to dribble some tea from his mouth. "Now look what you have made me do, Rishi!" Smiling, Bijay poked Rishi on the arm. Both men tried to contain themselves as Sanjay cast a critical gaze in their direction.

Bijay clasped his hands together as in prayer. "Please excuse us, Sanjay. Rishi is being a monkey's ass. I am but his lowly victim."

Sanjay took a sip of aromatic white tea before continuing his report. "The software developed by Rishi and Hari provided us with reams of data. The supercomputer, so adroitly constructed by Bijay, allowed Sudhir and me to work through the data with very good results." Pausing for another sip of tea, Sanjay looked at Sudhir and smiled. "Our most interesting finding is that we have competition in our endeavor to find these special children. We discovered a group in the States has a similar study underway. They could become serious competitors. But as they lack our most excellent computer network, they have identified only two of the children that we have located: the girl in Stockholm and the boy in Denver—none of the others. I believe Denver is in the State of Colorado, is that correct Rishi?"

Everyone knew Rishi completed advanced degrees in the United States, prompting Sanjay's inquiry. Caught with a succulent piece of mango in his mouth, Rishi struggled to speak. "Yes, yes, that's correct. Actually, I visited Denver with a group of skiers. The mountains of Colorado are as breathtaking as the ones here."

Sanjay smiled, pleased that he caught Rishi with his mouth full. *Now we are even, my friend. Do not toy with your elders.* "Excellent. And, now back to our subject." Sanjay moved towards the seated group and struck an actor's pose. "Gentlemen, it is time to act. Although our competition has not identified the girl in New Delhi, Sudhir and I believe we should move to acquire her first. She's in our backyard. Easy access, as I see it."

"What do you mean by *acquire?*" Hari asked.

"Hari raises a good point." Sudhir spoke, taking charge of the discussion. "We have committed both capital and labor to this venture. It's time to reap some profit. To do so, we must control these special children."

"And how do you propose to take control of them?" Harshal asked the question that others in the group were thinking.

Sudhir slapped the arm of his chair. "Damn it, let's get serious. We must have control over these assets if we are to benefit from whatever special skills they possess. It is clear now that the boy may be a math genius and the girl here in India may have talent that we cannot begin to measure—some say she is a living deity. These are very valuable assets! We must do whatever is necessary."

"Okay, then. What is your plan?" Abhay demanded. "Do we kidnap her? Can she be purchased from her family—perhaps as a bride?"

Bijay sat quietly listening to the exchange, and then stood. "Come, come, gentlemen. Let us accept that our actions must be quick and decisive. If you agree, I shall arrange to take control of the girl in New Delhi. Best leave the details to me. I have contacts with men that—for a few American dollars—will do whatever is necessary."

Each man looked at Bijay, giving his blessing to the unspoken plan. Bijay would make the necessary arrangements. The fate of the child was in his hands.

Chapter 28

Location: The Overseer's Cottage, Carrington Farm, Northern Virginia
Time: September 2034

Lieutenant Jenkins rose from his chair. "That's it, I'm fried! Let's take a break and get something to eat. Think we can get something up at the Carrington house?"

Jenkins' words were music to Mitzi Weaver. The morning had taken its toll; she was hungry and needed a break. "Oh, yes. You'll love it. They have a nice buffet for lunch."

"Well, that's fine with me." Jenkins looked to his colleague. "What do you say Cox? Are you hungry?"

"Yeah, I could eat something. Let me hit the john first."

Weaver reached for a light jacket. "Let's walk up. It's lovely outside. I'm sure we could all use a little fresh air. What do you say?"

Both men agreed. Cox placed the recording equipment in "sleep mode" while Jenkins retrieved their jackets.

The red cinder walkway that lead from the Overseer's Cottage to the mansion passed by a long, narrow pond enclosed by an earthen dam. As the group walked past the pond, Special Agent Cox stopped. "Is that where it happened, Doctor Weaver? Did the children disappear from down there?"

"Over there, near the tree." Weaver pointed towards a small evergreen near the edge of the lake.

The two men studied the area, creating mental images of the shoreline and surrounding area. As professional investigators, the pond was the crime scene.

"Hey, Cox, enough with the interview stuff," Jenkins grumbled. I don't have my lapel cam turned on. Even if she admitted that she drowned them kids in that pond, we couldn't use it without an audio recording. Besides, it's lunchtime. Let it rest!"

❧

The food, delicious as promised, included home-fried chicken, tender pot roast, mashed potatoes with real cream gravy, and a medley of oven roasted root vegetables and squashes. For dessert, there was a deep-dish apple pie baked in an iron skillet four inches deep and twenty-four inches across. Jenkins demonstrated how he managed to maintain his two-hundred-plus pounds by having a generous helping of each item, including the apple pie.

While dining, Mitzi was conscious of the stares coming from the clergy whose retreat was still underway. Apparently, word spread among them about the disappearance of the children. She studied the clerics and their religious garments—a Buddhist monk robed in saffron cloth, a priest in purple vestments, and a rabbi wearing a black felt hat with long locks of hair in front of each ear. *Who are these people, anyway? Guess they never heard the saying, 'Judge not, that ye be not judged.'*

Special Agent Cox took the linen napkin from his lap and dabbed his mouth. "This is a nice place, and the food is excellent. No offense to Sheriff Jones, but it sure beats his interrogation room."

Chuckling, Jenkins said something that neither Cox nor Weaver understood, as the Lieutenant's mouth was full. The three managed light conversation during their meal, being careful not to talk about the disappearance of Ethan, Chetana and Sara. Mitzi chose to ignore the stares of the other guests in the dining room.

After eating, Mitzi and the two men started back to the cottage. The noonday sun was bright and unseasonably warm. The group walked slowly. No one seemed in a hurry to return to the task that lay ahead.

As they reached the cottage, Cox stopped to admire Mitzi's Tesla sports car. "You won't believe this, but I'm still driving a Chevy Volt. Bought it after leaving the FBI Academy." With a sense of pride, he added, "The damn thing just will not die—has almost two hundred thousand miles on it!"

Entering the cottage, Cox checked the recorders while Jenkins visited the bathroom. Mitzi did not sleep well last night and felt drowsy after her large lunch. *God, I could use a nap about now. Not much chance of that happening!* She sat down in the overstuffed armchair where she spent the morning session and watched as Cox adjusted the audio and holographic recording equipment.

An unmistakable sound came from the direction of the bathroom. Weaver and Cox looked at each other and tried to muffle their laugher.

In a hushed voice Cox said, "Either Jenkins has terrible gas or he accidently discharged his weapon. Tell you the truth; I'm not sure which it was!"

Mitzi grinned and shook her head in agreement. "I think you're right, but it sounded more like a cannon than a pistol."

Cox and Mitzi chuckled like a couple of school kids until the bathroom door began to open. Both struggled to wipe the grins off their faces. Cox returned to his task of adjusting the recording equipment and Weaver closed her eyes and pretended to doze.

Jenkins sat down in the chair facing Weaver and fiddled with his lapel camera. "Well, is everything ready, Agent Cox?"

"Yes, sir. Everything looks good to me."

"Okay folks, let's get to it." The Lieutenant removed the spiral notepad from his shirt pocket and flipped through several pages. Satisfied that he was ready, he started the interview. "Doctor Weaver, before lunch you told us about the time you met young Sara in Stockholm. You said when you left there that you planned to meet the boy named Ethan. You wanna pick it up from there?"

"Okay. Well, when I returned from Stockholm, my plans were to visit Emily and to meet Ethan in Colorado, but Emily changed that. Shortly after I returned, she called to say that she and Ethan would be in Baltimore the following week."

"What caused her to visit you?" Cox asked.

"Emily knew that Ethan was special. She had begun checking on schools that catered to talented and gifted children. She learned that Johns Hopkins offered one of the best programs in the country, the Julian C. Stanley Study of Exceptional Talent. The program helped high IQ children to achieve their full potential through specialized instruction."

Cox nodded several times, then said, "So, Doctor Lake decided to visit Johns Hopkins, saving you a trip to Colorado. Why'd she think that this program was right for her son?"

"Well, it served children with high math and verbal skills. A child under thirteen with a score of seven hundred on the math or verbal parts of the old SAT exam could enter the program."

"Seven hundred!" Cox whistled in amazement. "I took the SAT to get into college. I scored almost six hundred on the math section. If I remember correctly, that was above average."

Jenkins took a sudden interest in the discussion. "So, you're saying kids in this program were real geniuses? And this Ethan, he got into the program?"

"Yes. Eventually, all of the children did, Sara, Chetana, and Ethan."

The two men sat quietly for a minute before Cox said, "Okay, Doctor Weaver, let's get back to when you first met with Ethan and his mother. How'd that go?"

"That was over ten years ago, but that day is so clear in my mind." Mitzi paused and licked her lips to moisten them. "I think that I remember it so well because Emily was there. We were such close friends in college and I had not seen her for five years." Weaver repositioned herself in the overstuffed chair and thought of that day when she first met Ethan. *What should I tell these guys? How cute little Ethan was? How smart? Of course, there was that damn visit from the Secretary of Health and Human Services!*

102

Chapter 29

Location: Office of Mitzi Weaver, Johns Hopkins University
Time: April 2023

Mitzi Weaver came to work early. There was much to do before she went to the airport to meet Emily and Ethan. As she scanned DNA reports, her cell phone rang; it was not good news. The director of the McKusick-Nathans Institute of Genetic Medicine called instructing her to attend a special meeting arranged for that morning. The Secretary of Health and Human Services decided to visit the campus to review federally funded projects. He was particularly interested in the Institute's progress to identify genetic markers associated with Type I diabetes. Weaver supervised a significant portion of the research. She had no choice but to meet with the Secretary. This was a command performance.

"Charlie, help," Mitzi called to her graduate assistant in the office next to hers.

In an instant, a young man dressed in blue surgical scrubs appeared at her office door. "Yes, ma'am. What do you need?"

"Aren't you scheduled to pick up biologicals at the airport this morning?"

"Yes, ma'am. I'm going around lunchtime."

"Oh, thank goodness. My friend and her son are due in from Colorado on Continental Flight 249. Would you please meet them at Gate 52B for me? They'll be in around one o'clock."

"Of course. No problem. I'll just have lunch out there. They have great pizza in the terminal—deep dish with everything on it."

"Excellent!" Weaver took her wallet from her desk. "Here, pizza is on me."

❧

By the time Weaver freed herself from the meeting with the Secretary and returned to her office, Emily and Ethan were there. "Hi!" she said enthusiastically, her arms outstretched. "I see you found the place. You're looking great!"

Emily stood and embraced her friend. "You're being kind. As you see, there's a little more of me now than when we were at UT—but I'm feeling good—just haven't been able to lose these extra pounds from my pregnancy. Enough about me; how about yourself? Trim as ever, I see. Bet you run every day. Wish I could find the time to run!"

Mitzi sat down on the couch next to Emily. "Well you're a busy mom with a daughter and this handsome young man. I'm not that blessed." She reached out and touched Emily's shoulder, then turned to the child. "And what's your name?"

Ethan was large for his age. Mitzi surmised that Emily's nurturing and Kevin's genes accounted for his size. She could see traits of Emily and Kevin in the boy—grey-blue eyes, rusty brown hair, and ears that angled away from his head, a gift from his father.

The child slid off the couch and stood in front of Weaver. "I'm Ethan. What's your name?"

"Mitzi." Weaver bent at the waist to be face to face with the child.

"Momma told me you're a scientist. I guess you like math?"

Weaver recognized that Ethan did not possess Sara's language skills, although his language skills were quite good for his age.

Without waiting for Mitzi to reply to his first question, Ethan began to ramble. "I like math and baseball. I 'specially like to figure things out. Know how many eggs you would have if you had six dozen eggs, but you broke two dozen and Mr. Fox stole eighteen eggs?" Again, not waiting for the answer, he continued. "I also like baseball. Do you know how far a player runs if he hits a homer? Three hundred sixty feet! That's ninety feet between each of the four bases. Wanna know how many feet per second a baseball travels if the pitcher can throw it at eighty-five miles per hour?"

"Okay! That's enough," Emily ordered. "We understand you like math and baseball." Turning to Mitzi, she smiled and said, "That husband of mine has loaded his head with every conceivable bit of baseball trivia you can imagine. Actually, I think Kevin ran out of 'numbers' for the boy. Ethan's a math sponge—he loves the stuff."

Weaver was astounded. She experienced the same sense of disbelief she felt when she met Sara. *He just turned four! A four year old should be in pre-kindergarten learning to use crayons, not doing math problems in his head. Maybe he's just a math savant. Maybe his abilities have nothing to do with the cosmic fallout. Gotta get him tested this afternoon. That should tell us more.*

❦

Before Weaver left the campus that evening, she received the answer to her question: Ethan possessed the highest math IQ ever recorded for a four year old at the Julian C. Stanley Study of Exceptional Talent. Although only four, Ethan received an invitation to participate in the summer program the following year.

Chapter 30

Location: Office of Bijay, Mumbai, India
Time: June 2023

"Damn it man, I'm telling you they took the bloody girl to the States!" Bijay shouted into the webcam. "I hacked the airline manifests. They left New Delhi this morning and won't return until next Thursday."

"It does not matter my friend," replied Rishi, half-yawning. "We can still implement your plan. The girl will be ours."

Bijay studied Rishi's video image. "Are you in your underwear?"

"Yes. I'm getting dressed. Your message was coded 'urgent' so it came to my home. I have you on the monitor in my bedroom."

"Enough of this." Bijay crossed his arms and frowned. "You agreed to help me. What are we going to do? How can we stay on schedule if the girl is in America?"

"Not to worry," Rishi responded in a pacifying tone. "You said that they are due back on Thursday. The first phase of the plan does not happen until Saturday. Remember? That's when this Kapur fellow attends the reception for his boss. He's not going to miss such an important event. Leave it to me. We have our best men handling everything. And of course, I'll be there."

"Okay, but if you need anything, let me know." A smile formed on Bijay's face as he started to close the video link. "Please get dressed, my friend. Your manliness is hanging out in the front—what little there is of it!"

The screen went blank before Rishi could respond. *Bijay, you piece of monkey dung! I'll get you. Just wait!*

Chapter 31

Location: The Overseer's Cottage, Carrington Farm, Bath County, Virginia
Time: September 2034

Special Agent Cox looked at Jenkins, who was "resting his eyes" for the moment. *Looks like I lost Jenkins. Better take the lead. She told us how she met Ethan and Sara. What about the other girl?* "Doctor Weaver, as I recall from yesterday, the other child came from India. Kumari was her name—no, that's her mother. Chetana, that's her name. How'd you come to meet her?"

"Fate, that's how." Weaver hesitated for a moment. "Ram, Chetana's father, happened to be in New York to visit banking clients. I was in the city to do an interview on one of the network morning shows. Do you remember those old shows?"

Lieutenant Jenkins, opened his eyes, suddenly revived by Weaver's question. He was old enough to remember national broadcast networks. "Yeah, that was before the cable conglomerates took over. I recall how my wife would watch those shows every morning."

Mitzi smiled at Jenkins. *The old fart was married. Bless that poor woman's soul!* "You're right. Lots of folks started their day that way. The shows were popular back then. Anyway, a producer at one of the networks called me about doing a follow-up piece on my research on the effects of Ross-Katsura."

"Let me guess. Chetana's father saw the story and contacted you—right?" Cox asked.

"That's about it. Ram was watching television that morning and happened to catch my interview. I mentioned my hope to conduct a study to determine if there were any positive genetic links to Ross-Katsura. After my interview ended, Ram called the television station and managed to get me. I was fascinated by what he said and agreed to meet him."

Intrigued, Cox asked, "What made Ram think you were talking about his daughter?"

Weaver leaned forward, smiled, and gently shook her head. "Well, that's a story all by itself. You see, Ram and Kumari were trying to deal with Chetana's unique skills but they could not agree on what to do. As Ram put it—quite some time after we met—Kumari and her mother wanted to make Chetana a 'religious sideshow,' as he called it. He, on the other hand, felt Chetana should have a normal life—go to school, have friends—normal stuff." Weaver paused, as if to collect her thoughts. *Damn, I'm tired. Haven't slept much the last couple of nights.* She stretched, placing her hands behind her head, before continuing her story. "Anyway, back to how I originally met Chetana and her family."

Jenkins interrupted, "Hey, before we get to that, let's take a break. Nature is calling! Guess I ate a bit too much for lunch."

As Jenkins headed to the bathroom, Cox began making coffee; San Remo blend for Jenkins and Ethiopian dark roast for himself.

Weaver plugged in the teakettle to prepare a strong cup of tea. *Never was a 'tea sipper' before I met Ram. He introduced me to the joy of tea.* Waiting for Jenkins to return, she thought of that first meeting with Ram and his family. *Chetana was such a pretty little girl. Large, dark eyes, beautiful wavy hair, and such a sweet smile.*

When Cox and Jenkins returned with their coffee, Weaver recounted the events of that first meeting over a decade earlier.

Chapter 32

Location: Edler's English Tea Shoppe, New York, New York
Time: June 2023

Mitzi Weaver experienced mixed emotions as she entered Edler's Tea Shoppe. Ram Kapur asked to meet for "high tea" at Edler's, which was located in the financial district near his hotel. As the shop door closed behind her, she began to have second thoughts. *What am I doing here? I have no idea who this man is. He sounded English but that doesn't mean anything. He could be a local nut job! Yet, he sounded so earnest. I shouldn't have mentioned the new study on-air. Stuff like that brings out all kinds of weirdoes. What the hell! I'm here, might as well see it through.*

The boutique teashop looked like most gourmet coffee shops—the smell of coffee replaced with the scent of flavored teas. The aroma of each tea evoked its unique taste: Scottish Breakfast tea with its malty flavor; Darjeeling from India, the "champagne of teas," with its delicate natural bouquet; and, Earl Grey, made of China black tea flavored with the oil of bergamot oranges grown in southern Italy. A row of wooden boxes lined the wall behind the service counter; their clear fronts revealed the loose tea leaves within. All around were the accoutrements of tea connoisseurs—kettles, quilted cozies, strainers, and porcelain tea services.

To the left of the service counter, Weaver could see a backroom filled with soda shop tables and bentwood chairs. In the rear corners of the room were overstuffed chairs and couches setup as conversation areas. The massive furniture, characteristic of eighteenth-century English roadhouse décor, stood in stark contrast to the adjacent soda shop tables and chairs.

"May I be of service," the silver-haired man behind the service counter asked.

"Oh, I'm here to meet someone. I'm a bit early." Mitzi smiled graciously then looked to the shop entrance as the door opened.

A well-built, Indian gentleman wearing a tailored Savile Row suit entered. At his side stood a beautiful woman with luxurious, shoulder length hair that framed a delicate face. Dressed in an ivory colored suit and a raw silk blouse, she was a fashion plate of perfection. Snuggled tightly to the woman's leg was a child; a little girl with jet-black hair woven in a French braid. Her brown eyes twinkled with the happiness of a child on a grand adventure. A new dress and matching socks bearing the monogram of a famous mouse were evidence of recent trip to a Disney Store.

Weaver studied the man. *Is this who I'm supposed to meet? The person I spoke with had a distinct English accent. This guy looks Indian. Why am I so poor at remembering names? I never listen when people introduce themselves. He said he saw me on the "telly," so he would be able to recognize me. Mitzi, you're a damn fool! What are you doing here?* As she waited, unsure, the man removed a business card from his vest pocket.

"Doctor Weaver, it is so good of you to come. I am Ram Kapur," he said as he offered his card. "I do appreciate your kindness in taking time to visit with us. This is my wife, Kumari, and our daughter, Chetana. Let us take a seat in the back. It is quiet there."

Instinctively, Weaver pulled a business card from her purse and handed it to Kapur as she glanced at his.

Mr. Ram Kapur, MBA
Executive Director and Chief Economist
Federal Bank, New Delhi, India

Ram led the way into the back room, nodding to the silver-hair shop assistant as he walked past the counter. Both smiled, obviously known to each other.

At the conversation area, Ram invited Weaver to take a seat. She chose to sit on one of the massive couches; its high, padded back and oversized wooden armrests, made her feel very small. The smartly dressed woman sat at the other end of the couch with the child between the two of them. Before Ram sat down, a man wearing a full-length cotton apron appeared.

"Mr. Kapur, good to have you with us again." The waiter spoke with a working class English accent, hardly the educated voice of his customer.

"George, my man, it is good to see you. This is my guest, Doctor Mitzi Weaver."

"Good to meet you, ma'am. It'll be my pleasure to serve you today."

Still standing, Kapur turned to Mitzi. "Doctor Weaver, may I presume that you have enjoyed a traditional English 'high tea' in the past?"

"I'm afraid I haven't had that pleasure."

"Then, may I order for you?"

Mitzi smiled her acceptance. She did like hot tea, but only on cold winter nights when she curled-up with a good book.

"Fine, then." Kapur proceeded to order for the four. "Let us have Darjeeling, piping hot, some of your tasty cream cheese finger sandwiches, and an order of vanilla biscuits. That should do us." When the waiter departed, Kapur sat down in a chair facing Weaver. "I do hope you like my choices. The biscuits are not American biscuits, only simple sugar cookies." He turned toward the child. "Chetana, say 'hello' to Doctor Weaver."

"Hello, Doctor Weaver. I am pleased to meet you."

Mitzi grinned, "I'm happy to meet you, Chetana." *She is precious! Has her mother's features. Certainly speaks well for a child her age. She must know at least two languages, an Indian dialect and English.* "Your father told me that you are very special."

"He's my father. Don't all fathers think that their daughters are special?"

"I guess that is true."

"Father told me you are a scientist. I want to be a scientist or a physician when I grow up. Did he tell you that I like plants and bugs, and things like that? Do you work with bugs and things?"

"Well, in a way. I'm a microbiologist. I study small living things."

Ram Kapur was obviously very proud of his child; he beamed as he said, "Chetana has some very special talents. She tells us that she communicates with everything around her. Apparently, she can. Watch, if you will." Taking a pink Gerber daisy from a vase on the end table by his chair, he handed the flower to Weaver. "Examine the flower, please. Observe its sad condition. See how the leaves and petals are limp?"

Weaver examined the flower. *What's this about? Okay, the flower is on its last leg.*

Kapur turned to his daughter and asked, "Chetana, would you speak to the poor flower?"

The child scooted closer to Mitzi, who started to hand the flower to the child.

"No. You hold it," the little girl instructed. The child looked intently at the flower and then gently cupped the petals in her hands.

Weaver could not believe her eyes. *What's happening? The stem is growing firmer. It's regaining its natural turgor. The pedals are growing more vibrant. How's this happening! Must be a trick.*

Kapur cleared his throat to gain his guest's attention. "Doctor Weaver, I believe you see why I called this morning. Wouldn't you say that our daughter has a special gift?"

Mitzi Weaver sat speechless, dumbfounded by what she witnessed. *She's a special child, all right, and the right age for Ross-Katsura. Can't imagine how she did that thing with the flower? Could be an illusion. If it was, it was a damn good one.* "I don't know what to say, Mr. Kapur. You must forgive me. I haven't come to grips with what I think I just saw. But if it wasn't a trick, yes, your daughter does have a remarkable gift!"

❧

Kumari Kapur sat on the edge of the bed as she watched Chetana read a book about plants. *She's so lovely. I only want the best for her but I don't know what to do. Maybe I should talk with Doctor Weaver. Where's that card she gave Ram? It has her cell number. I'll call her.*

The sound of her cell phone startled Mitzi Weaver as she lay on the bed in her hotel room. *It's late evening. Who could be calling at this hour?* She reached for the phone. "Hello, this is Doctor Weaver."

"Good evening Doctor Weaver. This is Kumari, Chetana's mother. Am I disturbing you?"

"No, no, not at all." Mitzi was a bit surprised to hear her caller's voice.

"I'm sorry to trouble you. You said that we should call with any questions. My husband is attending a business dinner tonight, which is good because I wanted to speak with you personally. Ram, well, he can be so—you know—a man."

"How may I help you," Mitzi asked, hearing the distress in Kumari's voice.

"I must confess: Ram and I do not always see eye-to-eye when it comes to what is best for Chetana. He sees her as a brilliant child who should have every opportunity to receive the finest education—to make the most of her talents. I am not sure that is what she is here to do."

"I'm sorry. You said 'what she is here to do.' What do you mean?"

"It is difficult to explain. You must understand our Hindu beliefs. We believe in reincarnation and that our religious deities return to help us." Kumari paused to summon courage to continue. "I know you will think me strange, but there are those who believe that Chetana could be a reincarnated deity."

Weaver was a scientist. When asked, she would say she was Methodist, but religion was not part of her everyday life. "Kumari, I'm not sure what you mean by a deity? Certainly, what I saw this afternoon might be called 'miraculous' but hardly god-like."

"I know that it is hard for a westerner to understand our beliefs. We believe in many gods, not just one. As I explained, our deities come back to help us deal with our problems. My mother and her friends are convinced that Chetana is such a reincarnation and she should share her gifts with those in need. You saw what she did with the flower. She can speak with poisonous snakes and revive injured animals with her touch. I want her to be happy, but I also want her to serve the purpose for which she was sent to us." Sobbing softly, the distressed mother continued, "Ram believes my mother and her friends would place Chetana on public display, or worst, place her in a monastery. I don't wish to lose her. She's only a child. My child!"

Mitzi could feel the woman's pain. "I am sure you want the best for Chetana. Maybe, I can help. If she could be tested, we may be able to explain what is happening."

In a tearful voice, Kumari said, "You are right. It's best to find out what we are dealing with. I'll speak with Ram. He will call you. Thank you for listening to my concerns."

The phone went silent. Weaver pondered Kumari's words. *I can't imagine what it is like to have a child, much less a gifted child, like Chetana.*

Chapter 33

Location: The Overseer's Cottage, Carrington Farm, Northern Virginia
Time: September 2034

Jenkins and Cox appeared perplexed as they tried to digest what they heard. The two men looked at each other; Jenkins shook his head in disbelief.

Mitzi could see the skepticism on their faces. *Lawmen deal in "facts," what happened with Chetana in the teashop must sound like pure fantasy!*

"Now, Doctor Weaver," Jenkins said in a patronizing manner. "Are you saying this child could revitalize plants by just touching them?"

Mitzi knew that the two men were experiencing the kind of incredulity she experienced the day she met Chetana.

Cox studied Mitzi. His years of training and experience did little to prepare him for an interview like this one. He wanted to tear at Mitzi's story, but instead, he summarized what he heard as professionally as he could. "Okay. Let's take a moment and review what you have told us about these three children. The boy, Ethan, was a math prodigy and liked baseball. Sara, the Swedish girl, was some kind of a language savant. And, this Chetana, she was—what can I say—an illusionist? Is that about it, Doctor Weaver?"

Mitzi disliked Cox's glib tone, but remained calm. "I guess that's about it." Her response communicated her distain for what Cox said. *These guys think I'm feeding them a bunch of bull. What can I say?* She waited a moment to allow the tension in the room to wane. "Ram did call later. I asked if he would allow Chetana to undergo testing at Johns Hopkins. He seemed pleased that his daughter would have the opportunity to demonstrate her special abilities. I arranged to have her tested before they left the States. Of course, she impressed everyone and was accepted into the summer program along with Ethan and Sara."

"Let me get this straight. When you met the children they were around four years old?" Without waiting for a reply, Cox continued his questioning. "So, they were around five that first summer they went to Johns Hopkins for an in-depth evaluation?"

Mitzi nodded, "Yes, that's right." *How different they were then. They were little children just learning who they really were and what they could do!*

"Okay, I have heard enough of this." Jenkins waved his hand motioning Cox and Weaver to stop talking. As he did so, he removed his notebook from his shirt pocket and flipped through several pages. "Yesterday, you said that you started your professional work with these three children that first summer at Johns Hopkins. Tell us about that. And please, be as factual as possible."

Weaver was uncomfortable with how things were going. *I'd like to tell you what I really think. Best bite my lip and do what he wants.* "Yes, I obtained a National Institute of Health grant which supported the travel of the children and their parents to Baltimore. While they participated in the summer program, we ran a series of clinical studies to assess their genetic and physical characteristics."

"You thought they were different from ordinary humans and wanted to prove it," Jenkins said in a deprecating tone.

Weaver became defensive. "I wouldn't say that. Our goal was to determine if they had unique physical or genetic differences. That's all."

Jenkins was deliberately testy. "Doctor Weaver, let's be truthful. You're a research scientist. Weren't these kids kinda like your lab rats?"

Mitzi weighed Jenkins' words: his words came too close to the truth. "It's sad, but you may be right. All their lives people wanted to take advantage of them. We may not have been any different. We wanted our pound of flesh like everyone else."

Cox, who had been silent, asked, "What do you mean? Who wanted to take advantage of them? And, how?"

Weaver hesitated. "Each child was, in some way, a victim of those around them."

Jenkins was a lawman: he thought like a lawman and responded to hot button words. "Victim—victim of what? And who were the perpetrators?"

Mitzi's mind pounced on his statement. *Perpetrators? Yes, there were perpetrators, like those guys in India. But were we as bad? Did we cause these precious children pain just to satisfy our curiosity?* Her mind drifted to the time right after meeting Chetana. *Yes, there were real villains!*

Chapter 34

Location: A Rural Road Outside of New Delhi
Time: July 2023

Ram Kapur and Kumari returned from New York just a few hours ago, neither felt well, but custom demanded that they attend the anniversary reception to honor his supervisor, Mr. Bhatt. Due to a weather delay, the airlines cancelled their original reservations for the return trip to New Delhi. The only seats on the next available flight were in coach—seats far too small for a man of Ram's size. He slept very little on the flight, compounding his jet lag. He was in a grumpy mood as he drove to the reception—everything seemed an irritant.

"Be careful Ram," Kumari cautioned. "The traffic is terrible enough without you driving like a madman!"

"It's these bloody lorry drivers. They think they own the road. They shouldn't allow them on these narrow roads.

At that moment, a dilapidated two-ton lorry, idling on the side of the road, pulled in front of Ram's vehicle. Stomping the brakes of the compact SUV, he yelled, "You bastard!"

"Ram, watch your language. You sound like my father's warehouse workers. Besides, he can't hear you!" *Men are too aggressive! They should allow only women to drive!*

The offending lorry suddenly sped up. Ram followed; his anger escalating. As both vehicles gained speed, the lorry suddenly stopped in the middle of the road. To avoid striking the larger vehicle, Ram turned sharply. The SUV left the road and came to rest in a shallow ditch that paralleled the roadway.

A bit dazed, Ram turned to check on his wife. "Kumari! Kumari! Are you all right?"

Kumari struggled to talk; her head lay against the passenger's window. "Yes. Yes. No harm done—just a bit shaken."

Ram surveyed the situation. The SUV came to rest at an awkward angle, tilted into the ditch. *The airbags didn't deploy. Thank goodness. I'll need a tow to get out of this. Damn it, we're going to miss Bhatt's reception!*

As the couple struggled to right themselves, a tapping noise on the driver's window drew their attention to a well-dressed man standing beside their vehicle. Behind the man was a white, Bentley limousine.

"Do you need medical assistance?" he asked.

Ram labored to lower his window. "We are fine, but I'm afraid my motor car is in a bit of a pickle."

"Certainly looks that way. It's getting late. I doubt you'll get a lorry to assist you before morning—not out here anyway. Perhaps, I could give you a lift to the next village."

With the man's help, Ram struggled to get out of the SUV. "That is very kind of you. We are on our way to the Devonshire Country Club, just six or eight kilometers up the road. Would it be possible for you to take us there?"

"Devonshire? I'm headed there myself. I'm happy to give you a lift."

"You are too kind." Ram wiped his hand and extended it to the man who had come to his assistance. "Thank you so very much. I am Ram Kapur. My wife, Kumari, and I cannot begin to repay your kindness." He paused, and then asked, "And to whom am I indebted?"

"Call me Rishi, all my friends do. Now let's get your lovely wife out of there."

Kumari called to the men. "I am fine. All I need is a hand." With remarkable grace, she eased herself out of the car.

Ram and Kumari entered the well-appointed limousine. Inside, white leather seats, blonde burled wood and polished chrome blended in a testament to design and functionality. Neither of them had ridden in such luxury before.

As the chauffer driven limousine pulled away, Rishi asked, "I hope I do not offend, but may I offer you a glass of champagne? It's French—very delicate."

"Thank you, I believe both of us could use a glass of wine." Ram turned to his wife for confirmation. "What do you say, Kumari?"

"Yes, a little wine would be nice."

Ram watched Rishi pour the champagne. "And what takes you to Devonshire?"

"Oh, a reception given by a new banking acquaintance, I'm afraid. He's such a gentleman. I couldn't say no to his invitation."

"A reception?" Ram was surprised at the possible coincidence. "Would that be for Mr. Bhatt—the Senior Manager for Federal Bank?"

"Why, yes. Yes, it is." Rishi handed Kumari a glass of wine and then gave Ram a glass. With a questioning look, he asked, "Do you know Mr. Bhatt?"

Ram was all too eager to explain that he was the chief economist for the international investment division of the bank and that Bhatt was his immediate supervisor.

"Most interesting. It is such a small world." Rishi expressed his interest in international business opportunities, an interest born of his days attending Massachusetts Institute of Technology.

Kapur sat up to face Rishi. "I can't believe that we have so much in common. I, too, lived in Massachusetts around the same time."

The men discussed life in the States and the good times they enjoyed as young students. A rapport quickly developed between the two men—a rapport that would not have surprised Bijay. He knew the two would hit it off; why else would he choose Rishi to carry out his plan. He reasoned that the two scholars would find a great deal in common; their bond was the key to future actions.

By the time the limousine arrived at its destination, Rishi felt things were going as planned. *Well played, my man. Be careful tonight—not too friendly, just be interesting. Work on Kumari. Find a way to talk about the child.* In the receiving line, Rishi smiled and said something charming to Mr. Bhatt and his wife.

As the evening ended, Rishi generously offered to take Ram and Kumari to their home. "Oh, it is no problem. I'm headed that way myself." While he said one thing, he thought another. *It won't be long before Kapur and his wife are in my pocket. And the child is ours!*

Part VI

EMPOWERMENT

Testing Their Special Skills

Chapter 35

Location: Mountain Condo of Doctor Hank Belo, Aspen, Colorado
Time: November 2023

Before Emily Lake left Baltimore, she invited Mitzi Weaver to Colorado for Thanksgiving. Although reluctant at first, Mitzi accepted her friend's invitation. A three-day vacation away from campus would be nice. The two had a lot of "catching up" to do. Rather than staying in Denver, Emily decided that they should go to the mountains for the weekend. Kevin and Ethan loved the idea. The ski season opened Thanksgiving Weekend and both of them had new skis that they were eager to try.

Emily waved to her husband and son as they reached the bottom of the ski run. As they skied toward her, she called out, "Mitzi and I are going back to the condo. We'll see you there. And, please, try to be careful!"

All morning, Emily and Mitzi, watched as father and son tested themselves on the mountain. The pair were intrepid, challenging the steepest slopes.

As the women entered the Cadillac SUV, Mitzi removed her coat and placed it in the backseat. "I'm ready for a cup of tea. How about you, Emily?"

"Sounds great. I'll make us some when we get back to the condo."

Mitzi smiled as she took Emily's ski jacket and put it with her coat. "I wish that I had a friend that owned a condo in a fancy mountain resort. Nice of your friend, Hank, to let us use his place up here."

"Yeah. Belo's a nice guy. Last year, he told me I could use the condo but we just never seemed to have the time. You know how that is. Work, work, work—what can I say?"

❧❧

Emily placed the kettle on the stove. "So, you like Aspen, Colorado—the village of the rich and famous?"

Spinning on a bar stool like a child, Mitzi nodded her head. "It's lovely. Although, I can't imagine living here."

Emily stopped her tea preparation and turned to her friend. "Yeah, it's like our cabin at Pikes' Peak, but not as remote. It's a beautiful place to visit but I couldn't live here. As much as I dislike the congestion of Denver, I need the city—the shopping and entertainment—can't live without them! Of course, Kevin couldn't live up here. It's too far from his beloved sports franchises. My God, what would he do without football and baseball?"

Mitzi chuckled and nodded her agreement. "Kevin hasn't changed much since our days at UT, has he? And I see he's passed his love for sports on to Ethan. They are a 'dynamic duo.' I was amazed at how fast they skied today—especially Ethan."

"He does like to go fast—and skiing is the worst. I don't see how he can control that much speed. I try not to be overly protective, but sometimes he scares me to death!"

"Well, I'm impressed by what Ethan can do. I can't believe that he's only four and a half."

Emily placed her hands on her hips and looked at Mitzi. "Hey, around Colorado, kids start skiing before they're out of diapers. Kevin put Ethan on skis when the boy was two!"

"My goodness. That young? But knowing Kevin, I can believe it." Mitzi stood and arranged the cups and saucers. "Speaking of the boys, when do you think they'll quit for the day?"

"Probably when they get hungry." Emily poured Mitzi a cup of tea. "Why do you ask? Do you want to do something?"

"Well, I thought we could go out for dinner—my treat. What about Antonio's? I noticed it on the way here. It looked nice."

"Oh, I can't let you do that. The last time Kevin and I came here with Belo and his wife, we ate there. It's way too pricy!"

"Now, Emily Sopko, don't be like that." Mitzi used her friend's maiden name to make a point. "We've worked our asses off to get where we are. Just because we were raised on chicken and chuck roast doesn't mean we can't have lamb and lobster, now and then!"

Laugher filled the room. Both women understood Weaver's comment. Each of them worked hard to be successful in their chosen fields.

As the pair finished their tea, Emily ran her finger around the lip of the cup. "Mitzi, you know that Ethan has special talents, but did you notice anything out of the ordinary about his behavior at breakfast this morning?"

Mitzi answered playfully. "You mean the fact that he ate three pancakes and drank two glasses of milk?"

"No, really." Emily's tone was serious. "Anything about his body movements?"

Aware of Emily's concern, Mitzi reflected for a moment. "No. Can't say that I did. Why do you ask?"

"Oh, I am probably just being foolish. You know, being a mother, but Ethan developed a strange tick a couple of months ago. He moves his head like there's a fly buzzing around him." Emily picked up the teacups and carried them to the sink. "At first, I thought it might be Tourette syndrome; I've ruled that out. He doesn't have all of the symptoms. I don't know—I'm just concerned there is something wrong."

"So, have you asked him about his behavior?"

"Yeah, of course. But each time he said the same thing—he thought he saw something. Apparently, he's very sensitive to light and shadows. I guess it's nothing, but like I said, I'm concerned. When he visits Johns Hopkins this summer, would you keep an eye on him for me?"

Weaver studied the angst in her friend's face. *She's really worried.* Judging Emily's uneasiness, Mitzi measured her words. "Certainly, I will. It's probably nothing, just a boy being a boy."

Chapter 36

Location: McKusick-Nathans Institute of Genetic Medicine,
        Johns Hopkins University
Time: Late July 2024

"Doctor Weaver is your communicator on?" the petite young woman asked as she stepped in the office doorway.

"Oh my goodness!" Weaver searched through the clutter of papers on her desk. "I turned it off to visit with Dean Allred and forgot to turn it back on. Did you try to call me, Shelly?"

"No ma'am, but Security tried. They called me in the lab when they couldn't get you. There's a woman downstairs who wishes to see you."

"A woman?"

"Yes ma'am...a Doctor Johansson, I believe. Do you want me to bring her up?"

"Oh, yes. Do bring her up. And thank you." As the assistant departed, Mitzi assessed the disaster area she called an office. *My God, this place is a pigsty.* Although fastidious in the laboratory, Weaver was not the domestic housekeeper her mother tried to make her. She began gathering books and binders from the desk, stacking them against the one wall not covered by a file cabinet or a bookcase. *When's the damn paperless society going to reach my office? There's just too much stuff in here. Chair? Need a chair.* Moving quickly, she emptied a chair of its computer printouts and placed it near the desk. *I hate to have anyone come here. I'll catch Christina in the hallway and take her to the Dean's Lounge.*

"Doctor Weaver. We're back." Shelly motioned for the woman and the child to enter.

Before Mitzi could turn around, a female voice, with a slight Scandinavian accent said, "Hello, Doctor Weaver. It's good to see you again."

Weaver turned to face her guests. "Christina! Good to see ya, too." In her enthusiasm, she momentarily slipped into her native Texas tongue. "And, look who we have here, and as beautiful as ever. How are you Sara?"

The child scrunched her face and grinned. In flawless English, she replied, "I'm fine. Thank you for asking. And, how are you?"

"I'm fine. Come on in."

Shelly interrupted her supervisor. "If you don't need me, Doctor Weaver, I need to get back to the lab."

"Oh sure, Shelly, and thank you. I certainly appreciate your help. Call me if you have any problems with the embryonic cultures; they should be pretty routine."

When the assistant was out of earshot, Christina said with an expression of concern. "I'm sorry to bother you this morning but I needed to speak with you before we meet with the assessment staff tomorrow."

Sara interrupted her mother. "They think I'm insane."

"What?" Weaver could not believe what she heard. "Who thinks that?"

Christina raised her finger to her lips. "Shhh. Not here Sara. Mitzi, is there somewhere that we may talk—perhaps have a cup of American coffee?"

"Sure. The Student Union. They have great coffee. We'll have the place to ourselves. Everybody's on break this week."

Walking to Java Joe's in the Student Union, the three caught up on what happened since their meeting in Stockholm. Oskar was at CERN, having joined the permanent research team there. Christina was now the Director of the Near East and Arabic Section for Swedish intelligence. She also worked with the newly formed Organization of Baltic Sea States, a response to the collapse of NATO following the withdrawal of all American troops from Europe.

When the three reached the service counter, the barista stopped washing a coffee pot and called over his shoulder, "What'll you have, ladies?"

"Two medium coffees," Weaver replied. "And what would you like, Sara?"

"I want chocolate milk."

With their drinks in hand, Weaver led her guests to a booth. Once everyone was seated, she asked, "Now, what is this about Sara having a mental problem?"

Before her mother could speak, Sara spoke. "I told them that I hear voices."

"Sara, please, let me tell Doctor Weaver what happened." At Sara's consenting nod, Christina continued. "This all started in the daycare center where I work. I enrolled Sara when she was six months old. Greta, the director of the early childhood section, became very interested in Sara's special language skills. She worked closely with Sara. A couple of years ago, Sara told Greta how she heard voices."

"It's true. I told you too, remember, before I told Greta. You told me that many little girls have imaginary friends—but I wasn't pretending—I could understand their questions. It's like I know what they're thinking."

Weaver was not sure what to make of Sara's assertions. "You know what they are thinking? So, you can hear their thoughts." Weaver's expression changed. "Can you hear my thoughts?"

Sara frowned; her small face showing her disagreement. "I can't read minds! I just get messages. They pop into my head. I told Momma and everybody that they're like—like...." Sara groped for a way to describe what was in her mind. "I guess they're like a picture."

"A picture that's a message?" Weaver asked, uncertain of what the child meant.

"I know this doesn't make sense but—oh, I know!" The child genius, found a solution to her communication problem. "Look at that window." Sara pointed to a large window not far from them.

Weaver took a sip of coffee and faced the window. "Okay. Now what?" Outside the window, she could see a courtyard. In the area were several wooden planters, each filled with brightly colored flowers.

Sara jumped from her chair and stood in front of Mitzi. "Now close your eyes real tight. Don't open them until I say so. After you open your eyes, close them again. Understand?"

Mitzi Weaver was a professional biologist, well versed in anatomy and physiology; she knew what would happen. She closed her eyes.

"Are you ready? Not waiting for a reply, Sara said, "Open your eyes. Now quick, close them. Do you see the pictures in your mind? Well, that's how I get messages. They're little pictures, not real words; somehow, I can understand what they mean. It's like hearing with pictures, not sound."

Mitzi kept her eyes closed, studying the green and purplish images in her mind. She understood. Everything about the window and the courtyard was clear in her mind's eye. "I see what you mean."

Christina, who had been silent, addressed Weaver. "She doesn't know who is sending the messages. The messages or thoughts—whatever they are—aren't about daily life, like feelings or the weather. Tell her, Sara."

"Well, they asked about me, who I am, and where I am. It's like they live in some distant country. Lately, we talk about 'right and wrong' and things like that."

"You said 'talk.' How do you talk to them?" Weaver was intrigued. "Do you speak out loud or do you just answer their questions in your mind?"

It's more like thinking, but I don't use words. They just know what's in my mind."

"Sounds like thought transference to me," Weaver blurted without thinking. Embarrassed, she glanced at Christina and then at the child. "And, you're sure these people never said where they are? Did you ask?"

"Yes, but I couldn't make sense of their answer. They say they're 'here'. I'm not sure where 'here' is." The child squirmed and looked about the dining room. "Momma, *jag måste kissa.*"

Mitzi did not need a Swedish dictionary to understand the child's request. "Oh, the restroom is down the hall."

Tossing their paper cups into a recycle bin, Mitzi escorted Sara and Christina to the restroom. The discussion quickly shifted from Sara's situation to topics that were more cordial. Sara visited Disney World in France last year and was eager to tell Weaver of her adventures there. Mitzi explained that tomorrow Sara would meet Chetana, another little girl that liked Mickey and all his friends.

When Sara entered the restroom with her mother, Mitzi thought about what little Sara had said and the way she expressed herself. *The intellect of an adult with the heart of a child. God bless her!*

Chapter 37

Location: SÄPO, Swedish Security Police, Stockholm, Sweden
Time: Late July 2024

The head of internal intelligence operations, Deputy Director Marvin Lundberg, oversaw domestic security for SÄPO. As usual, he arrived early. The time display on his monitor showed 06:13; it would be an hour before any of his staff arrived. *Peace and tranquility. Too bad it can't last all day.* A sip of dark roasted coffee, black with no sugar, helped clear the fog from his mind. *Let's see what happened last night.* Lundberg methodically scrolled through the overnight intelligence reports until a message caught his eye. *What's this? What has "big brother" found?*

The message was from Domestic Communications, the unit that monitored electronic transmissions throughout Sweden.

CHRISTINA W. JOHANSSON, Director, Near East and Arabic Section, Organization of Baltic Sea States; linguist, Swedish government intelligence: JOHANSSON, OSKAR J. (Husband); Physicist, University Stockholm, National Security Clearance-Atomic Energy Access.

Excerpt of transmission between Baltimore, MD, USA and Stockholm:

Christina: We made it okay. The flight was a bit bumpy. I'm staying at a hotel near Johns Hopkins. Oh, before I forget—you do have my return flight info, don't you? I need you to pick me up at the airport. It's important.

Oskar: Yes, I have your itinerary. I'll meet you at the airport. How's Sara? Did she handle the flight okay?

Christina: She's fine. I'm going to try to visit with Doctor Weaver before the session starts. I haven't made an appointment; I hope she can see me. I want her to know about Sara's problem before they do the testing. Maybe their specialists can figure out why she hears those strange voices.

Oskar: Sounds good. I'd like to know if we need to do anything for her—if she needs some kind of treatment. See if Weaver can give you some advice.

Christina: Okay. Take care of yourself. And please, watch what you eat! Stay away from that fish and chips place.

End transcribed transmission.
Issue: Security operative outside of country. No known mission.

Lundberg nursed his coffee and read the message a second time. *Christina Johansson. What's the head of the language intel section doing in Baltimore with her daughter? What kind of treatment does the girl need? Why must they go to the States for her to be treated?*

Lundberg finished reviewing the balance of the morning intelligence reports before handwriting a note to his aide.

> *Inga,*
>
> *Obtain the security folder on Christina Johansson. Also pull the security folder on her husband, Oskar Johansson. He's a physicist at the University of Stockholm. He worked on the Swedish nuclear energy program a couple of years ago. Both of them have high-level security clearances. Give me the folders when they are available. Thanks...ML*

Deputy Director Lundberg flipped through the material in Christina Johansson's folder. He liked paper files better than electronic ones. Examining documents appealed to him: the feel of the paper, even its smell. Eraser marks and smudges communicated facts lost on a sterile electronic screen. *Interesting. We collect the strangest info on ourselves. Hmmm. What's this? Sara's been evaluated by a psychiatrist for "hearing voices." What the hell does that mean? Is she schizophrenic or something? The psych evaluation states she's not nuts. So why take her to the States?*

Chapter 38

Location: Johns Hopkins University, Baltimore, Maryland
Time: Late July 2024

Mitzi Weaver awakened to a bright summer morning with unseasonably warm temperatures predicted. Raised in west Texas, heat did not bother Mitzi but she disliked the humidity that enveloped Baltimore in the summer months. There was much to do today; rushing about campus would leave her drenched with perspiration. As she dressed, she reviewed a mental checklist of the day's activities. *Need to give the parents an on-site orientation to the facilities and staff. Have to assure them that the children are in good hands. Then we have to get the kids settled into their dormitory. Glad that they hired a nanny for the children. Oh, supper tonight. The whole group is going out. Good time for the parents and staff to get to know each other. What do I have to wear tonight? Blue dress? Ah, it's at the cleaners. Hit the cleaners on the way home. Need to check on the transportation from the restaurant to the dormitory so the parents can tuck-in the children.*

Much to Weaver's surprise and satisfaction, the first day's events went off without any mishaps. The children spent the night in their rooms on campus as the adolescent care staff requested. They thought it wise to have a "dry run" to see how the children would react to separation from their parents. The children responded well when left for the evening. They would have time to say their goodbyes later this morning, after the parents completed background interviews with the staff psychologists.

Weaver was concerned as she drove to the campus to pick up the children. The initial NHS grant called for extensive genetic testing and comprehensive medical workups for each child. *Much to do, perhaps too much! Can't imagine what we'll find? Lord, let no harm come to these children. Did I just pray? That's not like me!*

The children were waiting when Weaver arrived at the dormitory. The nanny reported everything went well and the children enjoyed their breakfast. Mitzi loaded them into her car and drove to the building housing the Julian C. Stanley Study of Exceptional Talent.

Once in the center, Weaver advised the children, "Wait here a moment. I have to check-in at the reception desk."

The children sat quietly and studied the area around them. Glassed-in offices lined the outer walls of the large open space that served as a reception area. Outside of each office was a desk staffed by a clerical assistant.

Sara broke the silence. "What do you think that we going to do today?"

"I'm not sure," Chetana answered. "I think we are going to take some tests to see how smart we are. I don't like taking tests."

"Me neither." Ethan squirmed and made a face. "I like math but I don't like reading and stuff like that."

"You don't like language?" Sara was shocked. "I love languages and I love to read. I can speak six languages. You want to hear?"

"No. Not really," Ethan replied in a boyish manner with a turned up nose.

Chetana stepped between Sara and Ethan. "They expect us to play nice." She faced Sara, deliberately placing her back in Ethan's face. "I speak two languages, Hindi and English, but I prefer studying plants and animals. I want to be a biologist like Doctor Weaver."

For a moment, none of the children spoke. Energized by a mathematical fact, Ethan jumped from his seat and faced the girls. "Do you know we're all the same age?"

Sara assumed a superior air before responding. "Yes, that's why we're here. We were all conceived during some big cosmic thing."

"What's that mean?" Ethan was not knowledgeable about things like human reproduction.

Chetana gave Ethan a "know-it-all" smile, having studied reproduction and cell mitosis during the last semester at her school. "Oops! Guess you don't know about the 'birds and the bees' do you?"

"Boys are so dumb about these things!" Sara turned to Chetana and smiled. "Girls are so much smarter."

Before young Ethan could respond, Weaver appeared. "Get your backpacks. We have to go next door to the testing center. We're going to see just how brilliant you are. After you finish your tests, we'll have lunch with your parents so you can say goodbye. This afternoon you're scheduled to have scans and a few other tests."

"You gonna stick us?" Ethan asked. "I don't like needles."

Mitzi smiled and placed her finger on the boy's nose. "Nope. No needles, just a cotton swab and a ride in Doctor Misenheimer's supersonic space machine."

"What kind of machine?" Chetana asked.

"Oh, it's nothing to worry about—you'll see." Weaver directed her young charges toward the door.

ChapteR 39

Location: The Overseer's Cottage, Carrington Farm, Northern Virginia
Time: September 2034

Cox looked at Jenkins to see if he wanted to question Weaver. Jenkins crooked his head at an odd angle to convey his negative response.

Cox shrugged his shoulders in reply and turned to Weaver. "Tell us what you learned that first summer. Was the genetic make-up of the children different from regular kids?"

"The children were barely five years old when they came that first summer." Weaver avoided Cox's question. "Since they were so young, we didn't want to frighten them with invasive testing. We obtained only oral epithelia swabs. No blood was drawn."

Cox chuckled, amused by Weaver's comment. "Even research biologists have hearts. Sorry Doctor Weaver, just recalling something Jenkins said earlier about treating the kids like lab rats. My apologies."

Mitzi smiled half-heartedly. "I guess there's some truth in what you say. The scientific community has a bad reputation when it comes to using live specimens. Same is true with physicians. It seems that to treat a patient, they start by inflicting pain—a needle here, an incision there. Everyone should have Doctor McCoy's medical analyzer. Do you remember the doctor in the Star Trek series? He'd wave his little analyzer over the patient and get a comprehensive report. Too bad we can't do that—not even in 2034."

Redirecting the conversation, Cox asked his question a second time. "So, what did you learn from the samples you obtained that first summer?"

Weaver knew she was opening a can of worms. She hesitated. *They're not going to like what I have to say.* "Well, as you might suspect, we learned that the children were different. The children possessed some variations in their DNA and in the anatomical structures of their brains."

Jenkins suddenly sat up and asked a series of questions in rapid succession. "Different? What do you mean? How was their DNA different? What was different about their brains?"

Startled by the sudden interest of Jenkins, Weaver did not respond immediately. *Wow. Who stuck him in the ass?* She reflected for a moment on the revelations of that first summer. *The time has come. May as well tell 'em everything! They're not going to believe a single word of it!*

134

Chapter 40

Location: McKusick-Nathans Institute of Genetic Medicine,
        Johns Hopkins University
Time: Late July 2024

"Doctor Weaver, the DNA reports from yesterday are posted," Shelley announced as she entered her supervisor's office. "As usual, we don't have the reports on the MRI studies. I asked Radiology to put a rush on them but they gave me their song and dance about being backlogged."

"I'm sure they'll do their best, Shelley. Did you have a chance to review any of the DNA results?"

"Yeah, but I'm not sure what to make of it."

"What ya mean?" Weaver's response let her Texas upbringing temporarily show through, something that happened in casual conversations.

"Well, like you suspected, the children have unusual genetic profiles."

Her scientific interest aroused, Weaver asked, "What's most significant?"

Shelly gave that cute smile of hers that everyone liked. "It's their DNA strains. They're so robust—I mean the whole structure—like DNA on steroids?

"So, they're young, healthy children, why wouldn't their DNA reflect their youth."

"Well, it's more than that. You'll see. Everything tells me these young folks have defense mechanisms we don't have. And, another thing. Their telomeres are way longer than average. These kids could live until they're a hundred and fifty years old!"

Shelley's assessment of the DNA results and the way she gave her report caused Mitzi to chuckle loudly. Gaining her composure, she responded. "Sounds interesting. The detailed studies should tell us more. I've planned a comparative analysis of their genomes. What else did you find?"

"Tell you the truth, I haven't gotten my head around that yet. The early lab results aren't much to go on, but I have a hunch you're going to find some physical anomalies." The graduate lab assistant paused and her tone grew serious. "Just a guess, but I'd say some parts of their bodies are going to be as different as their DNA. If we had those radiology reports, we might know more. Anyway, whatever is different, it's certainly not visible. I have seen these little guys. They look like ordinary five year olds."

Weaver's phone rang interrupting Shelley's report. "Hello, this is Doctor Weaver."

A gruff voice answered with a derogatory demeanor. "Hey, Mitzi. What the hell are you up to?"

"Nothing really—and good morning to you to Dr. Misenheimer!" Mitzi recognized the voice of Phillip Misenheimer, Chief of Radiology. He did not sound happy. "And what's got you so upset his morning?

"I just read the results from those MRI's we did for you. One of my residents read them last evening. He didn't know what to think, so he sent them to me." The chief radiologist took a deep, audible breath. "So, you want to tell me why you played around with the images? Are you trying to get a rise out of me or something?"

"Phil, I'm sorry, but I don't know what you're talking about."

"Okay, that's enough. Fun's over, Weaver. What do you want me to do with these images?"

"Phil, slow down. I really don't know what you're talking about."

"Okay, Mitzi. I'll play you're silly ass game, but it'll cost you a deep dish pizza from Giovanni's. Get me a pizza with everything on it and be in my office at noon."

"I will buy you a damn pizza! But I'll say it again—I don't know what you're talking about. I'll see you at lunch." As the phone went dead, Mitzi considered her friend's comments. *Not like Phil to act like a horse's ass. What the hell—for the price a pizza I'll find out what's bugging him!*

❧

Weaver sat patiently in Misenheimer's office, a large pizza resting in her lap. *He better get his butt in here fast. This pizza smells too good to wait much longer.*

"Well, if it's not our little jokester," Misenheimer said as he entered the office. "I'm still amazed at how you did this. You must have gotten one of your graduate nerds to monkey around with the data files. Give me my pizza." Grabbing the pizza from Mitzi's lap, Phil sat down at his desk.

Mitzi handed her colleague a paper plate and watched as he served himself a couple of slices of pizza. "Well, are you going to show me something, Phil, or did you just want me to fetch your lunch?"

"Okay, if you insist. I'll show you your handiwork. Misenheimer took a large bite of pizza. A long string of cheese dangled down his chin. He wiped it with a paper napkin while he looked a Mitzi. "Go ahead. You can have a piece of my pizza."

Weaver answered in a coquettish voice. "That's awful generous of you, sir. Seeing as how I paid for it, and all."

Misenheimer grabbed a couple of napkins and wiped his hands before he took a remote control from a pocket of his lab coat. With a click, an array of images appeared on the large monitors that filled one wall of his office. "Take a look at these screens. See that. Now tell me that you didn't have one of your graduate nerds monkey around with these images?"

Mitzi Weaver was not a radiologist, but she and Misenheimer worked together on several studies that involved the use of tomography and magnetic resonance imaging. "Phil, you know I'm not an expert in reading MRI images. All I see is that you have enhanced different parts of these brain scans. Why did you do color them that way?"

Misenheimer blurted out, "I didn't do anything!" His curt response communicated his displeasure with Mitzi. "You can drop the act. I got my pizza. If you're not going to admit to what you did, just get the hell out of my office—and don't try this again. It was a costly trick that wasted everyone's time."

"Damn it, Phil. Enough is enough. I didn't do anything."

Misenheimer leaned back in his chair, his chin tucked down. He cocked his head at an odd angle and stared at Weaver.

Recognized for his contributions to the field of radiology and the academic community, Phillip Misenheimer spent two decades rising to the top of his profession. The sudden change in his demeanor alerted Weaver that something was happening within the compendium of images that filled his brain.

"Well, honey," Misenheimer said in a slow, resonating voice. "If you're not kidding me, we have something very special on our hands." He rose from his chair and approached one of the monitors. "I've never seen anything like this before. You see these enhanced colors." Misenheimer pointed to several images. "That's telling me that each of these children has a unique brain structure."

The two academic professionals concentrated on the brightly colored images before them. Misenheimer raced from one image to the next while shouting out his findings. With each image, the excitement in his voice and behavior increased. Misenheimer was certain that he was peering into the minds of a new generation of mankind!

Chapter 41

Location: McKusick-Nathans Institute of Genetic Medicine,
      Johns Hopkins University
Time: August 2024

Chetana and Sara sat on the edge of a couch in the patient waiting room, their feet not quite touching the floor. The two had grown close over the past two weeks as they endured medical, psychological, and intelligence tests. They had even begun to like that obnoxious boy from Colorado.

Chetana turned to Sara. "Is your mother coming for you tomorrow?"

"Yes. She's coming by herself. My father is in Switzerland at the lab. He can't come."

Ethan came into the small waiting room. "Well, that's that. I'm ready to go home!"

Both girls looked at their friend and nodded their agreement. The three sat quietly for a few minutes.

Chetana turned to Ethan. "Sara's mother is coming for her tomorrow. Is your mother coming for you?"

"No. My daddy is 'spose to fly in from Denver tonight. I'm flying home with him. I wanted to go by myself but they said I wasn't old enough to fly alone."

Sara looked at her two new friends. "Well, I've enjoyed visiting with both of you, but after two weeks, I want to see my dog, Sitka."

"I wanna go home, too," Ethan added. "I've missed a couple of baseball games with my daddy."

The three again sat quietly for a minute before Chetana spoke. "I know. Why don't we stay in touch? We can e-mail each other!"

"That would be nice," Sara agreed. After a pause to build courage, she continued. "Sometimes, I think I can hear the two of you."

Ethan did not understand what Sara meant. "Well, I can hear you, too. I'm not deaf."

Sara gave Ethan a stern stare. "You smart-off like that again and I'm going to slap you." She waited a moment for an apology from Ethan but received none and decided to continue what she had started. "You know that I can hear things that other people can't."

"Yeah, I heard that you got a problem," Ethan said in a sarcastic way to indicate that he understood Sara's mental health issues.

"You're not very nice." Sara struck Ethan's shoulder with her closed fist causing him to flinch.

"Ouch! That hurt!"

"Stop, you two." Chetana stepped between her friends. "Sara, what do you mean that you can hear us?"

Sara regained her poise. "Well, when we are close together, like now, I think I know what you're going to say before you actually speak. It's like a DVD where they dubbed in the words and you can hear the words before the character moves her lips."

Ethan gave Sara a strange look. "So? What are you saying?"

"I don't know. I guess what I want to know is if you can hear me that way?"

Chetana and Ethan looked at each other and shook their heads.

"I'm sorry," Sara apologized. "I guess I'm different, but I thought...."

"Wait a minute," Chetana interrupted. "Hold my hands. Form a circle and be still. Watch this! It might work."

The three stood and held hands. Suddenly, Ethan jerked his hands free and cried out, "What did ya do? You shocked me!"

Chetana smiled at Ethan. "Don't be a sissy. Hold our hands again."

The boy complied, although with some hesitancy. The three held hands.

"Sara, let's try it again." Chetana said as she closed her eyes.

"Okay. Everyone close your eyes and listen." Sara concentrated—her mind filled with one thought—*Are you there?*

"Yeah, I'm here." Ethan opened his eyes. "Who do you think is holding your stupid hand?"

Sara giggled and poked Ethan. "Look at me. Now listen." While Ethan stared at her, she thought. *Are you there? Are you there?*

"Wow, how'd you do that?" The boy's face filled with excitement. "You didn't move your lips."

"I thought that I could communicate with other people—like the people in my head—but I couldn't do it without Chetana's help."

Chetana nodded. "Sometimes when I touch a plant or small animal, something happens. They change in some way. That's what you felt, Ethan— that little shock."

Ethan could not contain his enthusiasm. "Fantastic! We're fantastic—like those guys in the comic book—but we're for real!"

The girls giggled, amused at Ethan's behavior. They looked at each other, and without words said, *"Boys. They're weird."*

A bond immediately formed between the children, delighted at their newfound ability. They agreed not to tell their secret to anyone, not even their parents. Until they left for home, the three enjoyed talking between themselves, fascinated that others could not hear them. When the time came to say goodbye, each of them shed tears of sorrow, even the tough little guy from Colorado.

Part VII

DISCOVERING NEW TALENTS

Confronting New Challenges

Chapter 42

Location: Johns Hopkins University, Baltimore, Maryland
Time: August 2024

Mitzi Weaver checked the connections from her computer to the forty-inch monitor on her desk for a third time. *This damn thing better work. Never done three-way video conferencing before. Can't have anything go wrong this morning. Too important!* An image suddenly appeared on the screen.

"Good morning, Mitzi. How are things?" Sandy Santini looked half-awake as he bit into a breakfast sandwich.

Before Mitzi could reply, the image of Celia Foxe appeared on the monitor next to Santini. "Hi, everybody."

Weaver could clearly see both of her guests. "Looks like everyone is on board. Thank you so much for taking time to visit with me."

"Glad to do it," Santini said. "How are you doing, Celia?"

"I'm fine. You look tired."

Santini nodded then took a sip of coffee from a paper cup. "Did an 'all-nighter' working on the cyclotron here at Fermi. Soon as we're finished here, I'm off to bed."

Foxe nodded her head. "Been there. Done that too many times." With scarcely a pause she continued. "And Mitzi—what's this big deal you want to discuss with us?"

"I have something I think both of you need to see. Give me a minute." Weaver loaded a file into her computer. "Check this out." A dozen MRI images filled the screen. "Here are the findings from our workup of the children. These are scans of their cerebral functions. See those brightly colored areas? Well, those areas are the portion of each child's brain that is enhanced—not normal."

Santini moved his face closer to his monitor. "I've seen stuff like that on the science channel. Those brightly colored spots show a high level of activity."

Mitzi giggled. "Chalk up one for public television! You're correct. And here's the interesting thing; these are 'resting' images. During the test, the children were blindfolded and listened to a white noise to block out the sound of the machine. You know how loud those damn MRI things can be."

"That is interesting." Celia looked at the right side of her monitor and waved her finger back and forth between herself and the image of Santini. "But what does all this have to do with a couple of physicists like Sandy and me?"

Weaver took a deep breath. *Now's the time to sell your idea. Get 'em onboard.* "In our original study, we determined that Ross-Katsura impacted embryonic cells but we concentrated on negative results, like birth defects and stillbirths."

"Yeah, I remember." Santini's words were barely audible, obstructed by a mouth filled with food.

"So, Mitzi. What's this have to do with these brain scans?"

"Good question, Celia. As I said a few months back, some of us think that Ross-Katsura may have had some beneficial effects on fetuses. These brain scans may be our first evidence of that. Which begs the question: how do we prove it? That's where you two come in. The NSF and the World Health Organization are willing to fund a study to isolate the composition of Ross-Katsura so we can understand its full impact. And, if possible, replicate the event."

"Oh, come on!" Santini leaned into the video camera creating a close-up of his face. "I'm pretty sure we can isolate the composition of the event—but replicating it—well, that's a whole different task."

"Sounds like the makings of a Nobel prize to me," Foxe said with a snicker. "I'd think that the 'Great Santini' would want a piece of this."

"Yeah, sure, who wouldn't? But how are you going to generate neutrons, tachyons, bosons and damn near the whole electromagnetic spectrum? That's what it could take!"

Before Foxe replied, Mitzi Weaver winked seductively. "Now, Sandy. If it was easy, I wouldn't need to ask for your help. Now would I?"

Celia laughed out loud, amused by Mitzi's use of feminine guile. Caught between Mitzi and Celia, Sandy acquiesced and began to outline how to conduct the experiment. Mitzi volunteered to draft the research proposal once Foxe and Santini identified everything needed. All agreed to talk again in three weeks.

After Weaver said her goodbyes to Santini and Foxe, she sat motionless for several minutes. *It's going to happen. I just know it.* The bell tower clock struck the hour. *Nine o'clock. Off your ass, Mitzi Weaver. Gotta get the children ready. Much to do today. Can't believe their parents take them home tomorrow.*

Chapter 43

Location: The Taj Mahal Palace Hotel, Mumbai, India
Time: September 2024

The Bombay Gentlemen chose to gather for their regularly scheduled meeting at the Taj Mahal Palace Hotel—the site of the first licensed bar in the city of Mumbai. Hosting maharajas and dignitaries from around the world since 1903, the hotel epitomizes the blending of Indian and Victorian architecture prevalent at the time of its construction.

The members of the Gentlemen's group spent the morning discussing business opportunities and enjoying the company of their friends. Now they would hear a report on the project to identify the Enlightened Ones described by Manish, the holy man. Over the past four years, they invested significant funds and labor in the project. Today, they hoped to hear good news.

"Gentlemen, gentlemen. Quiet, please. We have much to discuss," Harshal called to his colleagues. "As you know, our project is moving forward better than we hoped. Sanjay and Sudhir will give us an update."

Sanjay spoke first. "Each of us has contributed to the success thus far of our project. To Hari and Rishi, we are indebted for their development of the scanning software to sift through the massive amounts of data that we have collected. Data, that our friend, Abhay provided through his access to private files of the credit card companies served by his firm. But data that could not be obtained without Harshal's help when he successfully inserted a backdoor into the antivirus software of two major companies with which he works. Using this access, Bijay created a supercomputer by linking together a network of microcomputers around the world."

Sudhir rose, a laser pointer in his hand, which he used to direct everyone's attention to the material displayed behind him. "And now, gentlemen, let's get down to business. Our project identified several targets. As you know, one of them died in a house fire. A tribesman set fire to the house where the child lived. Remember?"

"Yes," confirmed Abhay, "and the child caused the death of the man using telepathy or something like that. Quite amazing!"

Sudhir acknowledged Abhay's comment before continuing. "Sadly, we lost another child who was showing potential in math and science. He dropped off the map about six months ago. He's Tibetan. We think the Chinese have him. Now, Sanjay will tell you more."

Sanjay used a remote control to display two photographs: one of a boy with a dark complexion, large black eyes and black hair; the other, a beautiful, young girl with amber hair and green eyes. "Here we have two other children that have little value to us. The Pakistani boy committed the entire Koran to memory before age four. Of course, the people in his village think he's a prophet or something. We're not likely to obtain him. The girl played the piano at age three and composed a full concert last month. Regrettably, after that she experienced a mental collapse. They say that she sits and rocks back and forth, as if lost in music being played in her head." Pausing to consider the loss of the two children, he continued. "Enough about what we don't have—here's the good news."

"About time," Harshal declared loudly. "I doubted that our venture was going to pay any dividends."

"Yes, my friend, I think it will," Sanjay said as Sudhir handed him the remote control. With a click, three photographs appeared. "Here are three children that may hold real promise. Just last month a prestigious American clinic evaluated them. Each child demonstrated great skill in either languages, math, or biology."

Sudhir faced Abhay and bowed in the traditional Hindu manner. "Before I say more, let me recognize Abhay for giving us complete access to the research files of Johns Hopkins University in Baltimore, Maryland. It is my honor to know such a devious little bastard as he."

Everyone laughed. The room filled with shouts of "Hear, Hear! Hear, Hear!"

"And now let's see what the fine people at Johns Hopkins found." Sanjay stood and displayed images taken from the university's computer. "These are brain scans of the children. First, the boy. The report states that he has highly developed parietal and occipital lobes. Parts of the brain that deal with vision. The parietal lobe controls how we see while the occipital lobe interprets what we see, like color, light, and movement. What is more important is that the boy's aptitude tests indicate exceptional skill in mathematics. We all know how important that is in our businesses."

"That is what I want to hear," Bijay stated forcefully. "Exceptional math skills equal cash in hand!"

"Yes, my friend. That is correct, but let me continue." A click brought up a second set of images. "Let us look at the test results for the child in New

Delhi. Her MRI indicates unique connectivity in her brain. It is as if every cell is connected. One report suggests that her ability to process information may one day outstrip our best computers. Another odd thing, she appears to radiate an aura, like some science fiction character." Sanjay laughed at his comment causing the others to follow suit. He concluded, "Her evaluation indicates that she is interested in biology."

Bijay injected himself into the Sanjay's report a second time. "I can't see how that's of much value—biology?"

Abhay looked to Bijay seated next to him. "Let us not be too quick to judge the value of this girl. With that unique brain, who knows what she could do." Abhay turned to Sanjay. "As neither the boy nor this girl possesses language skills, I assume that the Swedish child is the one that does?"

"Yes, she is fluent in six or seven languages; a trait she may have inherited from her mother, who works as a linguist. Her MRI shows significant enhancement of the temporal lobe—the part of the cerebrum responsible for language processing, comprehension, and hearing."

Bijay probed again, "You say this girl has superior hearing and language skills. Of what value are these skills to us?"

Sanjay raised his hand; his index finger pointed upward. He shook his hand rapidly as a parent does to scold a child. "My good friend, we are dealing with raw talent here. These are Enlightened Ones. Who knows what she may be capable of doing."

Sudhir jumped to Sanjay's defense. "Sanjay is correct. There is some evidence that she can hear the thoughts of others. They say that she hears voices."

"My good man," Bijay questioned in a smug voice. "Surely, this child can't read minds—can she?"

Sudhir looked directly at Bijay and winked. "Well, now. It hasn't been proven, but SÄPO, the security police of Sweden, are interested in this child. Apparently, they think she may have some intelligence value."

Having made his point, Sudhir sat down, not knowing how prophetic his words were. Director Lundberg had plans for little Sara—plans that would end badly.

Chapter 44

Location: The Overseer's Cottage, Carrington Farm, Northern Virginia
Time: September 2034

Phil Jenkins shifted in his chair and puckered his lips as he thought. He placed his hand on the back of his neck and stared at Weaver. After a moment of silence, he turned to Cox. "I need a short break. Why don't we step outside for a minute?"

Cox could see that something was troubling Jenkins. "That sounds fine. Could use some fresh air."

Weaver watched as the pair left the cottage through the French doors that opened on to the patio. *I wonder if Jenkins has something on his mind or just needs to fart. Look at them. It's chilly out there.* Through the glass panes of the door, she could see Jenkins and Cox bracing themselves against a brisk north wind. Brightly colored leaves danced about, coaxing them to go indoors. Weaver strained to hear what the men said. *Guess Jenkins is trying to figure out how to proceed with this thing. On the other hand, he may just think that I'm some nut job!*

In unison, the men nodded and walked toward the cottage. As Cox opened the door, a gush of wind raced in ahead of the two. "Sorry about that."

Jenkins made himself comfortable in the chair facing Weaver. "Well, we understand what was found with the kids' DNA and their other tests, but just for the record, did the boy have Tourette's syndrome? And, what did the folks at Johns Hopkins find out about Sara's mental condition?"

Jenkins' questions surprised Weaver. After he and Cox met outside, she prepared for the worst. She answered in a voice that reflected her relief. "Oh, Ethan didn't have Tourette's. After undergoing a battery of tests and several observations, everyone felt his twitching behavior was related to his extraordinary visual acuity. His field of vision was so wide he glimpsed things that other people don't see. That's why he moved his head quickly—trying to catch sight of everything around him."

"And what about Sara's condition?" Cox asked.

"All the psych specialists discounted any form of mental health problem. Her MRI showed that her temporal lobes were extremely active. Based on those findings, the audiologist felt she was trying to make sense out of sounds outside our normal range of hearing."

"Give me a minute." Jenkins wrote a quick note in the spiral notebook he carried in his shirt pocket. "That's enough about the children for now. What did Santini and Foxe discover about the composition of the stuff from that cosmic blast? Did they find what caused the children to be the way they were?"

Weaver looked at Jenkins and smiled. *About time, we got to that.* "Yes. Yes they did. But it took a while to gather the data. First, we had to obtain the funding to allow Celia and Sandy to work on the project. Once we received the funding, it took almost a year to complete their research. A half dozen top flight people helped them—astrophysicists, geneticists, and analysts."

"Okay, okay, but what did they learn?" Jenkins demanded, showing his impatience.

Weaver ignored Jenkins' demanding tone and deliberately sipped her tea. *Wouldn't you like to know?* "Well, a little over a year after the initial evaluations of the children at Johns Hopkins, Sandy and Celia called to say they were on their way to Baltimore. They wanted to share their preliminary findings with me." Mitzi took another sip of tea then sat the cup on the end table next to her chair. *Damn, that was a long time ago. I can't remember everything. The report was so technical. Besides, I doubt if Jenkins knows the difference between a tachyon, a boson, and his butthole!*

Chapter 45

Location: Mitzi Weaver's Townhouse, Baltimore, Maryland
Time: October 2025

Mitzi Weaver scurried about her townhouse as she prepared to receive Celia Foxe and Sandy Santini. She vacuumed the entry, dusted the main living area, organized a stack of professional journals, and straightened everything in sight.

Last evening, Celia called to say that she and Sandy planned to stop in Baltimore in route from Paris to Chicago. They wanted to share the results of their study with Weaver. A knock at the door announced their arrival.

"Come on in. I'm so happy to see you!" Weaver gave each of them a warm hug and invited them in. "Make yourselves at home. The teakettle is hot. I can make coffee, if you want some."

Once everyone sat down with a strong cup of tea, Weaver said, "So, tell me what's been happening with you two. It's been over a year since we talked."

Sandy spoke first. "You mean in our personal lives?"

"Of course. You can tell me about your research later."

Simultaneously, Celia and Sandy answered, "What personal life!" The two commiserated over their lack of a personal life; their professional life was the only life that they had while they worked on the project.

Mitzi understood; there was never time in her life for entertainment or the possibility of romance. She changed the subject. "I really appreciate you taking time to visit with me. I know it must have been a tiring flight."

"Yes, but we both slept on the plane," Celia said. "Love those *Business Class* seats."

Santini looked at his watch. "Can't stay long, but we wanted to tell you what we found. Have a tight schedule. From here, we're off to Chicago to publish the findings"

"When do you have to leave?" Mitzi asked.

"Our flight is later today. Celia and I meet with the publication folks at Fermi Lab tomorrow morning."

Mitzi put her cup down, sat up straight, and asked with a sense of eagerness, "Well, tell me what you found. I've waited a year to hear this!"

Santini laughed softly as he nodded his head. "Okay. Here it is. Let me begin by saying that we had unprecedented access to a tremendous body of data—data collected from around the world. When NOAA announced that the blast would occur, every professional and amateur scientist with any kind of equipment prepared to gather data."

"Let me start." Celia removed a micro-tablet from her shoulder bag before rethinking her action. "What am I doing? I'm not going to read to you! You can read it later." She shoved the tablet back into her bag. "Simply put, Ross-Katsura was a hell of a nasty brew. It's evident now that something cataclysmic did happen in deep space—a supernova or something like it—that released a unique combination of particles."

The two physicists explained what happens in a supernova. Celia started, "Typically, here's what you need for a supernova. First, you need a star that is about three hundred times as large as our sun. When this massive star runs out of fuel to support nuclear fusion—the process that makes stars shine—it will collapse from gravitational pressure. When gravity compresses the star to a certain point, the gases within the star explode. Bang! You got yourself a supernova. We're not sure if that is what happened, but we are certain that a supernova—or even a hypernova—caused the eruption."

Santini giggled in reaction to his colleague's folksy explanation of how a supernova occurs. "If I might continue. When the star explodes, a tremendous amount of matter and radiation is ejected into space. The material generated by the supernova associated with Ross-Katsura was so incredible that it disrupted a vast area of space-time. And, more to the point, we think that it shredded what we know as dark matter and dark energy."

Feeling overwhelmed, Weaver said, "Dark energy and dark matter, I don't...?"

"You're not alone," Foxe interrupted. "Both of these things are still a mystery to most of us. Santini works in this area. You want to add something, Sandy?"

Santini smiled, pleased to share his knowledge. "Without going overboard, here's what we know. The visible universe—what we can actually see—represents only four percent of the total matter and energy in the universe. Dark energy and dark matter make up the rest—over ninety-six percent. So, we basically don't know squat about most of the material in our universe!"

Celia could not restraint herself and added, "Dark matter is not like regular matter. While regular matter is uniformly distributed throughout the universe, that's not true for dark matter. It's kinda clumpy. It usually clusters around galaxies and nebulae. While it has mass and can bend light waves, it does not display the same properties as regular matter. When two galaxies collide, their associated dark matter does not react the way the regular matter in the galaxies react. The dark matter just continues to move in a straight line unaffected by the surrounding stellar matter. It's as if dark matter can pass through regular matter the same way trillions of subatomic particles past through you and me every day. Some theorists believe that dark matter and dark energy actually bind galaxies together."

"What we're dealing with in Ross-Katsura is not just dark matter and dark energy," Santini added. "There is also a broad spectrum of electromagnetic radiation—common things like radio waves, microwaves, infrared radiation, visible light, ultraviolet radiation, X-rays, gamma rays—and a bunch of not so common things. Our eyes see only a small portion of the available wavelengths. What we see, we call the visible spectrum. If the electromagnetic source does not emit photons, then we can't see it—just like we can't see dark matter."

Weaver shook her head and raised her hand. "Wait. Wait. All that sounds great, but how'd it affect the children?"

"Well now. That's the interesting part!" Foxe licked her lips and smiled. "'In a nutshell, we believe a supernova created a massive number of subatomic particles. Everything from neutrinos, to tachyons, to Higgs bosons—trillions and trillions of the little buggers—far greater than the number we normally encounter. Physicists have identified many new subatomic particles over the past three decades. The days of talking about atoms as the building blocks of matter are long past. Today, we subdivide electrons, protons and neutrons within the nucleus of the atom—and subdivide them again. We have a whole lexicon for such things as bosons and fermions. We know that these are the basic ingredients that form everything around us—inanimate things and living creatures."

Santini added, "The Earth is constantly bombarded by these particles and all types of electromagnetic energy. What made Ross-Katsura different is that the volume of these particles and rays was significantly increased. And here's the kicker—as best as we can tell—all of this material interacted with a massive cluster of dark matter and energy. We learned this from sifting through all that data I mentioned a moment ago. Measurements indicate that particle density in our little part of the galaxy increased by thirty percent. That's amazing! We're theorizing that a lot of this new matter and energy struck the Earth. Actually, it just passed through the Earth—and us!"

Caught up in Santini's excitement, Foxe explained, "You see, our atmosphere shields us from most damaging rays, but some get through every day, like gamma rays and neutrinos. In Ross-Katsura, the volume of electromagnetic radiation and subatomic particles increased significantly."

Foxe stopped abruptly and touched Mitzi's knee. "And that, Doctor Weaver, is what we think happened to Ethan, Sara, and Chetana."

Weaver looked confused, uncertain about what Celia meant by her last comment. "What do you think happened? What do you mean? Are you saying that this material changed their genetic make-up? But if that's so, why have we not found many more affected children?

"That's what stumped us for a while," Foxe responded, nodding her head in agreement. "Then someone asked, 'what's so damn different about these kids?' Which led us to the question, 'what do they have in common?' Those two questions sent everyone back to the data. Sure enough, last year when the parents visited Johns Hopkins, someone recorded an extensive medical history of the parents, including the conditions of the children's conceptions. Can you imagine that! One of your folks asked, 'where and when was your child conceived'—damn nosey if you ask me. But thank goodness that they did. That's how we found the connection between your three kids—just two key variables, timing and elevation." Celia Foxe waited, as if she had cast bait into the ocean and expected a sudden strike.

Mitzi Weaver mulled over Celia's words. "Timing? Timing of what? Their conception? And by elevation—you mean altitude?"

"You got it!" The bait taken, Foxe continued. "Where were the parents when the children were conceived?"

Mitzi chuckled. "I guess that they were in bed with each other!"

"Okay, smart ass." Foxe could not help but laugh along with Mitzi.

Mitzi controlled her laughter and said, "You mean the type of locations—where each conception occurred? I think I remember something about that. If I'm right, they were all visiting mountainous areas. That came up one time when I visited with them. I didn't think much of it at the time."

With an impish smile on his face, Santini responded. "That's right—mountains above ten thousand feet. You might call it the 'two-mile' high club! Remember, the Earth's atmosphere protects us from most harmful radiation. Whatever caused the change in the children must have dissipated quickly."

"And timing," Weaver added. "Now you are in my backyard. Fetal development is my field. I'll bet that you found that the zygote, the embryonic material for each child, was in the first week of gestation—a time when the cells are most vulnerable. So you're saying that some form of radiation or subatomic particle altered the structure of the children's genes in this very formative stage of development?"

Celia Foxe and Sandy Santini nodded, acknowledging Weaver's description.

Foxe summarized. "So, some form of matter or radiation interacted with dark matter and dark energy to release subatomic particles that moved at the speed of photons. But, unlike photons that don't have mass, these unique particles had mass and were able to penetrate human DNA."

"That's about it. Every day, we're bombarded by all sorts of particles and rays that pass through our bodies—gamma rays and neutrinos. The geneticists on our team theorize that the particles involved were so infinitesimally small that they could pierce the nucleotides of chromosomal tissue and change them without damage to the cell structure. We haven't precisely identified the particle involved. I like to think of it as 'God's little scalpel'—one of his tools for shaping mankind!"

The three continued to discuss the implications of the study. Are there more children affected by the fallout, not yet identified? What methodology might identify other effected children? There was much to consider but very little time before Santini and Celia had to leave for the airport.

Mitzi Weaver rested that night, content in the knowledge that she was working with three of God's special creations. As the years passed, she would learn just how special they were.

Chapter 46

Location: Beach Estate of Sanjay, Colombo, Sri Lanka
Date: October 2025

Sanjay stood in the marble arch that formed the entry to his home, ready to receive the Bombay Gentlemen. Over five years passed since the group last visited his splendid estate in Sri Lanka. The limousine service from the airport was not dependable, but a call from Harshal alerted him that his guests were on their way.

Today, the group would receive an update on the Enlightened Ones, as Manish, the holy man, called them. Sanjay and Sudhir would again be giving the progress report. For over seven years, the Gentlemen invested labor and equipment in their effort. There was hope that the time had come to reap some dividends for their efforts.

As two stretch limousines halted and their occupants emerged, Sanjay bellowed from the steps leading into his home, "Gentlemen, gentlemen, come in. Welcome to my humble abode!" The jet-black vehicles stood in stark contrast to the brilliant white stucco portico and the adjourning arches. "Food and refreshment are inside. Ask if there is anything that you wish; my staff will be happy to assist you."

Inside the luxuriously furnished home, the men were ushered into a theater room with overstuffed recliners. At the front of the room was a screen measuring twenty feet across. A well-stocked wet bar filled the back of the room. As the men entered, they gathered at the bar for drinks before taking their seats.

Harshal rose, finished the last swallow of his tropical fruit drink, and proceeded to the front of the theater. He paused for a moment to allow a mahogany podium to emerge from the floor. "Gentlemen! We are here to work, but please continue with your refreshments. We would offend our host if we did not sample the fine beverages and the other delicacies he has provided." With a smile to his face, he continued, "Of course, this does not include his young servers. They are his private stock."

The men in the room chuckled. They knew Sanjay was very fond of young women, especially the fair-skinned ones of mixed British and Ceylonese heritage.

After Harshal reviewed the agenda for the meeting, he invited Sanjay and Sudhir to come forward. "Gentlemen, the floor is yours."

Sanjay and Sudhir approached the podium. As they did, Sudhir said, "We have much to discuss, my friends. This is an auspicious day. We have been successful in obtaining a most important document, the unpublished report of a group that has been investigating the Ross-Katsura event. As you know, the birth of the Enlightened Ones is related to that event."

"And how, might I ask, did we obtain such a prestigious document before its publication," Harshal asked, obviously soliciting personal recognition.

Sudhir bowed towards Harshal and then towards Bijay. "My dear friends, we are again indebted to Harshal and Bijay for their illustrious work. Harshal's antivirus software modification and Bijay's network of computers, gave us easy access to the Publications Department at Fermi Lab in the United States. The Lab, may I say, *generously* allowed Bijay to download a copy of the report from its mainframe." Sudhir turned to Harshal. "Is that adequate my friend or does each of us need to kiss your bulbous ass?"

Laughter filled the room, which prompted Harshal to stand and offer his bare buttocks to his colleagues. The group responded with moans and catcalls.

"Enough fun and games. Let's get serious." Sanjay raised a bound document. "Here is a copy of the unpublished report prepared by Santini and Foxe—two highly respected physicists. Let's review their findings."

When Sanjay and Sudhir completed their presentation, the group discussed the findings in a scholarly exchange. As the discussion waned, Rishi stepped up to the podium and assumed a matter-of-fact pose. "For over a year, I have worked to befriend Ram Kapur in our effort to gain access to his daughter, an Enlightened One. He and his family are now regular guests at my home and aboard my personal jet. And while I do not mind maintaining the relationship with this chap and his lovely wife, I question where we are going. When do we take control of these children?" Rishi paused and studied the faces of his colleagues.

Sanjay spoke first. "I appreciate the contribution you are making, my friend, but I feel the time is not right for us to act."

"I concur," Bijay said. "We should wait to see how the children develop—to see what skills each demonstrates."

Harshal quickly added, "Yes, yes. Why show our hand until we know exactly how their special skills may be utilized?"

The group agreed; they would wait a while longer. In the meantime, Rishi would stay in touch with Ram Kapur and his family. Harshal would formulate plans to make contact with the family of the American boy. Kevin Lake seemed an easy target; he was in the brokerage business—highly approachable by men of wealth. They would continue to watch the Swedish child. If she developed talents that could turn a profit, they would devise a suitable course of action to take her under their control.

Chapter 47

Location: The Overseer's Cottage, Carrington Farm, Northern Virginia
Time: September 2034

Mitzi Weaver and the two lawmen sat on the patio behind the cottage, enjoying a momentary burst of warm autumn sun. Jenkins agreed to a short a break to make fresh coffee and allow everyone to get some fresh air. As they drank coffee and enjoyed the pastoral setting, the three found themselves interacting on a social level.

"Don't you love the mountains in the fall," Weaver said as she stretched her arms to her side. "The colors are beautiful and the weather is so pleasant."

Jenkins looked toward Mitzi, nodded, and winked. "It's kinda strange, but what I like is the occasional smell of burning leaves—brings back some good childhood memories. Folks still do that up here. They're not too concerned with all the new air pollution restrictions we have back in Richmond"

Cox chuckled, amused by Jenkins. "Well, there weren't many leaves to burn when I was a child. I grew up in the panhandle of Oklahoma; a stand of trees was a rarity out there. Besides, when I was a boy, late September meant harvest time. My daddy had us kids cutting and hauling grain."

"Well, this is nice, but we best get back to it." Jenkins collected everyone's cups before he added, "I'd like to get home tonight."

The trio entered the cottage and Cox said to Weaver, "Santini and Foxe seemed to have pinpointed how the children came to have special qualities. Was there a formal study to follow the development of these kids or did you just informally stay in touch with them?"

"Initially, there wasn't a formal study but I did stay in touch with them and their parents."

"The reason I ask, is that I'd like to develop a personality profile for each of them. Did they show any signs of extraordinary potential as adolescents? Were they pretty normal kids or did they act out? What can you tell me about their childhood years?"

Jenkins frowned. "Hold on there, Cox. We need to get your questions on the record. My lapel cam wasn't on. Let's take our seats 'fore you get started."

Returning to the living room, Mitzi and Cox sat down while Jenkins fiddled with his lapel cam and its remote recording device. "Okay Cox, give us your questions again."

Cox obliged by repeating his earlier questions to Weaver.

Weaver deliberately stared into Jenkins' lapel camera. "As I said earlier, there wasn't an ongoing study of the children. We wanted to follow them annually, but the funding just wasn't there. After publishing the initial findings, interest in the project started to wane. It was hard to find funding for a long-term study that covered three kids—a rather small study group. For the second part of your question, I'm not sure what you FBI guys use in creating a personality profile, but a couple of things come to mind. If they aren't what you need, I'm sure you'll tell me."

"That will be fine," Cox responded. "If I need something more, I'll follow-up later."

Mitzi Weaver searched her memory. "I guess I know more about Ethan than about Sara and Chetana. Emily and I kept in touch more." Leaning back in her chair, she began, "Actually, each of them experienced some trying situations as juveniles. It's hard enough being a child, much less one with very special gifts."

Chapter 48

Location: Franklin Elementary School, Denver, Colorado
Time: November 2026

Ethan Lake, as a seven-year-old, attended Franklin Elementary, but he seldom joined his second grade classmates. His only contact with them was during recess and lunch. The remainder of the school day he spent in upper grades: fourth grade for social studies and writing; fifth grade for science; and sixth grade for math, his favorite subject.

On this particular afternoon, Ethan was not interested in math nor any other subject. This afternoon, there was only one thing on his mind. It was the final period of the day. Sitting on the edge of his chair, staring at the hands on the old fashion clock, he was poised for action. *Only five more minutes and I'm out of here. Gotta run straight to the bus parking lot. Teachers will be there.* He gripped his backpack and posed himself for the dash that lay ahead.

The moment the bell rang; young Ethan scurried down the hallway and out the front door of the building, walking as fast as he could across the playground. *Don't run, don't run. Can't run on the playground. Teachers are watching.* Suddenly, three sixth grade boys appeared in front of him. *Oh no! It's Max.* Before he could react, the largest of the three boys spoke.

"Geek butt! Yeah, you, shithead. Where do you think you're going?"

Ethan studied Max and the two other boys. He wanted to run but he knew it was hopeless. Looking up at his antagonist, he asked in a trembling voice, "What do you want, Max?" Although large for his age, Ethan did not wish to confront a sixth-grader almost twice his weight—and Max's two friends.

"What do I want?" Max Donnelley repeated. "I wanna teach you a lesson. That's what I wanna do. I'm gonna kick your smart ass."

"What did I do to you?" Ethan knew that Max was angry about what happened in math class earlier in the day, but he feigned ignorance.

"I told you this morning you'd better cover your ass. Nobody makes a fool of me."

Ethan knew what Max meant. In math class, Mr. Dugan, the math teacher, asked Max to give the numerical value of *Pi*. When Donnelley could not answer, Mr. Dugan called on Ethan to answer the question, an easy task for the young math whiz.

Ethan could see that Max was angry. *Why's he mad at me. It's not my fault he didn't know the answer.* Before he could finish his thought, Donnelley swung his fist in a powerful uppercut aimed at Ethan's stomach. Without thinking, Ethan jumped back, to avoid being hit.

The force of Donnelley's thrust caused him to spin halfway around, nearly losing his balance. Righting himself, he screamed, "You, asshole! Now you really pissed me off." The words barely left his lips before Max swung a second time targeting Ethan's face.

Again, Ethan dodged his assailant's blow causing Donnelley to nearly fall. Only the quick reactions of his companions kept him from hitting the ground.

Ethan saw Max hanging in the arms of his friends. *Run! It's only thirty yards to the buses. Run!* Before he could move, the three ruffians lunged toward him in unison. As they did, Ethan spun to one side and caused his attackers to land in a disheveled heap with Max Donnelley on the bottom, blood flowing from his chin. With his tormentors on the ground, Ethan sprinted to the bus lot and the protection of Ms. Zobel, the teacher on bus duty.

⁂

Principal Stevens stood to greet Emily Lake as she entered the principal's office. "Thank you for coming here on your lunch hour, Doctor Lake. I apologize for calling your home last evening, but I felt we needed to deal with this issue immediately."

"Certainly. But I am not clear what this is about. Last evening, you said it was urgent that we speak. Has Ethan done something that I need to know about?"

"Yes, there is. It appears that Ethan was in an altercation yesterday. I'm advised by our school nurse that a sixth grade student visited our clinic shortly after school was dismissed yesterday." Stevens consulted notes in a folder on his desk. "It seems the student sustained an injury to his chin and mouth. A rather nasty cut on his chin required a couple of stitches. Which leads me to ask: Is Ethan enrolled in martial arts classes?"

Emily, stunned by the question, did not know what to say; she hesitated. "No. He's too busy with his school work and sports. Why do you ask?"

"There were several witnesses to the incident that stated Ethan inflicted the injuries to the student in question."

Emily laughed aloud. "You must be kidding! You expect me to believe that a kid who is only seven beat up a twelve or a thirteen-year-old."

"Not only that, a couple of children that observed the event stated that he also knocked two other sixth grade boys to the ground. Fortunately, neither was hurt."

"Come now, Mr. Stevens. Does that make sense to you? My son is scarcely sixty-five pounds. Granted, he is large for his age, but accosting three boys at once—I doubt that!"

Stevens shook his head. "I know. I know. That's the reason I asked about the martial arts training."

"Well, he's no Kung-Fu master—that I can tell you!" Emily assumed a mother's protective posture. "So what are you planning to do regarding this incident?"

Principal Stevens collected his notes. "I'm placing your son and the three other boys in detention for thirty minutes each afternoon next week. The detention will be served during the children's scheduled activity periods."

Emily stood and gave Stevens a stern look. "I understand you must take some action, although I disagree with your decision. Be assured that I will speak with my son this evening." She grabbed her purse and placed it under her arm. "If that's all—then good day to you, sir."

Walking down the hallway to the parking lot, Emily replayed what Principal Stevens said. *I can't imagine how this happen? It's ridiculous. I need to hear his side. Kevin's meeting clients tonight. He won't be home for supper. I'll take Ethan for burgers at the ice cream shop. Best way to talk to him. Can't imagine how he took on three sixth grade boys and didn't get pulverized!*

❧❧

That evening, as Emily and Ethan enjoyed burgers and ice cream sundaes, Ethan recounted what happened at school. "Momma, I'm telling you. I didn't hit anyone. All I did was get out of the way when Max tried to hit me."

"You mean he tried to strike you? With what? His fists?"

"Yeah. But he's not very fast. I just got out of the way."

"But Mr. Stevens said you threw three boys to the ground. And one of the boys needed sutures to close a cut on his chin."

"Yeah, Max was bleeding when I ran, but I didn't do anything to him. He and his buddies just fell all over each other."

"I don't understand, Ethan. Why did they fall?"

"They were trying to jump on me, but they move real slow, Momma. I could see what they were going to do and just got out of the way. They must've tripped on each other when I stepped aside. All I know is that they fell down and I ran to the bus."

Ethan paused to sip his drank. As he finished, his hand shot towards his mother's face. Startled, she jolted to one side. Her son grinned and slowly opened his hand to expose a fly. "Flies aren't all that fast either. Are they Momma?"

Chapter 49

Location: Home of Ram and Kumari Kapur, New Delhi, India
Time: April 2027

"Damn it, Kumari, I don't want your mother and her bloody friends in my house, ever again!" Ram Kapur was upset over the recent actions of his mother-in-law. "Do you understand me? I'll not hear of this...."

"Please Ram, settle down. My mother only wants what is best for Chetana, but she sees things differently. She and her friends are devoted to the goddess, Saraswati. She believes that the deity returns to the Earth, from time to time, to help humanity reach Nirvana. Do not your Christian friends at Harvard and Cambridge speak of Jesus Christ coming back to earth? How is that different from my mother's belief?"

"The difference, my dear wife, is that Jesus Christ is not my child. Chetana is! And I'll not have a bunch of zealots turn her into a religious sideshow! I don't care if your mother and her friends are convinced that our daughter is the reincarnation of some goddess. The whole thing is bloody madness."

"Ram, please. All they ask is to allow the holiest monks of the temple to question Chetana. What harm could there be? If she is not the reincarnation of Saraswati, then so be it. But if the child is who they believed her to be, who are we to stand in the way of a divine plan?"

"Enough. I'll hear no more." Ram shook his head rapidly and stomped out of the room.

৵৵

That evening, Kumari lay next to Ram, her fragrant skin pressed against his. In a soft voice she asked, "My love, is it too much to ask that our child be examined by the holy men?"

Ram was physically strong, with even stronger convictions, but he was no match for Kumari as she softly caressed his chest. "Okay, okay, if that is what it takes to put an end to this foolishness."

Kamari kissed him on the chest. "Thank you, my husband."

Chapter 50

Location: Temple to Goddess Saraswati, New Delhi, India
Time: April 2027

Malati, Chetana's grandmother, rose early to allow time for prayers and a breakfast of fruit, yogurt, and delicate pieces of bread with honey. Malati, which means "flower", had become a thorn in the side of her son-in-law, but she prevailed. *Today, my beautiful granddaughter will stand before the holy men of the temple. There is no doubt in my mind that they will declare Chetana the embodiment of our goddess, Saraswati. What other outcome could there be? Everyone knows that my lovely grandchild possesses powers reserved for the holiest of beings.*

As Ram Kapur and his family entered the temple, a group of supplicants greeted them, each seeking blessings from the holy child. Ram pushed his way through the group and proceeded to the front of the temple where sat several monks with clean-shaven heads.

The senior monk, draped in a saffron silk robe and seated on a satin pillow, nodded to Ram but spoke directly to Chetana. "Welcome, my child. Thank you for coming."

"You are most welcome," Chetana responded politely.

The elder monk studied the child while three monks dressed in simple cotton robes looked on. He said, "I am told that you are a very special person. Is that true?"

"Some say so."

"And what do you say?"

"I am who I am. A little girl, no more."

"Is it true that you possess powers that other little girls do not?"

"If you say so."

The holy men studied the child and listened closely to every word she said. A great deal was at stake—more than their personal reputations—the very future of the temple of was at stake. Offerings had fallen off in recent years.

The once brilliantly painted murals that depicted the magnificent deeds of the goddess were in need of retouching. Tapestries and carpets showed years of wear. If this child was the embodiment of their beloved goddess, she would fulfill to their prayers and the prayers of many devout believers.

Malati and her friends watched as the monks put question after question to the child. Some of the questions upset Ram; his mind raced. *Who are these men to ask a young girl if she is a virgin? Or, if she had ever taken the shape of a serpent in this life?* When the senior monk finally rose to address those present, Ram was visibly relieved that the ordeal was over.

"Dear friends, we have heard much today. The time has come to pray and to seek the guidance of our mother, Saraswati." Bowing deeply, the monk and his entourage, processed from the room.

"Well, that's over! I could use a strong drink." Ram spoke just loud enough for the faithful who abstained from alcohol to hear his words.

Kumari and her mother glared at Ram as they slowly exited the temple; their displeasure with what he said was obvious to all.

❧❦

In a private room behind the temple's altar, the holy men convened to discuss their findings. Several novices brought tea and small pastries and then sat where they could observe the deliberation.

The senior monk looked into the eyes of each of the six monks seated in a circle around him. "Brothers, we must decide if this child is the reincarnation of our goddess or a mere child. It is a grave burden that we bear—a burden not to be taken lightly."

The holy men felt the gravity of their task. In turn, they discussed the answers given by the child to each question. As the evening meal hour approached, they lacked consensus. A few asked for more time to pray while a larger faction called for action. To delay was not acceptable; temple aides reported that many of the faithful returned to the temple throughout the day seeking news of the decision. They were growing impatient.

One of the younger monks asked if he might speak frankly. "My brothers, I am not sure if this child is our beloved one, but what if she is? Think of the benefits she brings. Should we not err on the side of the question that most greatly benefits our temple?"

From indecision, consensus suddenly grew. Questions arose. What would be the next step? Why would anyone other than the most fervent believers accept the group's decision? There must be a test—a public display of the child's powers—a healing would do. Such a demonstration would not be too much to ask of a living goddess.

The chief monk spoke. "Here is what we shall do. First, we identify an afflicted person and arrange for him to come to the temple. If necessary, offer a small cash inducement. Once a date is selected, a novice should deliver a message to the parents asking that the child come to the temple. If there is resistance, just contact the grandmother for support. Lastly, this is a time for celebration. Let us decorate the temple and bring in flowers. Such an important event demands flowers and offerings to the goddess."

As the monks undertook each task, word of the planned healing quickly spread among the devoted; many of the faithful planned to attend the healing.

❧

Ram opened the note from the temple as Kumari looked on. He took care not to tear the delicate rice paper on which it was written. "They want Chetana to appear at the temple. Listen to these instructions: 'Come one hour before the midday meal on the first day of the period of *Vaisakhi.*' Have these monkeys heard of a watch or a real calendar? What's the first day…?"

Kumari reached for the note and read it herself. "These are simple instructions. We are just to go to the temple." She handed the note back to Ram. "You needn't worry about the date. My mother knows how to read the Hindu lunar calendar. She'll tell us the date."

"Your mother! She got us into this bloody mess."

"Ram, please. We have been over this enough. We are going. It is not just for my mother—I need to know."

Ram shook his head to show is disapproval. "I think it's a bloody mistake. But I'm wasting my breath; you will not change your mind."

❧

The day for Chetana to visit the temple arrived. As Ram and his family entered the temple, he repeated his displeasure one last time. "I'm telling you, this is bloody foolishness! I have said it once more."

His words brought the immediate wrath of Kumari and her mother—but only muffled giggles from Chetana.

The temple buzzed with activity. Many of the faithful hurried to place offerings of fruit and incense on the makeshift altar prepared for this special day. Others gathered at the rear and along the sides of the worship area to share their beliefs about whether this child was a living deity or a fake.

At the front of the temple, an ornately carved chair with a red velvet cushion sat on a raised platform. Before the chair lay a palette, like that used by invalid beggars, but draped with velvet that matched the chair cushion.

A chime rang and everyone standing took seats within the temple. After a few moments, a man around thirty entered the temple from a door to the right of the platform. Aided by two novice monks, he was lead to the palette and sat down facing the faithful—and the curious—in attendance. The novices removed the man's tunic to reveal a marked tremor in his right arm.

Whispers ran through the audience. Ram heard a man seated behind him say, "Yes, yes. I know this fellow. He is a beggar. He is unable to work."

Ram turned to Kumari. "What's going on? Did you know about this?"

"No, I didn't. I have no idea who that man is or why he is here."

The afflicted man sat for several minutes before the chief monk, dressed in an elaborately embroidered robe, entered and sat in the chair next to the palette. In a full voice he said, "Believers, followers of the divine one, Saraswati, we are here to testify to her presence among us." He summoned the child. "Chetana Kapur, come forward."

Malati gently pushed her granddaughter. "Go my child. Take your destiny."

A novice hurried to where the child was. When Chetana rose from her seat, he bowed toward her, and guided her to the platform. A rumble of voices emanated from the faithful that filled the temple.

"Chetana Kapur, if you are the embodiment of our beloved Saraswati, remove this affliction from your servant, Isha, who lies before you."

The faithful murmured among themselves, "Can she cure this man? Is she really our beloved goddess?"

Chetana stood quietly for a moment. A hush fell over the crowd as she took a step toward Isha and looked into his eyes. The child turned to her parents and then turned to face the chief monk. "May I touch your hand?" she asked, as she extended hers and moved towards the seated holy man.

The monk reached out, hesitated a moment, then gently grasped the child's delicate hand.

In a strong voice that resonated throughout the temple, Chetana asked, "Are your motives pure?"

Amazement, followed by disbelief, covered the holy man's face. He did not speak, stunned by the apparent accusation.

Chetana's gaze turned from the monk to the assembled group. She spoke in a deliberate voice. "If I do this thing, you will make me into what I wish not to be. If I choose not to do this thing, you will say that I deceived those around me. Of this, I am not afraid. For by not acting, I will remain with my father and my mother. I choose my parents." Chetana faced the senior monk, and again, spoke in a firm voice for all to hear. "Before I go, I testify that your outward acts of piety are but a sham to hide your transgressions against those that you claim to serve. I know your sins. Now, leave this place and do not return or I will tell the people who you truly are!"

The monk stood and started to speak but stopped before uttering a word. His jaw clinched, he hurried from the altar area amid cries from his once faithful supporters, "Speak! Tell us who you are. What are your sins?"

Chetana stepped off the platform and ran toward her parents. When she reached them, she asked, "Did I do right, father?"

Ram reached for his daughter's small hand and the hand of his wife. "I think we may leave now." With the swagger of a vindicated man, Ram proudly led his family from the temple.

The chief monk did not return to the temple. Temple worshippers sought to learn what the child meant when she said he sinned against those he served. Gossip said he stole from the temple. Several weeks after his departure, word came that he died under suspicious circumstances. After a short investigation, authorities closed the case for lack of evidence.

A rumor persisted that Isha moved to a nearby village where he worked his small farm with two strong arms. When asked what became of his tremor, he would only say, "It was the will of the goddess that I am no longer afflicted."

Malati and her friends never again spoke of Chetana as being a living deity. The child chose to be with the ones she loved. After all, love is the greatest blessing.

Chapter 51

Location: Indoor Tennis Club, Stockholm, Sweden
Time: February 2028

Christina Johansson directed the personal transportation vehicle onto the computer monitored roadway. After she entered the address of the tennis club, she released the steering wheel. "There everything is programmed. We can relax and talk." Christina enjoyed the trip to the club; it gave her time to visit with her daughter.

Sara was in a particularly talkative mood, fueled by excitement. "Momma, I'm so nervous. It's my very first juniors' tournament. Oooh, I hope I win!" As if struck by lightning, she reached into the back of the vehicle and feverishly searched through the pile of equipment bags, towels, and knapsacks. "Did I bring my good racket? I have to have it. I can't play Olga with a clunky club racket."

Christina placed her hand on Sara's shoulder. "Settle down. I got your racket. It's in the back. Now sit down."

Once at the club, Sara went to the dressing room and Christina found a place on the aluminum bleachers overlooking the court on which Sara would play. The bleachers were cold, prompting her to look for a thermos in her knapsack. *Just as I thought. This place is always cold.* She retrieved a large thermos and poured a cup of hot chocolate. *Now that's better. Ah, there's Sara now.* Before she could take a sip of chocolate, a familiar voice called to her.

"Good morning, Doctor Johansson."

Christina looked behind her to see a middle-aged man dressed in a tailored, blue sport coat that fit his uncharacteristically wide shoulders and thick neck. "Deputy Director Lundberg, so nice to see you here." Slightly intimidated by the presence of a senior executive from her office, Christina did not know what else to say. *What's he doing here?*

The questioning look on Christina's face prompted Lundberg to say, "My wife's a member of the club. We ate breakfast here this morning. I'm not fond of tennis, but I do like the breakfast. Nice, very nice." Changing the subject, he continued, "So, your daughter Sara is playing this morning? Which one is she?"

Christina pointed to a nearby court. "She's on court three, in the yellow outfit." *How does he know Sara's name? What does he want?*

"Oh yes, I see her. She takes after you, blond hair and all. I understand she has your gift for languages."

"Yes, she likes studying languages. Guess Oskar and I are to blame for that." *Where's he going with this?*

A short time passed before the start of Sara's match. Lundberg watched the match, grinning broadly when Sara served an ace or won a rapid volley. "Well, I must go. I have a meeting downtown. Let's talk on Monday. Say around nine?"

Christina knew that this was not an invitation that could be accepted or rejected; Lundberg was directing her to appear. "Oh, okay. I'll see you then." *My God, he's up to something!*

∾

Oskar was not able to watch Sara play that morning. When Christina arrived home, she explained what happened—how Deputy Lundberg approached her.

"Christina, you're making too much of this. There could be a dozen reasons for him to visit the club. After all, he said his wife was a member and that he liked eating breakfast there. As for him knowing that Sara likes languages, he probably heard it from someone at work. It's not like you keep it a secret. Maybe he wants another language specialist! Like mother, like daughter."

"Oh, Oskar, don't be silly! Sara is only nine years old. She's not going to work in an intelligence unit."

Oskar put his arms around his wife and hugged her. "It's Saturday morning. Less than two days from now, you'll see Lundberg and this great mystery will simply disappear. Now stop worrying."

∾

"Christina. Welcome. Come in," Marvin Lundberg boomed. "So pleased that we could talk this morning. This weekend was miserable—I'm still working on that Turkish-Iraqi border issue. But enough of that. May I offer you a cup of coffee? Fresh brewed. Dark roasted Arabica beans from Ethiopia. Doesn't get any better!"

"No, thank you, Director Lundberg, I've reached my limit for this morning. I must admit this meeting had me up early."

"Oh? I'm so sorry. I didn't mean to trouble you. And what's with this 'director' stuff? We have worked together many times. We are friends."

"So, what did you wish to talk about," Christina asked, trying to move the meeting forward and allay her concerns.

Lundberg took a chrome thermos from the credenza behind his desk and poured himself a cup of black coffee. A pungent aroma filled the room. "Christina, I wanted to speak with you about Sara. She's ten now, isn't she?"

Christina Johansson was not a newcomer to the intelligence field. When Lundberg asked a question, he probably knew the answer. *Yes, she's almost ten. Yes, she speaks several languages fluently. Hell, I don't doubt you know the last time Oskar and I had sex!* Straining to maintain her composure, Christina politely responded. "Yes sir, she'll be ten in March."

Lundberg stared at the woman seated before him and realized to whom he was speaking. *No more cat and mouse games.* "We're professionals here, Christina. Let me get to the point. Sara is a very special child. She possesses certain talents. I believe you know what I mean. We think she could be an asset for our organization."

"An asset?" *He means an operative. A spy!*

Lundberg took a swallow of coffee and then traced his lips with his index finger. "Christina, I'm sure that you've heard of remote viewing, haven't you?"

"Yes sir," Christina answered inquisitively. "The Russians and the Americans played around with the technique back in the cold war days. Some individuals were supposedly able to see or feel what a subject was doing. I don't recall it ever being utilized—not effectively anyway. Why do you ask?"

"I've spoken with some people who are knowledgeable about these things. Based on what I know of Sara's gifts, I believe she might be able to do something similar. Call it 'remote listening' or whatever you wish."

"Are you kidding?" The words tumbled out of Christina's mouth without thought.

Lundberg, noticeably shocked by Christina's outburst, collected himself for a moment. "I'm quite serious. I know Sara is just a child, but children that possess special skills need to learn to use them. Look how she has learned languages. If you did not encourage her, she certainly would not speak so many languages. What I am proposing is nothing more than adding dance or piano lessons to her schedule. Think of it as a personal development activity."

Christina Johansson withheld the anger growing in her. *Piano lessons, my ass. I know what happens downstairs. Careful now. Remember who you're talking to.* "So, Director Lundberg, exactly what would this entail? I can't see Oskar agreeing to Sara spending hours in some testing lab."

"Oh, no, that's not what I have in mind!" Lundberg leaned forward in his chair and repeatedly shook his head. "No, no. no. I don't wish to change her life. Children need to enjoy their childhood—play tennis, be with friends. Besides, we may be getting ahead of ourselves. Let's begin by having little Sara evaluated. Nothing elaborate—definitely, nothing frightening."

Christina gave no indication that she supported Lundberg's idea. After a moment, she asked, "How soon do you wish to conduct these tests?"

"Let me see what can be arranged. Please, believe me; we will not disrupt Sara's life. She may even enjoy it. It may help her to understand her special gifts."

You asshole! You and SÄPO don't give a damn about Sara. "Well, Director, I will speak with Oskar about your proposal. I'll be in touch in a couple of days."

"Lovely! Let me know what you decide. Again, I promise; I'll not allow any testing that will cause her discomfort."

On the way to her office, Christina thought about what Lundberg said. *Maybe he's right. Why not have Sara evaluated? She's very special. Who knows what she could do? Wonder what Oskar will think about all of this.*

⋘⋙

That evening after Sara was asleep, Christina told Oskar about Lundberg's proposal. Oskar let out a boisterous laugh, amused by Lundberg's request. "I can't believe this. The whole idea is ridiculous. Where do they get these pseudo-scientists that concoct such crazy ideas!"

Christina did not find anything amusing about the situation. "You can laugh if you wish, but I afraid of what the testing might entail."

The two spoke at length that evening, outlining the pros and cons of allowing Sara to participate in the evaluation. They finally agreed to Lundberg's request to test Sara, not knowing the consequences of their decision nor the dangers that lay ahead.

Chapter 52

Location: Overseer's Cottage, Carrington Farm, Bath County, Virginia
Time: September 2034

Jenkins waived his hand at Mitzi Weaver; he did not like what he just heard. "Whoa! Hold your horses! Are you telling me that this Sara was trained to spy for Swedish Intelligence?"

Mitzi rocked back in her chair, uncertain about what to say. *I told him earlier that I knew very little about the testing and training Sara received. Christina only gave me a few snippets here and there.* "Well, I really don't know that much about what happened. Apparently, Sara spent a couple of months working with Swedish Intelligence. The initial test results must have been encouraging. She received some training to focus her natural talents."

"Focus her talents?" Cox seemed interested by what Weaver said. "What do you mean? Are you referring to Sara hearing voices or her language skills?"

"I guess her hearing ability. Christina mentioned remote listening. Like I said, neither Christina nor Sara told me exactly what was involved. Besides, the training only lasted a few months—around the time that Sara attended the ten-year evaluation at Johns Hopkins."

"So that's it? That's all you know?" Jenkins quipped.

"I told you, I didn't have many details."

A bit peeved at Weaver's response, Jenkins continued, "Okay then. Let's get back to what you told us yesterday. You said that the children were evaluated twice, once at age five and again at age ten. Is that right?"

Mitzi did not appreciate Jenkins' tone; she answered in kind. "Like I said, we wanted to follow them annually, but couldn't get the necessary funding. We only received funding for a follow-up evaluation when they were ten years old."

Cox looked at Jenkins; he could see that the senior lawman was upset with Weaver's tone and her vague answers. *Let's see if we can lower the tension here. Need to get her back on the findings at the lab. She's more comfortable there.* "Doctor Weaver, tell us what was learned when the children came back that second time."

Weaver cocked her head to one side, gave Jenkins a "go-to-hell" glance, and then turned toward Cox. *Play nice Mitzi. Cox is doing his best.* "Mainly, we confirmed our initial findings." *To say the least. That second session shocked all of us. That's when we knew how truly different they were. Too much to cover. Anyway, they're not ready to hear everything. Not yet.*

Chapter 53

Location: Johns Hopkins University, Baltimore, Maryland
Time: June 2028

The children were to arrive today for evaluation by the staff of the Julian C. Stanley Study of Exceptional Talent. Weaver rushed about her office handling last minute details to receive the children and their parents. Like everyone at SET, she was eager to see how the children would score on the new intelligence and aptitude tests designed especially for them.

Melody Atkins, Weaver's current graduate assistant, stepped into the doorway of Weaver's office. "So what's the game plan for today? After everything you've told me, I'm looking forward to meeting these kids."

Weaver looked up, surprised by Melody's sudden appearance. "Oh good. You're here. Come in. I was about to check the schedule myself." Weaver waved her hand over the user identification device on the corner of the desk. A wall monitor lit up. "Shazam, display schedule for today." A detailed agenda for the day appeared.

"That's a great name for your computer concierge. I address my concierge as 'dumb butt'—can't deal with the fact that it's smarter than I am."

Weaver laughed at her young assistant's remark. "Okay, Melody. Enough of that. Let's see what's on the schedule. There's a lot to accomplish in the next couple of weeks."

Melody moved toward the illuminated wall. "Looks like everyone gets picked up at the airport around one o'clock."

"I arranged with campus transportation to send a van for them. Best check on that—can't have any screw-ups."

"Consider it done." Melody wrote a note on the palm of her hand.

"Did you just write on your hand?" Weaver asked rhetorically.

"Yeah. Can't get out of the habit. It's quick. Besides, I think it's rude to talk to your communicator when someone's talking to you." Melody skimmed the agenda again. "So, will the parents be staying for two weeks like the kids?"

"No, only long enough for the psychology staff to collect some background info—family history and such. They're going to do a work-up. You know, that 'in-depth, pseudoscience' that they do. Ooops! Gotta watch myself. The stuff that they do is not what I'd call true science." Mitzi looked at her young assistance, who had a large smile on her face. "And, if you repeat a single word of what I just said, I'll flunk you for this semester!"

"You don't have to worry. I know what you mean. They look for linkages between things that have no real relationship. Tell me how that is science? You can't replicate it."

Mitzi chuckled in agreement. "Spoken like a true biochemist." Weaver liked Melody who was very much like herself. "So, back to work. Have you confirmed my appointment with radiology and nuclear imaging for tomorrow?"

"Yep, got it covered. Doc Misenheimer insisted that he be present during the imaging. Said he read the original MRI and CT scans and wanted to see if there were changes. And, he said to tell you that he'd buy the pizza this time. Don't know what he meant by that? Does it make any sense to you?"

"Yes. It does! He made me buy him a pizza last time the kids were here—thought I faked their scans."

"You'll have to tell…" Melody stopped as the sound of a croaking frog came from her lab coat. "Better take this. It's the guys in the lab—the frog ring tone is for them. Seems right don't you think?" She retrieved a micro-tablet from her pocket and skimmed the incoming message. "Looks like the genetic testing you requested is set up in the lab. They'll run the tests when they get the samples."

"Excellent, Melody. We had better get moving—lots to do. Please check on that transportation. I'll call you when the kids arrive. You'll love them—but be on your toes—they're sharp as tacks."

Chapter 54

Location: Reception Center, Julian C. Stanley Study of Exceptional Talent
Time: June 2028

The university van delivered the children and their parents to Johns Hopkins as planned. The children were happy to see each other; their voices rang out above everyone in the room. Although the three communicated regularly by video conferencing and social networking, it was not the same as seeing each other in person.

Before the discussions died down, several individuals entered the room, led by a woman in her early forties. "Ladies and gentlemen, and of course, Chetana, Sara, and Ethan. I am Doctor Mildred Foley. I will be your program coordinator. If you would please be seated, we will begin our introductions."

The coordinator did a round robin introduction of the children and the parents. She then asked the staff members to introduce themselves; some noted that they participated in the original session five years earlier. "It is such a pleasure to have you children with us again. Now, let's review our schedule for the next two weeks. Tomorrow morning, parents will meet in the Psychology Department. The staff is keen to gather observational information about the development of each child." She stopped to catch her breath and review her notes. "At the same time, the children will begin intelligence and aptitude testing. For the balance of the two-week session, each child will receive specialized instruction based on the results of his or her test results." Foley looked toward Weaver and smiled. "And not to overlook an important part of our work here, Doctor Weaver will oversee the examinations to assess changes in the physical traits of the children."

After Foley finished her remarks, the staff visited with the parents. They had so many questions about the children but that would come later. Tomorrow there would be time to get to know each of other better.

"Okay, everyone. May I have your attention?" Foley waved her hand in a circular motion to get everyone's attention. When everyone quieted down, Foley thanked the staff for coming and dismissed them. With only the children and parents remaining, she reminded them, "Now don't forget. We're scheduled to dine with the University President this evening!" The joy in her voice indicated that this must be a rare opportunity for her.

⊷⊶

When Mitzi, the children, and parents arrived at the President's private dining room in the administration building, Foley met them—not the matronly dressed individual from earlier in the day but someone who was trying to impress. She wore a snug fitting, black cocktail dress that accentuated several unsightly aspects of her figure and far too much makeup.

Mitzi spoke first. "Doctor Foley, how nice you look."

"Oh, thank you, Doctor Weaver." Foley glanced at her watch. "Oh, look at the time; we need to hurry. Can't keep the President and his staff waiting." She led the group into the dining room as a mother hen leading her chicks.

When Foley stepped away, Weaver touched Emily on the arm and whispered in her ear. "My momma used to say that some folks need to invest in a full length mirror. Guess Foley never bought one. One look in the mirror and she would not have worn that dress." Both women snickered, fighting the compulsion to laugh aloud.

The President and key medical school deans were excited to meet the children. The introductions did not last long before the President asked everyone to take a seat.

After eating, everyone milled around and chatted. The adults seemed more interested in talking among themselves than with the children who gathered in a corner of the room.

At ten years old, the children were slightly larger than their age group, with Sara and Chetana starting to show early signs of puberty. Sara looked at Ethan and gently pushed his shoulder. "You're not as big as I expected. Couldn't tell how short you are in our video talks."

"It's 'cause you're girls. My momma is a pediatrician. She told me girls grow faster than boys do, but I'll be bigger than either you. Just you wait and see."

"We're not dummies, Ethan." Chetana, who was pursuing her interests in biology and chemistry, stepped in to defend the girls' position. "Everyone knows the growth rates of boys and girls are different."

"Oh, just ignore him, Chetana." Sara deliberately turned her back to Ethan. "What do you think they are going to do to us? I don't like being tested. I've had enough of testing this year. Those nerds where my mother works...."

Chetana interrupted, concerned for Sara. "What kind of tests—medical tests?"

"Oh, no, just stupid stuff. I'm being tested to see if I can hear people who are far away. I've done these exercises—like mind games. I sit in a room and one of the weird guys will ask me if I know what someone in another room is thinking."

"You mean like we can do when we hold hands?" Obvious apprehension appeared on Ethan's face. He pushed his way between the two girls. "Hey, you're not listening to me now are you?"

"No," Sara replied, in a less than convincing tone and a smug look on her face.

There was a reason for Ethan to be concerned. Like boys his age, he was beginning to notice girls. Like all boys, he spent a lot of time thinking about the opposite sex. If they knew what he was thinking, he would be embarrassed.

Chetana's large, dark eyes lit up. "That was fun—talking without moving our lips. Why don't we do it now?"

"I'm not sure that..." Ethan frowned and did not finish his statement.

"What's wrong? Are you afraid? Are you hiding something? Like we don't know that boys are always thinking about sex?"

Ethan's face reddened; his secret was out. He did not know if he should be embarrassed or relieved.

Sara questioned the young man, "What if I could hear what you are thinking, Ethan? Would it matter that much?"

"I don't know. Do you remember last time? I could hear you and you could hear me. It was as if everyone was talking at the same time. Seems kinda scary now."

"Oh, don't be a wimp, Ethan." Chetana looked at the adults who were still talking. "Grab my hands. Let's do it again!"

"I don't think we need to hold hands." Sara's words carried a sense of uncertainty.

"Whatcha mean?" Ethan asked; his use of nonstandard grammar revealed his association with other boys his age and that language was not one of his strengths.

"Remember, I said that the people who work with my mother had me do some exercises to test my listening skill. Well, I think the exercises made a difference."

Before Sara could explain, Doctor Foley called to them. "Sara, Chetana, Ethan, it's time to go."

That night, the children stayed with their parents in University guest quarters. Later, they would stay together in a group house with a housemother to look after them. As they went with their parents, they wished that they could have stayed together, to see what Sara meant. Could they communicate without holding hands?

Chapter 55

Location: Radiographic Imaging Department, University Hospital
Time: June 2028

Mitzi Weaver hurried down the long hallway that led to the radiographic imaging department. When she reached Misenheimer's office, his receptionist greeted her. "Hi, Doctor Weaver. Please come in. Doctor Misenheimer is on his way; and so is the pizza he ordered. Why don't you have a seat in his office? It shouldn't be long."

Monitors covered three of the walls in Misenheimer's office; each monitor displayed brightly colored images. Weaver recognized the images as the children's original brain scans. *Just like Phillip, always doing his homework. Had to review everything. Can't wait to see their new scans.*

"There you are. See you've come seeking pizza." Misenheimer entered the office and dropped onto a well-worn couch. "Come, sit here. Lunch is on its way."

Weaver sat down and then asked, "What did you find, Phillip?"

"About what I expected."

A young man carrying a large pizza box appeared in the office door. "Got your order, Doc."

While the two ate, Misenheimer displayed recent images of the children, manipulating his remote control with the speed of a video gamer. Image after image appeared only to be replaced by the next image. Between mouths full of deep-dish pizza and catching stringy cheese, he explained how the brain tissue of the children did undergo significant changes in the past five years.

"Phil, this is almost too much to absorb. Can you give me an abbreviated version?"

"Okay, let me sum it up. The early scans showed heightened activity between the two hemispheres of the brain in each child, but that activity is greater now, three or four times greater—well beyond what you'd find in an average person." Misenheimer took a swallow of pink lemonade. "Chetana, by far, has the greatest level of activity. Although her overall activity is higher, Ethan and Sara exceed her in a couple of areas. The cerebral cortex of Sara and

Ethan shows an immense development since their first visit. As you know, that part of the brain controls sensory perceptions—seeing and hearing—as well as muscle control and intellectual functions like speech and memory. Hell, what can I say? The brain structures of these three children are beyond amazing!"

When Mitzi Weaver left her colleague's office, she knew her life would never be the same—the children were evolving so fast. What could lie ahead for them?

Chapter 56

Location: Reception Center, Julian C. Stanley Study of Exceptional Talent
Time: June 2028

Two weeks passed quickly, filled with activities. Having completed a rigorous program of intelligence and aptitude tests, decision-making exercises, and physical examinations, the children were ready to leave. The specially designed testing proved inadequate to evaluate their true potential; the children easily completed each test and exercise. Never had such intellectually advanced children been evaluated by the Julian C. Stanley Study of Exceptional Talent. This morning, the children and parents would hear recommendations of the staff. Only Oskar Johansson and Ram Kapur attended the presentation in person. Video conferencing allowed the other parents to participate in the meeting.

The conference room was abuzz with conversation when Doctor Foley entered carrying three folders and placed them on the conference table. "Good morning. So pleased to see that all of our parents could be with us." Foley looked at each of the three monitors, acknowledged the viewing parents, and sat down. "I asked everyone to come today to hear the recommendations of the educational placement staff. Based on the test results of each child, the staff feels that each is ready to enroll in university programs targeting their unique talents. Our recommendations considered the expressed interest of each child." Foley looked at Ethan and then to the monitor that displayed Emily and Kevin. "Our recommendation for young Ethan is straightforward. He should enroll in the Stanford University on-line mathematics program. Additional tutoring is available in the Denver area to assist him." Foley closed Ethan's folder and nodded to a woman at the opposite end of the table. "Doctor Milford, will cover the educational plan for Sara."

"Good morning." Milford spoke with a British accent. "Our recommendation for Sara considers her residence and her special interest in paranormal activities. As the liaison for European education, I contacted the University of Stockholm. They agreed that Sara should enroll in their advanced linguistics program. With respect for Sara's desire to study psychic phenomena and clairvoyance, the academic evaluation team is uncertain as to whether she would benefit from formal study in these areas. Although not broadly supported, the evaluation team suggests that Sara enroll at the University of Derby located in the East Midlands region of England. Derby offers a lecture and research program in the Psychology of Paranormal Phenomena. The proximity of her home in Stockholm to Derby would allow visits to the campus when required." Milford looked towards Foley. "That concludes the team's recommendations for Sara."

"Thank you Doctor Milford. Before I give the recommendations for Chetana, I must say that recommendations for her proved most difficult. We spoke with several American and European universities—each of which was very interested in having her attend. In discussions with her parents, we learned that they want her to remain in New Delhi. Although New Delhi has several fine institutions, none offered a suitable program in bio-molecular chemistry. Therefore, Doctor Weaver agreed to coordinate Chetana's academic work through Johns Hopkins. The University of Delhi shall provide suitable laboratory space for her experimental work." Foley closed the folder that contained Chetana's material and paused to look about the room. "We shall miss you all."

৵৽

The children returned to the group house where they spent the last two weeks together. They did not know when they would be together again. While the adults attended to travel details, Chetana, Sara and Ethan sat silently on a bench outside. Soon a van would come to take them to the airport. No one that passed by thought much about their lack of conversation—or the cause for their occasional outbursts of giggles and laughter.

"*I'm gonna miss you girls.*" Ethan's lips did not move, a sad smile frozen on his face. Studying the faces of his friends, he knew that they could hear his thoughts, but even so, their faces still spoke volumes. "*I won't be able to talk to others girls like I talk to you. It's easier when you don't have to hide what you think.*"

"*I know,*" Sara agreed, her sadness evident to her friends. *I wish everyone could be as open as we are. I wonder what it would be like to communicate with our parents like we do. Sometimes, I wish I knew what they were thinking.*"

Ethan butted in, "*I don't know if I'd like that. Parents shouldn't know everything that a kid does!*"

"Oh hush, Ethan," Chetana scolded. "*Sara, do you think that we will be able to hear each other when we get back to our homes? We live so far apart.*"

"*I'm not sure—but I think so. Wouldn't that be nice? We could talk whenever we wanted.*"

"Will you continue doing those exercises—the ones with those guys at your mother's office?" Ethan raised his left nostril in a boyish frown to show his displeasure with Sara's situation.

"Yes, for a little longer, but I think they're ready to give up. I'm not able to do what they want."

When the University vans arrived, the children strained to hold back tears. They did not know if or when they would see each other again, but, there would be time to visit in the van.

Chapter 57

Location: Baltimore-Washington International Airport, Baltimore, Maryland
Time: June 2028

There are things that happen in life, call them coincidences, fate, what you will. On this day, a random set of events would ultimately alter the lives of Mitzi Weaver and the three children.

The University shuttle bus arrived on time to take everyone to the airport. There was some light discussion but the children seemed remarkably quiet. Mitzi, Ram, and Oskar shared their dislike for travel. After the bus dropped Chetana and Ram at the British Airways terminal for their flight to London, Oskar Johansson received a call on his wrist communicator. Everyone could hear the automated call broadcasted from his communicator:

> *Due to inclement weather, Scandinavian Airlines, Flight 2308, Baltimore to New York with connections to Stockholm, will now depart from Terminal 3A, Gate 12 at 12:09 PM. We regret the delay.*

Ethan almost screamed, "That's our terminal! You guys are coming with Dr. Weaver and me."

During the ride to Terminal 3A, Ethan and Oskar engaged in a discussion of physics and mathematics. The discussion continued through airport security and the terminal gate area. By the time the two settled into their seats in the terminal, they sounded more like colleagues—not professor and student.

"Doctor Johansson, Sara told me you are working on the behavior of the graviton particle. What's that about?"

The child's question surprised Oskar. "Yes, that is correct. I have been struggling with the problem for over a decade. I'm an experimental physicist you know, not a theoretical one. While I am certain of the theory underlying my work, I hope to prove it experimentally. That's why I am working at CERN. Actually, we've made important progress in the past ten years, but I'm afraid that we haven't achieved our final goal."

"What's that?"

"To put it simply, I want to know where gravitons go when they disappear. We smashed a lot of atomic material and watched the gravitons disappear and reappear. We're certain they move between dimensions. For many years in quantum mechanics, we've known of this behavior. As you may know, the standard laws of physics don't apply in the world of the infinitesimally small. In quantum mechanics, a particle can be in two places at the same time or disappear and reappear. That's cool, don't you think?"

"Yeah, sounds kinda crazy." Ethan's demeanor hinted that he was toying with a problem, suddenly his head bounced rapidly. "Doctor Johansson, you said that gravitons travel into another dimension. Where's that? Is it way far away or nearby?"

"A very good question. String theorists predict that our universe consists of more than the three dimensions that we can experience, you know, height, length, and width. Of course, we need a fourth dimension to describe where we are, like now, sitting here in this terminal. That's time. It does not help to know that we are here, if we don't know when we're here. We are here, at this time, as measured by some universal clock."

"That's one of Einstein's theories. Isn't it? But where do you think your gravitons go when they disappear?" Ethan sought a more definitive answer to his question.

Oskar shifted his position and twisted his head slightly, impressed by the young man's persistence. "I'm getting to that. May I assume that you know something about *M-Theory?*"

Ethan nodded. "Yep. I read Doctor Witten's work about string theory. Didn't he kinda prove that there are ten or eleven dimensions that make up the universe?"

"Very good! Well, that's pretty much accepted now as fact. Our universe is comprised of eleven dimensions. Six of these dimensions are very small and tightly folded together. We believe that's where our gravitons go, but we don't know for sure. That's part of my research problem—what I'm trying to prove."

Returning to his thought, Ethan was quiet for a moment. "What's in these other dimensions? Are there just gravitons or could there be little biddy people?"

"Who knows, young man. That's something for you to discover. Cosmologists tell us that ours is not the only universe. We are part of a multi-verse comprised of many membranes on which an infinite number of universes coexist. I know it may be hard to imagine, but the theoretical work is widely accepted."

Ethan began rocking in his seat and then jumped to his feet. "Excuse me, Doctor Johansson. I want to talk to Sara. I'll be right back." Dashing across the terminal, he called, "Sara, Sara."

As he approached the young woman she raised her hand, and without looking at Ethan asked, "What do you want? I'm reading the *International Business Times* in German and in Chinese to see how closely they are translated."

"Well, excuuze me!" Ethan contorted his face to convey how he felt about Sara's response. "If you could break away from what you're doing, I want to ask you something. It's about what your father said."

"Oh, okay, this is getting boring anyway. I don't understand what I'm reading; I just like comparing the languages. What's a *debenture* anyway?" She turned to face Ethan. "So, what do you want?"

"Your father and I have been discussing his work with gravitons. Do you know what he's trying to prove?"

"Yes, I help him translate his work into different languages. Why do you ask?"

This was the first time Ethan questioned whether his visions may be real. Was it just flashes of light in his peripheral vision or something else that flashed around him—perhaps something in another dimension that only he could see?

Part VIII

THREATS ARISE

Confronting Foes

Chapter 58

Location: Carrington Farm, Northern Virginia
Time: September 2034

The day was growing long. Mitzi Weaver felt that she could not tolerate many more questions. Hours of questioning left her mind and body fatigued. Jenkins and Cox showed the strain of the past two days. By now, they knew she was not directly involved in the disappearance of the children. What remained was to gather sufficient information to complete their report. Weaver dreaded the prospect of spelling out each detail for them.

Jenkins fidgeted in his chair. "Doctor Weaver. This is taking way too long. Can't you just summarize what happened to these kids?"

"Nothing I'd like more." Weaver leaned toward Jenkins and looked straight at him. "Here goes! When the kids arrived here two weeks ago for me to evaluate their decision-making skills, they were the intellectually superior beings Misenheimer knew they would become. The minute they started their university programs at age ten, they excelled at everything they did. At age fifteen, they were making breakthroughs in science, math and communications that scholars twice their age could only hope to accomplish. Then they disappeared! There, you got it all. Let's get the hell out of here." Weaver fell back into her chair, a self-satisfied look on her face. "How's that, Lieutenant?"

Cox bolted upright, throwing his arm across the chest of his colleague to restrain him. "Hey, let's take a breather here! Just because we're tired, doesn't mean we have to get all bent out of shape."

Weaver lowered her head, apologetically. She knew that fatigue had gotten the best of her. She looked into Jenkins' eyes and confessed. "Okay, my fault. I'm tired. I realize you need to know about the dangers these young people faced. When you are that brilliant, everyone wants to control you—to use you."

To lower the tension level, Cox asked in a soft voice, "So who were these folks that wanted to gain control of the children?"

Weaver did not respond but slowly stood up and stretched. "I need a break." Before walking away, she added, "I know of two groups that sought to use the children. You know about Lundberg and Swedish intelligence. Well, he didn't stop pursuing Sara—certainly not after he discovered that she was enrolled in the Derby University parapsychology program. That was right up his alley. The main threat to Ethan and Chetana came from a group of influential Indian entrepreneurs. Apparently, they tracked all of the gifted children from Ross-Katsura. They had a hell of an organization—better than we had. Let me take a tinkle. I'll tell you more." *Oh, so much more. Best start with that bunch in India. That's a good tale!*

Chapter 59

Location: Airspace Over the Himalayan Mountains, Northern India
Time: June 2030

In route to Germany, Rishi relaxed in the comfort of his private jet. The flight provided time to consider the events of the past several months. Last year the children attended a scheduled evaluation session. Since then, the children amazed their professors by consuming course material at three times the rate of the very best students. *The children are eleven. We've waited long enough. It is the time to act! Let's see what Bijay has to say.* Rishi took the gold plated satellite phone from its wall-mounted holder and said, "Call Bijay." The phone dialed.

"Good morning, my honorable colleague," Bijay said, "And just where are you?"

"Crossing over the Himalayan Mountains. Bloody beautiful up here—every peak is snowy white. Hate like hell to be down there, even this time of year. The Americans would say, 'It's colder than a witch's tit in a brass bra.' Don't know creates all those American sayings, but they seem to love them. Anyway, I just wanted to confirm that your man is in place and ready to go."

"Of course, my friend! For the money he's receiving, he'd screw his mother on the steps of Windsor Castle with the King and the whole of Parliament looking on. I think we chose well—an Englishman and his demure little Indian wife. No one will pay them any attention."

Bijay was cautious not to reveal too much information over an open satellite phone. Everyone from the Russians, to the Chinese, to the Americans monitored every word transmitted.

"Very well done. I've arranged to gather up Kapur and his family on my return trip, and then we'll head south. They're eager to visit the tiger sanctuary. I've arranged for us to stay in one of the guest bungalows. I used my special patron status to get us the best accommodation. Considering all the money I've donated to that bunch, I should get some bloody privileges."

"I'm sure everything will go as planned, but should you need assistance, the Gentlemen are ready to help. Call when the task is completed and everyone is safely in Sri Lanka."

"Okay, Bijay. By the way, Sanjay called last night. He's at his villa in Sri Lanka. He's arranged to meet the Englishman at the airport in Colombo. We'll need Sanjay's help with the local customs officers...."

Bijay interrupted, "Must run. I have an important call coming in. Call me back if there is anything else?"

"Okay, my friend. Don't forget to tell the others. I shall see that our 'profit' is collected before the end of the week!"

The anticipation in Rishi's voice was obvious to Bijay. "It's about time! Twelve years is a very long investment period! Be safe. I must leave you now. Goodbye, Rishi. Have a good flight."

As he put the receiver away, Rishi reached for the bottle of champagne chilling in a sterling silver ice bucket. *All is ready. Every detail addressed. Nothing left to chance. By Friday, Kapur's daughter will be ours!*

Chapter 60

Location: The Western Ghat Mountains in the Southern Tip of India
Time: June 2030

"Oh, Rishi, it's lovely down there. So lush and green." Kumari strained to see out of the window of the jet as it passed over the semitropical mountain range below.

Here, within the Western Ghats, lay one of the world's most biologically diverse ecosystems. Classified as an UNESCO World Heritage Site, the mountains contained several enclaves dedicated to the preservation of a portion of India's dwindling wild tiger population.

Ram, Kumari and Chetana could scarcely contain their enthusiasm. Like most Indians, they looked forward to seeing tigers roaming freely. When Rishi, arranged a tour of the Deccan Plateau Tiger Sanctuary, they were ecstatic. Although, he could stay only one night because of business in Sri Lanka, he arranged for Ram and his family to remain for a full week.

The Hospitality Manager of the Tiger Sanctuary met Rishi and his guests when they arrived. "Good day. We are so pleased to have you with us. If you will take a seat in our courtesy cart, I will take you to your accommodations. You will be in the Queen Victoria bungalow. It's our largest and best furnished accomodation."

Located in a secluded grove of trees, the design of the bungalow allowed it to blend into the surrounding jungle. Directly behind the structure was a gently flowing stream. Although secluded, the bungalow was but a short walk away from the main building that housed the grand dining room and lounge.

When the party arrived at the bungalow, they received tropical refreshments and a light lunch. While they ate, the manager proudly outlined the agenda for the next few days and arrangements for dining. "The Deccan Plateau Tiger Sanctuary offers four-star dining with breakfast served on the bungalow's terrace and lunches provided in the field. Adult guests may expect a scrumptious, five-course dinner in our main facility each evening. Younger guests will dine in their bungalow. Parents need not worry, as a chaperon is available to attend to our young guests at mealtime and anything that their parents are away. And, now to the reason you have come. Tomorrow, you will go into areas frequented by tigers—atop our elephants, of course. Guides and game attendants will ensure everyone's safety and enjoyment. However, within the compound, I encourage you to be vigilant: tigers do wander through the residential areas from time to time."

❧

That evening, Rishi and his guests waited while room service laid out dinner for Chetana and her chaperon. Rishi smiled, as the attendants placed a china teapot on the table. *What a lovely spot of tea and so nicely favored with a strong sedative!*

Leaving the bungalow with Ram and Kumari, Rishi looked into the darkness. A well-worn British Land Rover rolled to a stop some eighty feet from the bungalow. *Right on schedule!* "Well, Mr. and Ms. Kapur, are you ready to dine? I assure you. You will not forget this evening!"

A surly looking man and his wife watched the three adults walk away from the bungalow before exiting the vehicle. "Get the medical bag," directed the man. Dressed in a safari outfit, his clothing and sunburned face suggested he was a jungle guide, but tonight he was playing a different role.

His wife, a small Indian woman, only five feet tall, reached for a black leather bag on the floorboard. "I have it." She started to open the vehicle door.

"Wait. Wait. It's not time. Let's go over it again. We need to give the sedative time to work. When it hits them, we go in. After you draw the girl's blood, I'll take her to the Rover and get the tiger paw sandals. Give the woman the injection. Just enough to keep her down for fifteen minutes, no more. We want her to think she just dozed off. Don't forget to take off the child's shoes and tear off a piece of her dress. Wait on the porch 'til you see me put the child in the Rover, then put on the child's shoes. It's critical you make it look like she left the bungalow on her own. Walk toward that flowerbed there—the ground's damp and will leave good prints. Have the blood ready. Squirt it—like blood from a torn artery. I'll walk over to you in the tiger sandals. From the flowerbed, I'll drag you to the stream. Remember, it is important that only the child's shoes touch as I drag you—we need to leave a good scent trail. The dogs and trackers will follow our trail to the stream. Thank goodness, big cats like the water. The dogs and the trackers will lose the trail at the stream. That should do it. You have any questions my love?"

"You do your part, Hubby, I can handle mine."

"If we pull this off, Lambkin, we can retire to Africa for the rest of our lives. Okay, let's go." The man and woman stepped out of the vehicle and moved cautiously towards the bungalow.

In less than ten minutes, the pair completed their tasks and returned to the Land Rover, their feet wet from walking two hundred yards downstream. A rope hung from a large tree limb earlier in the day provided an escape from the stream, leaving no trail for the dogs to follow.

"She is gone. The child is gone." The chaperon was frantic as she entered the dining room.

Rishi, Ram, and Kumari were just starting to eat when the chaperon called out. They rushed back to the bungalow as the manager called the local police. Ram and Rishi made a quick search of the area with the help of the resort staff. Kumari and the chaperon waited in the bungalow in hopes that Chetana would return. When the police arrived, they conducted an exhaustive search. Even in the darkness, the evidence was clear.

The Chief Inspector delivered the bad news. "We have done all that we can do tonight. I'm afraid that when the chaperon dozed off, the child left the bungalow. Not a wise move in this area. It appears that a tiger took her. The footprints are clear. We'll return in the morning, but I am not optimistic."

Rishi watched as the local police drove away. They did not see him smile. *The plan worked just as we thought. Had there been an obvious kidnapping or the death of a parent, the local authorities would have undertaken an investigation. However, a poor child taken by a tiger is an entirely different situation. A tragic event, true, but all too common around here. The authorities will return but will soon close the case. A good plan indeed!* Rishi walked back to the bungalow to comfort Kumari and Ram. *It is a sad thing to lose one's child.*

Chapter 61

Location: Aviation Services Terminal, Ratmalana Airport,
         Colombo, Sri Lanka
Time: June 2030

"Sound planning, that's the key to success," Sanjay said to the customs officer standing beside him on the tarmac at Ratmalana Airport. At the smaller of the two international airports in Colombo, the arrival of a small plane would go unnoticed. Not coincidentally, the local customs authorities at Ratmalana were Sanjay's friends, having benefitted from his generosity in the past. Today, they would assist him with the arrival of a special guest who did not wish to pass through customs.

"Ah, there's our bloke now." Sanjay pointed towards a twin-engine An-32 cargo plane lumbering across the tarmac. An-32 aircraft are common in India, purchased in large numbers from the Russians. A short takeoff and landing aircraft, it is the airplane of choice for smugglers of contraband.

Sanjay led the customs officer towards the approaching aircraft, pausing to hand the official an envelope—a small token *for services <u>not</u> rendered!* As the rear door of the aircraft opened, a man with a deep tan stepped out. Sanjay took a second envelope from his linen jacket and handed it to the man. "How is the child?"

"Hungry, I'd say," responded the man in a distinctive British accent. "My wife's bringing her now."

As the woman approached, she called to her husband. "She's just coming out of it. Still a wee bit groggy."

"Hi, Chetana. I'm, Sanjay, your host. I'm so sad about the loss of your parents. What do you remember?"

"Nothing. What happened to them?" The child shivered standing in the propeller wash of the idling aircraft.

"Oh, my dear child," responded Sanjay, trying to show concern in his voice and manner. "There will be time for that later. Let's get you somewhere warm. I'm sure you are hungry."

Signaling to the executive Mercedes parked near the terminal, Sanjay and the customs man moved away from the aircraft. When the car arrived, the man and his wife boarded the plane. The engines accelerated and the aircraft pulled away.

Sanjay assisted Chetana into the limousine and smiled as a woman seated inside wrapped a shawl around the child. "Thank you, Mrs. Worthington. This is your new charge, Chetana. She recently lost her parents in a tragic accident."

"Don't worry, my child. I will take very good care of you."

"Take us to the rented villa," Sanjay said to the driver. "And call the housekeeper; tell them to prepare food for our guest."

As the limousine started, Sanjay could hardly contain his pleasure. *We've waited so very long for this day. Finally, some return on our investment! Our very own, Enlightened One! What might this child be worth? Priceless!*

Little Chetana did not know the man she was with, nor did she care. She only wanted to know what happened to her parents. Tired from her ordeal, she fell asleep.

Chapter 62

Location: Carrington Farm, Northern Virginia
Time: September 2034

Lieutenant Jenkins shook his head. "No. No, ma'am. Doesn't make sense. If these Indian fellows took the girl, how'd she windup here at Carrington with you?"

Mitzi responded emphatically, "She escaped. That's how!"

"She escaped?" Jenkins sought clarification.

"That's a whole separate story." Weaver signaled an unwillingness to say more.

Cox leaned toward Weaver. "Well, I'd like to hear how a child of eleven or twelve managed to free herself from a group of—what would you call them—international criminals?"

Weaver reconsidered. "Okay. It'll probably help explain what the children were capable of doing. She didn't do it by herself. Sara helped her."

"Ah, come on." Jenkins half rose from his chair, then sat back down. "You're telling me another kid raced to Sri Lanka and rescued her friend?"

"Well, not exactly, but Sara did have a direct hand in rescuing Chetana."

Jenkins eased back into his chair. "Well, I'd like to hear how."

Weaver took a deep breath and audibly exhaled. *Here we go again. He's not going to believe any of this!* "Following their second evaluation at Johns Hopkins, the children learned they could communicate with each other telepathically...."

"Ah, horse hockey! You don't expect us to believe that these kids were mind readers. Do you?" Jenkins was visibly upset.

"Sir, you may believe what you wish! I can only report what I know. If you don't believe me, ask their parents."

Cox moved quickly to calm the tension between Jenkins and Weaver. "Okay, folks, let's settle down." He waited a moment for the pair to cool down. "So, tell us what happened. How'd Sara help Chetana?"

"Okay. But you have to remember, I didn't learn any of this until much later. Everything I tell you, I learned from other people—what you guys call 'hearsay'— so there may be some gaps in what I say."

"Whatever." Jenkins smirked, not trying to conceal his animosity towards Weaver.

Chapter 63

Location: Johansson Family Home, Stockholm, Sweden
Time: June 2030

Sara Johansson was in her room reading. Suddenly, she leaped off her bed and shouted, "Mother, Mother! Where are you?"

"I'm in here Sara. In the kitchen."

As Sara hurried to the kitchen, she spoke in an urgent tone. "Chetana's in trouble. We have to help her!"

"What are you talking about?"

"Chetana is somewhere—she doesn't know where—but she's afraid."

"Afraid? Afraid of what? How do you know this?"

"Mother, I just know." Sara tried to explain. "It's like when I hear the voices. Some people have taken her."

Uncertain about what she should do, Christina listened as Sara implored her to act. *She's serious. It's not a game.*

"Hurry, Mother. You have to do something. She's afraid. She doesn't know where she is. We have to find her!"

"Okay, okay. If you are so certain, I'll call Chetana's mother. I'll bet you that Chetana is at home, happy as a lark."

Sara began to cry. "No, no, she's not! Call her mother. See what she knows."

Christina called the Kapur home in India. The housekeeper answered the video call.

"Hello, this is the Kapur residence."

"Is Mrs. Kapur available? This is Christina Johansson."

Sobbing, the young woman explained that Chetana was missing, reportedly taken by a tiger. "Master Kapur and his wife are in southern India at a placed called the Deccan Plateau Tiger Sanctuary. That is where it happened. I do not expect them to return for several days. They hope to find Chetana's body and bring her home."

Sara listened to the video call. When her mother ended the call, tears began welling up in the child's blue eyes. "Mother, she isn't dead! Chetana is alive. She's is in a large house. I know it." Sara's voice quivered with each word she spoke.

"Sara, you heard the housekeeper. How can you be so sure?"

"Mother, I just know. She's alive! Some people took her on a plane. Now, she's in a house overlooking the ocean. It's warm there. She's so frightened. We must help her."

"Sara! Stop. Stop this, right now! How can you know this? India is six thousand kilometers from here."

The child slumped to the floor and pulled on her mother's pant leg. "Momma, sit down, please." Between sobs, Sara explained how Chetana, Ethan and she could hear each other's thoughts.

Christina sat quietly and listened. *My God! I know Sara is special. But telepathy?* Convinced that Sara could communicate with her two special friends, she thought about the action that she could take. *How do you go about finding a single child on the Indian subcontinent? We don't even know if she's in India, just that it's warm and near an ocean. Warm and near water! That narrows it to half the globe. Check the traffic! Of course, check the traffic. Damn it woman, you're in the intelligence business. Surely, someone said something. If they did, someone heard it, like the Americans. Pretty sure the Americans are still monitoring the area around the Arabian Sea. They cover everything from Yemen to Iran to southern India. They must have something. Air traffic. That's it! If the abductors used a plane, there will be air to ground communications. Start with what flew in and out of the tiger refuge or near there. I must call Marley at MI-5. The Brits and Americans share Arabian Sea communication files. Marley owes me!*

Chapter 64

Location: Swedish Intelligence Headquarters, Stockholm, Sweden
Time: June 2030

"*God morgon*, Marley, have you been keeping up with your Swedish?" Christina called on a secure line to British MI-5 from her office in SÄPO headquarters.

"*God morgon* to you, Christina. Sorry, but my Swedish is rusty. Mind using the Queen's English?"

"For you, my friend, anything. So, did you find what we discussed, yesterday?"

"Actually, it was rather easy. In the last forty-eight hours, there were only two flights originating within one hundred kilometers of that tiger sanctuary. One was a corporate jet—some computer services fellow—Indian citizen. The other is a bit more interesting—British expat—works in India and Africa. A big game hunter and guide, or at least that's what he claims. His records show a couple of run-ins with Interpol, smuggling animal parts mainly. So I ask you, Christina, what are the odds that both of these flights were headed for Sri Lanka—and to the same airport. The Brit went first. Landed at Ratmalana Airport. Only stayed for a minute. Took off almost immediately. The corporate jet left the sanctuary airfield just a bit ago. Its flight plan calls for a layover in Mumbai for fueling before heading south. I'm sending you the file now. Does any of this help you? And why does SÄPO need this intel?"

"Now, Marley, you know better. If I told you why, you'd think I was putting you on. But trust me, it may save a life. Why don't we call this one, professional courtesy? 'I owe you one,' as you fellows say. Many thanks. Bye now."

Christina studied the leads Marley provided. *A British citizen and his wife flew an An-32 from a small airstrip near the tiger reserve to Colombo, then immediately departed. They didn't take on any fuel in Colombo. Why did they stop there?* She skimmed the jet's flight plan that Marley sent. *Now this is strange. The flight plan indicates that it departs Mumbai for the Ratmalana Airport in a few hours from now. It's going to same place the Brit went! Can't be a coincidence, can it?*

Her curiosity aroused, Christina ran background checks on the Brit and the owner of the corporate jet. Using SÄPO computers, it did not take long to find what she needed. *Interesting. The Indian fellow that owns the jet rented a villa outside of Colombo last month. Wait a minute.* She searched the electronic files gathered on Rishi and found a picture of the villa. *Ah, there it is. And what do you know, it has a seaside view. Could be where Chetana is? Need some eyes on the ground. Swenson! He's at our embassy there. Good old Swenson. Saved his ass a few years ago. He can't say no.*

Swenson was a good man, with good contacts in Colombo. It did not take him long to check out the villa and the people staying there. Late that evening, he called Christina. "I'm not sure what you are working on, but here's what I got so far. I checked out the villa. An Indian national, Sanjay Nayar, an Australian woman, and a girl are staying in the villa. Strange thing happened shortly after I got to the villa. An EMT vehicle arrived. They took that Indian fellow, Sanjay Nayar, to the local hospital. I called a fellow that I know at the hospital. Seems that Nayar suffered some kind of mental collapse."

"And the girl? What about the girl?"

"Now this is where things really get weird. The girl is in police custody. The report gives her name as Chetana Kapur, from New Delhi. The Australian woman claimed the child was a witch. You know they believe that stuff down here. Anyway, the child is supposed to have cast a spell on Nayar causing him to fall into a fit."

"You are a jewel, Swenson. That's what I needed. When you are back in Sweden, drop by. Dinner is on me!" Christina checked the time. She had stayed in her office from the time she started her inquiry into Chetana's whereabouts, almost fourteen hours. *It's near midnight. Sara's probably asleep. I'll wake her when I get home. She'll want to hear the good news.* It was early morning when she arrived home and spoke with Sara, but Sara insisted that they call Chetana's parents.

After the initial surprise and disbelief waned, Ram thanked Christina for the information. "You cannot imagine how grateful we are. Kumari and I will leave for Sri Lanka immediately. But before I ring off, may I ask how you learned that Chetana was missing?"

"I think it best that you ask Chetana that question. Her answer may surprise you—but then, nothing our two girls do should ever surprise us. Isn't that right?"

Reclining in a leather lounge chair aboard his private plane bound for Colombo, Rishi listened to the white noise of the jet engines. He was weary;

he needed to sleep, but there was no time for that now. The past thirty hours had been hectic, starting with his return to the bungalow with Ram and Kumari after the girl's abduction. He strained to play the role of consoling friend to the two of them. Begging their forgiveness, he reminded them that he was due in Sri Lanka on urgent business. Leaving Ram and Kumari, he assured them he would return as soon as possible. The buzz of the intercom interrupted his thoughts.

"Sir, sorry to trouble you," Curtis, the co-pilot said, "but I have an incoming call—a woman who insists on speaking with you. She said it's urgent. Something about your friend, Sanjay."

"That's fine, Curtis. I'll take the call. Put her through." The video display lit up; the face of a middle-aged woman appeared. "To whom am I speaking?"

"This is Mrs. Worthington." The woman was on the verge of hysteria. "I was hired to care for that child—if you can call her a child. Sanjay gave me this number in the event of an emergency. Well, this is a bloody emergency if there ever was one!"

Rishi listened to the woman's rambling tirade. She feared for her safety and was at Ratmalana International, waiting to board a flight to Australia. "I'm telling you, sir, I have to get as far away from that demonic child as possible. There is something terribly wrong with her—an evilness. When that evil creature touched Sanjay, he fell to the ground—curled up in a fetal position, he was. All he kept muttering was, 'I didn't mean it. I won't touch you. Don't hurt me.' The doctors say he's gone mad, but I know better. She cast a spell on the poor man."

Worthington repeatedly demanded additional compensation in payment for the stress she endured and airfare out of Sri Lanka. Rishi listened to her demands. "Mrs. Worthington, you need not worry. I'm sure that no harm will come to you. I will check on my friend and see that arrangements are made for your travel to Australia." He ended the called and thought of his friend's situation. *The whole plan fell apart because of one man's weakness. The one weak link in our plan. Dammit, Sanjay, why didn't you keep your bloody hands to yourself. Years of investment pissed away over a perverted fetish for young girls!*

Rishi pressed the intercom; the co-pilot answered. "Yes, sir."

In a sad voice, Rishi said, "Curtis, please tell Wilson to turn us around. We have to return to Mumbai. There has been a change in plans." On the return flight, Rishi called each of the Gentlemen. His message was clear: the investment had collapsed. Harshal's efforts to obtain the American boy should cease. The Enlightened Ones possessed powers beyond what they could conceive, much less, hope to control!

Unknown to Rishi, a naval listening station, picked up his conversations with Mrs. Worthington and his call to the other Gentlemen. The following morning, when Christina Johansson checked her encrypted messages, there was one from Marley.

> *Morning Darling: Thought you might like to see the attached transcript. I was curious about that corporate jet that flew out of the tiger sanctuary. Seems the Brit and the computer tycoon were connected. The jet never made it to Sri Lanka, turned back halfway there. Transcript tells it all. He contacted a bunch of big money men in India on the way back. Looks like they are all involved in something, but you probably know that. Next time you call an embassy agent, use an encrypted phone. The Yanks copied us on your calls to Sri Lanka. What were you thinking? You owe me. ...Marley*

Chapter 65

Location: Carrington Farm, Northern Virginia
Time: September 2034

Mitzi Weaver stared into the faces of Jenkins and Cox, anticipating their next question. *Don't ask. Don't ask!*

"Now, Doctor Weaver," Jenkins began in one of his more pronounced southern drawls, "I know ya said this Chetana could do strange things—like that flower in the teashop—but could ya explain what she did to the Indian guy. If there is an explanation?"

Weaver cleared her throat then rolled her bottom lip over her lower teeth in a calculated effort to stall. When convinced that Jenkins was about to say something, she spoke. "Chetana's abduction was a turning point for me and everyone involved. When I learned what occurred in Sri Lanka, our research protocols for the children changed—we went back to page one and started rewriting everything." Weaver rubbed her temples. "Up to then, we studied the children. After that, we knew we would learn only what they wanted us to know."

"Okay, I can understand that, but what did Chetana do to the Indian guy," Jenkins demanded.

Without emotion, Weaver spoke clinically. "Molecular disruption of the synaptic structure of the temporal lobes within the cerebral cortex."

Jenkins looked at Weaver; his face telegraphed the disgust he felt.

Before Jenkins could respond to Weaver, Cox played his role as mediator. "Excuse me, Doctor Weaver, but what does all that mean?"

Jenkins bobbed his head in agreement. "Yes, just what does all that mean?"

Weaver cast a smirk to Jenkins and then turned to Cox. "We learned Chetana could alter molecular structures at the subatomic level. When abducted, she was beginning to excel in biology and anatomy. She knew the parts of the brain that controlled emotions. With her touch, Chetana modified Sanjay's brain structure causing his emotional collapse."

"Holy chit," Jenkins avoided a vulgarity but made his feeling clear. "So this little girl could kill you just by touching you?"

Mitzi reflected for a moment. *How do you explain the unexplainable?* "By the time Chetana disappeared, she could alter matter at the quantum level—where things like gravity and space-time no longer exist. If that bunch in India had her, they could have used her to develop a quantum computer, although they didn't fully understand her potential at the time."

"A quantum computer; can you tell me what a quantum computer is?" Cox asked. "The NSA and FBI just got one—it costs a fortune."

Mitzi shrugged and began, "It's a computer that uses the power of atoms and molecules to perform storage and calculation tasks. The idea is not new, significant progress toward such a machine started around 2010. A regular computing device operates in a binary world, representing all numbers and letters using only two digits—'ones' and 'zeroes'—which equates nicely to a switch being 'on' or 'off.' Quantum computers work by observing the state of quantum bits that might represent a one, a zero or a combination of numbers between zero and one. Simply put, the thing can perform calculations many, many times faster than a silicon chip. The key to creating a quantum machine is being able to understand and observe the molecular process. That's what Chetana could do—she could sense or communicate with these quantum structures. But like I said, the Indian guys didn't know that at the time."

"Wow," Cox remarked, "A breakthrough like that would be worth billions to a company."

Jenkins leaned his head into his hand and slowly shook his head. He did not understand Weaver's scientific explanation but he understood motive. The group had a strong motive to control the children. He raised his head and nodded toward Weaver. "Okay, I think we understand why she could've been valuable to them. So after this incident, did the kids display other powers? I guess that's what you'd have to call them—dang sure not ordinary human talents."

"You are right. When we learned that they could communicate telepathically, it knocked us over. As far as we know, they never tried to communicate telepathically with anyone else, except once. From that point, the children immersed themselves in their individual areas of interest. Ethan pursed math and multidimensional space concepts—and of course baseball. Sara's language skills grew as expected. Her real joy came from work with the paranormal lab. Chetana continued her studies with the microbiology department at Johns Hopkins. She loved biology. For her, everything was alive, even rocks! Regrettably, each of them did deal with some unpleasant problems in their young lives."

"You said they communicated telepathically with someone. Did it have to do with the troubles they experienced?" Cox asked.

"Yeah, I'm sad to say it did. It involved Sara."

Weaver knew she opened the door too wide. There would be more questions from the two officers. It was time to reveal everything.

Chapter 66

Location: SÄPO Headquarters, Stockholm, Sweden
Time: June 2030

Director Lundberg arrived at his office late; the previous night he helped to entertain members of Riksdag, the Swedish parliament. He and his boss knew that the best policy was to keep members of the intelligence oversight committee happy. Fine wine, fine food, even the occasional woman, served the purpose. Of course, should something unmentionable happen to a member of the committee, SÄPO could always make it disappear.

Like iron drawn to a magnet, Lundberg went straight to his coffee maker when he entered the office. As he started a pot of coffee, there was a knock on the doorframe his office.

"*God morgon!* How are we today?" the young woman asked as she suppressed a snicker.

Lundberg turned to see Inga, his aide. "My dear woman. I spend my night protecting your miserable employment, and this is how you treat me?"

With an insolent smirk pasted on her face, Inga replied, "Oh, in that case Director, thank you." She placed a folder on Lundberg's desk. "Here's the transmission file from last night. There is another entry on Christina Johansson. I flagged it for you as you asked. We haven't received anything on her in a while. What is she doing calling MI-5?" Not waiting for an answer, she called back as she stepped out of the office, "I'll let you get to it. And, don't forget your eleven o'clock meeting with the budget office."

Lundberg gulped several swallows of the rich coffee before opening the transmission file. *I don't understand Christina. Doesn't she know we monitor all calls to and from citizens with ultra-top secret clearances?* Lundberg's interest grew as he flipped through the transcripts of Christina's calls. *What's this, a call to an MI-5 agent? And, what business does she have with our embassy in Sri Lanka?* He quickly skimmed the last transcript. *Now this is interesting, two calls to some Indian bank executive.*

A good field agent, Marvin Lundberg possessed the knack for sensing facts. His eye locked in on a single exchange.

CHRISTINA WILMA JOHANSSON, Division Director, Near East and Arabic Section, Organization of Baltic Sea States.
TO: RAM KAPUR, Indian National, Senior Economist, Federal Bank, India. Recorded: 11:33 P.M., excerpt of transmission; Stockholm to Mobile Phone, ping Southern India, WorldCom Tower.

> **Kapur:** *Before I ring off, may I ask how you learned that Chetana was missing?*
>
> **Johansson:** *I think it best that you ask Chetana that question. Her answer may surprise you—but then, nothing our two girls do should ever surprise us. Isn't that right?"*

Lundberg remembered the results of the remote listening project. *Sara can do it, I know she can hear or at least sense where someone is. How did those eggheads downstairs miss it? Maybe she just grew into it. Whatever it is, I'm damn well going to find out! This is could be the opportunity I've been waiting for, a career-maker for me! Imagine, Marvin Lundberg, Minister of National Security. I like the sound of that!*

Lundberg moved quickly to arrange a meeting with Sara and Christina for the next day. There would be no fooling around this time; he would demand that Christina explain how Sara knew of Chetana's situation.

⊷⊷

Marvin Lundberg did not have specific evidence that Sara Johansson possessed special communication or listening skills, but he was a man who trusted his gut. His gut told him there was something special about Sara. When Christina and the girl arrived, he got to the point. "Christina and little Sara! Thank you for coming. May I get you something? Coffee, sparkling water, perhaps?"

"No, we are fine," Christina responded. "But I am wondering why you asked us here this morning?"

"I'm going to cut straight to the chase; I have evidence that Sara has remote listening ability." Taking a sheaf of papers from a folder on his desk, Lundberg placed them squarely in front of Christina. Although he lacked real evidence, he knew how to use misdirection when questioning a person of interest. "These are transcripts of calls you made to MI-5 and to a Ram Kapur in India. I have proof that Sara is able to communicate with the child called Chetana. Do you deny it?"

Christina Johansson anticipated that her actions would lead to this moment; she was prepared. There was no need to dispute the obvious. The only course of action was to ensure that Sara did not become a cog in the Swedish intelligence machine. "So, what if Sara has some special talent? She does not wish to work with you or the geeks in the lab."

Caught off guard by Christina's frankness, Lundberg scrambled to regain control of the situation. He did not expect one of his loyal subordinates to challenge him outright. "Now Christina, did I suggest any course of action that would harm Sara or cause her to do something she did not wish to do? I only wish to confirm that such ability does exist. If Sara has this talent, then the Chinese or the Koreans could have someone with the same skill. We need to understand what we're up against."

Christina was about to confront Lundberg's sincerity when Sara spoke. "Momma, it's okay. I'll show him what he wishes to see. Don't worry. Everything will be fine."

"Excellent, young lady. That's more like it." The elation in Lundberg's tone was undeniable. "I think that you and the Indian girl should meet here. That way, we can see what you are able do. What do you say?" The Deputy Director's body language conveyed his pleasure with the way things were going. *Marvin Lundberg, Minister of National Security. Yes, yes, I do like the sound of that!*

"That will not be necessary. I can demonstrate my skill without Chetana being here."

Lundberg was not convinced but agreed. "Okay, let's see what you can do. We'll do it tomorrow here in the laboratory."

Sara smiled, as if she agreed, but then said, "Don't you think that you should see what I do before sharing the information with other people? Say, at my house?"

Lundberg considered Sara's request. *She's right. Why shouldn't I be the first to see her in action? That way, I can use the information to my advantage.* "Okay. Perhaps you're right. Best I see before anyone else. Tomorrow is Saturday. No one will miss us. Tomorrow morning it is!"

❧

Marvin Lundberg rose even earlier than he would any other morning, motived by what lay ahead. Today could be a major turning point in his career. After an austere breakfast of bread and black coffee, he mentally prepared for his meeting with Sara. When he arrived at the Johansson family home, he felt ready to observe the child. Sara met him at the door.

"*God morgon*, Mr. Lundberg. Please come in. If you would follow me to the kitchen, Momma has some coffee ready for you. She said you like coffee from Africa."

In the kitchen, Christina greeted Lundberg. "*God morgon.* I have that coffee you like. Shall I pour you a cup? It is fresh." Her tone and facial expressions concealed her distain for the man.

Following the usual amenities, and clutching a large cup of coffee, Lundberg followed Christina into the comfortable living room. Sara was there, seated on the floor. "I am not sure what Sara has planned. In fact, I know very little about the scope of her talents. But, I think you gathered that from my telephone calls, didn't you?"

"Momma, it is okay. I know what he wants to see. I will show him." Sara moved to the couch and beckoned to the Lundberg. "Come and sit here with me Mr. Lundberg."

"Okay, young lady, I would be happy to do so. Now, show me what you can do." Lundberg smiled in anticipation.

"You know I hear voices, don't you?"

"Yes, since you were a small child, I believe."

"Well, I guess that is when it all started. At first, I could only hear vague voices asking simple questions. Soon, it was easier to communicate with the voices—to understand what they were asking. Later I was able to communicate telepathically, but only with my two friends. They're special children, like me. That's how I knew that Chetana was in trouble."

"I gathered that you must have a connection with Chetana from your mother's call to Mr. Kapur. However, you said that you have 'two friends' with whom you are able to communicate. I know only of Chetana. Who is your other friend?"

"Oh, there's Ethan. He lives in Colorado. That's in the United States." Sara studied Lundberg for a moment as he sipped his coffee. "While the three of us are able to communicate, we can't read minds or anything like that. I have never communicated with anyone other than my friends, but I could try. Do you wish to try Mr. Lundberg?"

"Of course!" Lundberg set aside his cup. "So, we will hear each other's thoughts?"

"Yes, and more. Everything in your mind."

"You mean all of my memories?" The intelligence officer was not certain that a child should have access to his innermost thoughts; he did many unpleasant things as a covert field agent.

Sara did not respond immediately, her hand toying with the long blonde curl that graced her face. "Are you afraid of what I will learn about you?"

"Well, each of us has secrets that we don't wish to share," Lundberg admitted.

"In that case, you will never know what I can do. You cannot feel the warmth of the sun, if you are unwilling to expose yourself to its rays. You wish to hear what others are thinking, but are unwilling for them to hear your thoughts. I am sorry, but you can't have it both ways."

Obviously disgruntled, the seasoned intelligence operative weighed the alternatives of exposing himself to the mental scrutiny of an eleven-year old child. *I can't have her in my head. She will know everything that I did. But, I must know how it feels. Wait. What about the other two?* "Will I be able to share thoughts with your two friends?"

"Yes, if we are able to communicate, I think that you can do that. Momma warned me that you would not be happy unless you communicated with Ethan and Chetana."

Lundberg was torn; the stress he felt was evident in the reddish tint that spread across his face—the product of years of smoking, poor eating habits, and the overuse of alcohol. "Okay, I'll do it. Your mother is correct. I must experience what you and your friends share."

"Then, that is what we will do. Come closer. Put out your hands."

At the child's direction, the middle-aged man positioned his hands directly in front of her. He was a seasoned observer. If she tried anything—any trick or deception—he would catch her in the act. "What am I to do? Do I clear my mind or think of some special color that is supposed to relax me?"

Sara touched his hands and looked into his eyes. Without saying a word, Sara answered Lundberg's questions. *"It's not necessary. Nothing is required. See what I mean. You can you understand me, can't you?"*

Almost shouting, Lundberg responded. "Your lips didn't move, but I understood what you said. This is impossible—but I've done it." Concentrating, Lundberg conveyed his request telepathically, *"I want to speak with your two friends."*

"If you wish. Let me see if I am able to contact them. Ethan, are you there? Chetana, are you there?

Lundberg could not contain himself and said aloud, "I heard you call them. Will I hear them answer?"

Before Sara could respond, two voices spoke at the same time, *"Hi, Sara, it's me, Ethan. And me, Chetana."*

"Hello. I have someone with us, the man I told you about last night."

"You mean the man who wanted to make you a spy?" Ethan did not suppress his feelings toward Lundberg.

Chetana joined in, *"So this is the person who wanted to speak with us. Ah, I understand. Yes, yes, I am reading his thoughts. My word! He is a nasty individual."*

Not waiting for the interloper to communicate with her friends, Sara advised Lundberg, *"So, let's say goodbye to Ethan and Chetana. I have someone else for you to meet. Goodbye to both of you. We'll visit later."*

Lundberg looked to Sara, *"Who do you want me to meet? You said that you could only communicate with your friends?"*

"No, you forgot about the voices–they are here. Listen!"

Christina watched as emotion after emotion raced across the man's face—first, astonishment, then disbelief, and finally terror. His hands trembled, his posture grew rigid, and perspiration drenched his forehead. The once powerful individual degenerated into a pathetic figure before her eyes.

"Sara, Sara, what is happening? What are you doing to him?" Christina's questions went unanswered.

Sara stared into the eyes of her antagonist. *"You wanted to hear what I hear–now you do. I feel sorry for you–but then, it was your choice. I'll leave you with them now, my dear Minister of National Security."*

"Make them stop," Lundberg exclaimed aloud as he jumped to his feet. "You did this. Undo it!"

"I cannot. You see, they do not need me to talk to humans." A small tear formed in the corner of Sara's eye. She knew what she had done, but it hurt to see Lundberg in pain.

Powerless to resist, Marvin Lundberg ran to the door. Outside, the sound of a car spread away, its tires squealed against the pavement.

Christina stood speechless for a moment, bewildered by what happened. She then asked, "Sara, what happened? What did you do to him?"

Sara spoke in a manner unfamiliar to her mother, showing little emotion. "Everything will be okay. That is, except for poor Mr. Lundberg. The voices will not leave him alone. They are very powerful and very demanding. They must know everything."

Christina did not know what to think. Was Sara safe from Lundberg and men like him?

≈৩≈

The next morning Christina received the answer to her question. As she entered SÄPO headquarters, a familiar voice called out to her; it was Inga, Lundberg's aide.

"Doctor Johansson! Did you hear what happened on Saturday?" Inga hurried to Christina.

"No, Inga. What happened?" Christina feigned knowledge of what could have happened.

"Well, the word is that Director Lundberg went off his rocker! The details are sketchy, but the story is that Director Lundberg came into the building around noon acting strangely. He rushed through security and went to his office. Later, a janitor found him sitting at his desk watching a small fire in a metal wastebasket and called security. The janitor said it looked like he was burning a folder. By the time security arrived and put out the fire, there were only ashes left." Inga looked to her left and her right. She leaned closer to Christina and spoke softly. "Here's what is really strange. The guards called the emergency medical personnel. Can you believe it? They took Lundberg out of here in a straitjacket!"

Stunned by what she heard, Christina struggled to respond. "Are you sure, Inga? He was in a straitjacket. I can't believe he had a mental breakdown." *Oh, yes, I can. I'm afraid that I believe every word you said Inga.*

Confined in a mental health institution for patients who might disclose national secrets, Marvin Lundberg insisted that he was sane and that he could communicate telepathically. The attending psychiatrists ignored his claims.

No one in the Johansson household spoke of what happened that morning when Lundberg visited; that is, except when Sara told Mitzi the last week they were together at Carrington Farm.

Chapter 67

Location: Patio Area, Overseer's Cottage, Carrington Farm
Time: September 2034

"This is nice," Mitzi Weaver mused as she sipped a cup of jasmine tea. "Oh, not just the tea. I mean sitting out here. I loved to sit out here with the kids—talking, kidding around. It was so enjoyable. I already miss them so."

"What do you talk about with three super geniuses," Cox asked casually, and then glancing at Jenkins added, "Off the record, of course."

Jenkins nodded his acceptance to Cox and Weaver. "Yeah, it's okay."

Mitzi smiled, sipped her tea and answered. "You know, relationships with others, growing up, that kind of stuff. They may have been geniuses, but they were young adults dealing with pretty much the same things as other teenagers. You know, changes in body shape, the emergence of sexual arousal and parental pressure to conform. All teenagers are alike."

"Yeah, I guess we all went through it growing up." Jenkins' words surprised Weaver and Cox. "Have to admit, I can still recall trying to understand girls. Hell, can't even understand my wife after thirty-odd years."

Both Weaver and Cox smiled, partly because they could relate to what Jenkins said, but also, because he revealed a softer side they had not seen before.

Suddenly, Jenkins rose, as if shocked back into the reality of who he was. "Okay, can't sit here all day. There's work to do."

Returning to the living room, Cox said, "When we get settled, why don't you tell us about Ethan. You gave me some good information about the girls for my profiles. Could you tell me something about the boy—something I can use in building his profile?"

Mitzi Weaver gave Cox a large friendly smile, the ones she reserved for her dearest friends. "Actually, I can. I just thought about it while we were outside. Ethan reminded me of something that had a profound impact on him. It started shortly after the second session at Johns Hopkins. I told you about Ethan and Oskar talking on the way to the airport. Well, that's where it started."

Chapter 68

Location: Little League Field, Denver, Colorado
Time: May 2031

"You done good, young man," Kevin Lake said in his typical Texas style. He was proud of Ethan's performance.

As Kevin approached his son's dugout, Ethan agreed, "You bet. They actually let me hit a couple of times. Most teams just give me a walk. They don't let me hit the ball."

"Don't fret, my man. You have a near perfect batting average. So what do you want to do now? Ready for one of those really big milk shakes and a burger?"

"Yeah. Sounds good." Ethan struggled to carry his glove and baseball shoes out of the dug. He looked up at his father. "Would you grab my bat? And, where's the car parked?"

Once in the car, Ethan was quiet, immersed in thought. Kevin respected his son's special gifts: when Ethan was working on a problem, he did not disturb his son's concentration.

Without notice, the boy looked at this father. "Daddy, do you think I'm crazy? You know insane, like Sara?"

His son's question shocked Kevin. "Why would you ask that?"

"The kids at school say I'm crazy 'cause I'm always turning my head. You know, it's because I see things."

"Let me tell you. You are not crazy, or insane, or a nut job, or whatever else those numb skulls call you. What scares the hell out of them is that you're a lot smarter than they are. They are trying to find something to make them think that they are better than you are. Kids do that."

For the remainder of the ride, Kevin tried to reassure his son that everything was fine. Ethan went into detail about what the children at school said and how it made him feel. As the Cadillac Escalade pulled into the parking lot at the ice cream shop, the anticipation of tackling a giant milk shake replaced the seriousness of the previous moment—for boy and for man!

❧

"Ah, it's been a busy day." Kevin flopped down in his favorite chair. "First the game, then the yard, and that mess in the garage. That's enough for an old man."

"An old man? So you admit it?" Emily hassled Kevin. "Sit down. Make yourself comfortable. We deserve a little time together."

Ethan was in bed and his sister was spending the night with a friend. Emily and Kevin sat quietly with a glass of red wine.

"You know what our son asked me today?" Kevin asked.

"Let me guess!" A grin formed on Emily's youthful looking face. "I bet he asked if the speed of a ball off the bat was the coefficient of the velocity of the speed of the pitch."

Kevin shook his head. "Holy crap. You're starting to sound like him!"

"Okay, so what did he ask?" Emily giggled, amused by her attempt to sound like a mathematician.

Kevin paused for a second to allow Emily to recover: he loved to watch her laugh. "Ethan asked if he was insane. Evidently, some of the kids told him that only crazy people think they see ghosts. Ghosts! Isn't that strange. Why ghosts? Anyway, we talked. I think he's okay."

"It's his awful tic. Even though we ruled out Tourette syndrome, he still does that thing with his head."

"Yeah, yeah, don't go all doctor on me. I just thought you should know."

Upstairs, Ethan lay in his bed. He could not hear every word his parents said but he knew what they were discussing. *What are the lights? What causes them? Why am I the only one who can see them?*

Chapter 69

Location: The Lake Family Residence, Denver, Colorado
Time: August 2031

Denver area schools begin the fall term in late August. For Ethan, Little League baseball was over and ski season was just around the corner. Although he was only twelve, this would be his last semester to attend regular classes. He needed to complete only two courses at Lakeland High School to receive his diploma. He did not like regular school anymore and was happy this would be his last semester.

For the past couple of years, Ethan worked with Oskar Johansson and the Mathematics Department at Sanford on physics and mathematics. Today, he was busy completing a mathematics assignment in his room. Without warning, flashes of light raced about the room. *I'm not nuts. I see them. They're brighter than ever. What are they? Maybe they're just ball lightning? There's such a thing.*

"Ethan. Come to supper," Emily sung out. "You can study later."

That night, Ethan lay on his bed. He could not sleep. With school came a return of the taunting, probably with more intensity. As he stared into the darkness, he pondered how to confront his tormentors when the lights appeared, but only for a minute. Struck with insight, he sat up. *That's it, that's it! Gotta contact Sara!* His room was quiet. The digital clock on the nightstand announced 1:07 AM in bold red light. *What time is it in Scandinavia?* The math prodigy began a complex calculation in his head. *I don't care what time it is. Must be daytime. I have to contact her. Wait, wait. Clear your mind.* He tried to clear his mind of things he did not want Sara to know, but it was no use. He was twelve. She would understand. Slowly summoning his courage, he reached out. "*Sara. Sara. Are you there?*"

"*Ethan, is that you?*"

"*Of course it's me! Is there some other boy you can talk to this way?*"

"*You forget that I hear voices all the time. I never know when it is one of them.*"

"Sorry. Didn't mean to be rude, but that's why I wanted to talk to you. You said people used to call you crazy because you heard those voices."

"Ethan, "insane" is the correct English term, not crazy. And, yes, my preschool teacher was the first to think I had a mental problem."

"Okay, whatever." Ethan did not handle criticism well. He paused for a minute. *"So, I told you and Chetana 'bout the flashes of light I see. They're showing up a lot lately–brighter and more intense. You understand what I'm saying?"*

"Why of course. It's because you're crazy!" Sara laughed. *"I'm sorry, forgive me?"*

Although Ethan could not see Sara's face, he could sense her laughter. *"Okay, you've had your fun. I'm not nuts and I'm tired of people saying that I am. There must be some explanation for the flashes. What do think?"*

"Why didn't you ask Chetana? She's a science wizard like you."

The young man did not answer before Sara responded. *Ah, yes, you like her, don't you? You're afraid that you couldn't stop thinking about her body."*

"So what? Yes, I like her. Now are you going to help me or not?"

"Okay. Let me think." After a brief pause, Sara answered. *"Have you considered that it might be thin space? That's what it's called in Irish lore. We discussed it in my paranormal class."*

"What's thin space?" Ethan was eager to learn more.

Sara explained the ancient Irish belief about thin space, as she understood it. *"In Celtic Spirituality, thin space is that moment, that place, where the separation of this world and the next becomes thin; no longer opaque, but translucent, even transparent. Maybe you're experiencing something like that Ethan. Maybe you're seeing into the hereafter, or the future, or even into heaven. Now that I think about it, maybe my voices come from the same place. Do you think we can communicate with dead people? Even see them?"*

"Now I see why they call you a nut job. Thanks, but no thanks. You're telling me the same thing that the kids here say. They think I see ghosts. Just forget it." Ethan broke off contact with Sara but he could not stop thinking about what she said. "Do you think that we can communicate with dead people? Even see them?"

Chapter 70

Location: Carrington Farm, Northern Virginia
Time: September 2034

"There you go again!" Jenkins could not hide his disbelief. "Should have known. You told us the Indian girl could kill ya, just by touching ya, so why not have this girl and boy speak to dead people!"

Mitzi Weaver half-expected Jenkins' response. While he may have read about heaven, hell, and the joy of eternal life, he was a pragmatist, grounded in the reality of the here and now. In this reality, folks do not communicate with spirits.

Mitzi gave Jenkins a "go-to-hell" look. "You're forgetting what Misenheimer said about the part of Ethan's brain that controlled his eyesight. Remember? He had never seen anything like it. He predicted Ethan's visual acuity would increase, even beyond what it was when he was examined."

Cox jumped in, to avert a confrontation between Jenkins and Weaver. "So, Ethan's ability to see these images increased as he grew older. But, it appears that he was starting to come to grips with his situation. Did he solve his problem or did it trouble him until he disappeared?"

"I should explain. Emily told me that when Ethan was around eleven, he no longer excused his visions as flashes of light or images on the edge of his peripheral vision. He was certain that they were more."

Cox persisted as Weaver had not answered his question. "Did he solve the problem—you know—determine the source of the light?"

"In a way, maybe he did solve the problem. I know he talked to Oskar Johansson about it."

Jenkins sat forward in his chair and started to point at Weaver, but withdrew his finger. "And, what did Johansson have to say? Do you know?"

"Some of it. I told you that Oskar was studying the behavior of gravitons and was tutoring Ethan in quantum mechanics. That's why Ethan turned to him for help. I guess it started when Oskar invited Ethan to a physics conference in San Francisco."

Chapter 71

Location: International Conference on Subatomic Particles,
        San Francisco, California
Time: October 2032

Oskar Johansson stood near the entrance to the San Francisco Grand Hotel in anticipation of the arrival of Ethan Lake and his parents.

As the airport limousine pulled up and the trio stepped out, Oskar walked towards them. After he shook hands with Kevin and hugged Emily, he turned to Ethan. "Hello, young man. I'm so pleased you could attend the conference. You'll love it."

"Thank you for inviting me."

"My, you have grown since I saw you last. Sara would be impressed. You're taller than she is. You're almost as tall as I am."

"Yeah, Momma said I hit a growth spurt."

Oskar mussed Ethan's hair and grinned, "Well, it's good to see all of you in the flesh. Has it been almost two years since we were together?"

"Yes, I think so. It was when I visited the large accelerator in Switzerland. That was a fun time. Hope I get to go back and work with you."

"That would be nice. I look forward to working with you." Oskar smiled. He knew it would not be long before Ethan would receive an internship at CERN, even a position.

Ethan nodded his agreement. In a very business-like way, he said, "It's almost four. My parents want to have dinner at a fancy restaurant they used to go to before I was born. Since we have to register and everything, do you mind if we have dinner together?"

"You have grown!" Oskar marveled at the young man's adult behavior. "Certainly, let's have dinner together. I know just the place. It's not far from here." Looking at Emily and Kevin, he said, "You need not worry about Ethan. Go! Enjoy yourselves. We'll meet you in the main lobby after dinner. Say around nine o'clock?"

Kevin shook hands with Oskar. "That's great. "We'll see you then."

Following dinner, Oskar and Ethan sat in the main lobby of the hotel waiting for his parents to return. They discussed the sessions they planned to attend and talked about skiing.

Ethan did not ask the question that troubled him until the conversation waned. "I wanted to ask you something about the paper you're presenting tomorrow. I read the draft you sent. I was thinking…" The young man paused.

"What were you thinking?"

Gaining courage, Ethan said what was on his mind. "It's about your research. You've confirmed that gravitons disappear into another dimension, but you don't say where that is or what's there."

"That's because I am not sure where that is. We think they slip into one of the space-time dimensions described in string theory. I told you that at the airport in Baltimore."

"That's what bothers me. I understand that our universe is probably just a fraction of a much larger multi-verse. There must be billions of other universes, like there are billions of galaxies. If nature or some superior being created these places, there would be a purpose for them. Don't you think? Why create a universe that is void and uninhabited?"

"An interesting thought." Oskar nodded his head in agreement and then paused to consider Ethan's supposition. "Certainly they are not void. There must be matter. As for being inhabited, that's something else. Inhabited by what or by whom, I would not venture a guess. The laws of physics, as we know them, may not apply in these alternate dimensions. Quantum mechanics confirms that. What do you think is there?"

Ethan sat quietly, contemplating the question. "You know I see things—flashes of light. It's like when Sara hears things. Could we be getting glimpses of another dimension? What if heaven is just one of these dimensions and it's right here with us?"

Ethan's hypothesis amazed Oskar. "My word, young man. Science and theology! You never cease to amaze me. In fact, your question raises a number of other questions. I would ask, where does each dimension start and where does it stop? At what point does one leave this dimension and enter another?" Reflecting on what Ethan said, and thinking of his daughter, Oskar added, "I can't really say whether you and Sara have the ability to experience heaven in this dimension. I guess that only time will tell."

Ethan reflected on what Oskar said. *I need to talk to Sara. I don't believe that either of us is crazy!*

Chapter 72

Location: Atrium Dining Room, San Francisco Grand Hotel
Time: October 2032

The San Francisco Grand Hotel encompassed an expansive atrium that reached upward fifteen floors to a massive glass and steel skylight. Hotel rooms, each with a balcony, overlooked the open space. Tropical trees, potted plants and colorful flowers filled the atrium forming a microcosmic jungle, complete with tropical birds in ornate cages. In the middle of the atrium was a dining area enclosed by brass rails. The restaurant, decorated in the style of late nineteenth-century San Francisco, had four gas street lamps to mark its entrance.

"Isn't this beautiful," Emily said as she and Kevin entered the atrium and walked toward the dining area.

"Certainly is. Sorry we couldn't get into Ricardo's. I should have made reservations before we left Denver. I know how much you wanted to go there again."

As they approached the *maître d'* station, Emily grabbed her husband's arm. "It's okay. I love the atmosphere here and I'm sure the food will be fine."

"I hope so. I'm hungry." Kevin looked about the entrance for the *maître d'* but could not see anyone. From the shadows to his left, a young woman wearing a simple black dress appeared.

"Good evening. Welcome to the Atrium. Will there be two for dinner?"

⚬ᘓᕟ⚬

Emily and Kevin enjoyed dining together. Kevin ordered the "surf and turf" dinner with lobster and rib eye steak; Emily ordered the baked sea bass with drawn butter. A strolling violinist added a romantic touch to the evening, as did the bottle of wine that Kevin insisted that they have.

"Remember our last visit to San Francisco? When we ate at Ricardo's? We went back to the room and ..."

"Yes, dear. I remember." Emily smiled as she took Kevin's hand in hers. "That was then and we didn't have a teenage son with us." Patting the back of his hand, she added, "Enjoy your coffee."

The couple sipped cups of rich, dark roasted coffee flavored with sweet cream and raw sugar. They discussed the possibility of a visit to Fisherman's Wharf the next day.

As they talked, an uninvited man sat down at their table. "Good evening. How are both of you?"

Startled by the man's unexpected appearance, neither spoke a word. Finally, Kevin asked, in a tone reflecting his displeasure with the intrusion, "May I help you?"

The well-groomed man in a dark blue suit tilted his head in response to Kevin's question. "Actually, I'm here to help you, Mr. Lake, and your family."

"And how might that be," Emily asked. "And how do you know us?"

"First, let me introduce myself. I am Marion Diaz, Special Agent with the National Security Administration." Diaz handed Kevin an embossed business card bearing a government seal. "So, let me tell you why I am here. As you may know, NSA is responsible for defending the country against terrorist attacks. That includes internet hackers—in particular, Russians, Chinese, and rogue operatives. Here's the thing. Folks like the Chinese and Russians are recruiting their very best math and computer science scholars to staff their hacking operations. You must agree that it only makes sense that the U.S. would be doing the same thing. And that brings us to your son, Ethan."

"Wait!" demanded Kevin. "Are you saying that the NSA wants Ethan to work as a hacker?"

Diaz raised his palm towards Kevin. "Let's not get ahead of ourselves. Here's the deal."

Emily did not like people who used buzz phrases like, "here's the deal." It sounded like something a used car salesman would say. His choice of words only added to her dislike of the man.

"The Agency considers Ethan to be a national treasure—a treasure worth safeguarding. The Japanese call outstanding poets and artists, national treasures; well, we think individuals like your son are extra special. If his math skills are valuable to the defense of our country, wouldn't you want him to help protect the freedoms you have?"

Kevin did not like Diaz's attitude. "Hey, you're talking to a Marine combat officer. Don't come here waving the flag and give me that song and dance about protecting our freedoms. Why don't you tell us what all this means for Ethan?"

"Well, nothing is going to change. The Agency will continue to do its work without interfering with your lives. Actually, we've monitored Ethan for the past year without interfering with the family's normal routines. Bet you didn't even know that our agents were around." Diaz wiped his nose with his index finger. "Allergies. Can't stand San Francisco this time of year. Now where was I? Oh, yeah. So why are we talking to you now. Seems that Ethan's name surfaced on the watch lists of a couple of foreign governments. Someone up the ladder thought that you should know. Anyway, agents will continue to conduct surveillance to protect Ethan—make sure no harm comes to him. Of course, this protection extends to his family."

"Just like that?" Emily took the napkin from her lap and tossed it on the table. "You're telling us that we don't have a say in the matter?"

"Afraid not. You folks have a wonderful evening." With that, Agent Diaz, bid farewell to the couple and left their table as nonchalantly as when he arrived.

From that day on, Emily and Kevin found themselves looking over their shoulders to see who might be there, as did Ethan. The three agreed not to tell Ethan's sister—she was an active high school senior who would be leaving to attend the University of Texas at Austin.

Chapter 73

Location: Overseer's Cottage, Carrington Farm, Bath County, Virginia
Time: September 2034

Jenkins rose from his chair, stretched, and yawned. "Enough of this, Cox. Hope you have enough information for your profile."

"I think so. Won't be the best profile that I ever did but…"

"Well good then. We gotta get up to the Mansion and talk with those preacher folks. They'll be leaving soon." Jenkins placed his notepad in his shirt pocket and then looked down at Weaver. "Ma'am, when we get back I would like to skip to when you and the three kids got here. Would you please give that some thought so that we can move right along once we return? While the folks up at the Mansion prepare a fine meal, I have no intention of staying here another night."

Cox followed Jenkins' lead and yawned. "Wow, I guess I do need a stretch." As he gathered up the video recorder, he agreed with Jenkins. "I'm with you, Lieutenant. I need to get back to Baltimore. The folks back there probably have an APB out on me by now!"

Jenkins chuckled. "Yep, been here long enough. Let's go see them preachers." As he started toward the door, he took a parting shot at Weaver. "Gonna be nice to talk certifiable eyewitnesses."

Mitzi followed the two men to the door. "Call me when you're headed back and I'll make you some coffee."

Cox turned to Weaver and smiled. "We shouldn't be long. I'm sure we'll be able to wrap things up pretty quickly. I know you want to get Jenkins and me out of your hair."

As two men walked out of earshot of Weaver, Jenkins asked, "What do you know about NSA and this boy? Are you holding out on me, Cox?" Like most Americans in the middle of the twenty-first century, Jenkins was skeptical about the truthfulness of federal agencies. His face revealed his concern.

Cox did not look at his colleague. "Well, I don't know all that much. This fellow named Diaz from NSA contacted me before I left Baltimore. Said he would appreciate me giving him an update when I returned to DC. Never gave it much thought. We get calls from NSA all the time. Surprised me when Weaver mentioned his name."

"So, you haven't been in touch with him since we started this thing with Weaver?" Jenkins' tone conveyed his suspicion that Cox was not being completely honest.

"Nope! Nothing like that. Hell, you know me better than that. Diaz asked me to let him know what we found. I planned to call him when I got back to my office. I don't even have his contact info with me."

"Okay, then. I accept that." Jenkins' expression relaxed. He smiled and nodded his head. "Now that's behind us, there's something on my mind."

"Yeah, I think I know what it is." Cox adjusted his sunglasses and lowered his head to avoid the evening sun in his eyes. "When I heard Weaver say that stuff about Diaz contacting the boy's parents in San Francisco, I asked myself if it was possible that NSA kept the kids under surveillance here. And if they did, just what do they know that we should know? Is that about what you're thinking?"

"That's pretty dang close. Do you think that they have someone on the grounds here or did they use some high altitude spy gadget?"

Cox shook his head in the negative. "Can't say. But I sure would like to know."

Jenkins stopped at the steps of the mansion. "Got a favor to ask of you. Would you check with the manager and get us a room where we can have some privacy. And, ask him to roundup those preachers. While you're doing that, I'm going to call the Sherriff's office and bring them up to speed. Mainly, I want them to know that we'll be leaving tonight."

❧

Alone in the cottage, Mitzi took the Lieutenant's directions to heart, reviewing in her mind the events of the last year and a half that lead to her to bring the children to Carrington Farm. *Cox said that they wouldn't be long. Best think about what I'm going to say.* Mitzi drifted back to that day in her office that she called the children and told them the good news about meeting at Carrington.

Chapter 74

Location: Office of Mitzi Weaver, Johns Hopkins University,
Baltimore, Maryland
Time: April 2033

"Okay, you guys. You will get the research prospectus in the next day or so. Can't wait to see you." Mitzi Weaver checked the display on her new video communication headset. "End call," she said, and watched the telephone icon in the corner of the right lens blink three times before it disappeared. *Twenty years ago, I would never have thought that eyeglasses would be my phone and my computer. Back then, no one wanted to wear glasses.* Still uncomfortable with the device, she removed it and gently placed it on her desk. Her mind quickly turned to the subject of her telephone call. *It's going to happen! Can't believe I'm going to get to spend time with the kids again.*

Weaver relished the joy of the moment. She had just finished a joint call with the children to give them the good news about the grant. The four of them would spend three weeks together. If everything went as scheduled, they would meet in a little over a year from now. A knock at her office door interrupted her thought.

Shelia Rowan, Director of the Biogenetics Laboratory, stood at the door. "Hi, Doctor Weaver. Thought you'd like a cup of tea."

"Come in Shelia. I'd love a cup. I have some wonderful news. Thanks to the generosity of a very kind lady, I'm going to work with the children once more."

"You mean your whiz kids?"

Weaver took her sweater from the back of her chair. "Come on. I'll tell you all about it." As the two walked down the hallway, Weaver conveyed her good news. "It was one of those minor miracles. Mary Benton, the Chairperson of the Benton Charitable Trust, came by the other day. She was interested in how things were going with the children. She mentioned that she hadn't seen anything written about the children for some time. She went on to say that she was particularly interested in their potential to solve complex societal problems—like hunger, disease, and poverty—things most people see as being insurmountable."

Shelia shook her head and chuckled. "Boy that Benton thinks big."

"Yeah, we little people don't have the money to think big." Weaver pushed open the door to the faculty lounge. "Ah, the good old lounge. What would faculty do without this place?"

"I know what you mean. Our very own little *sanctum sanctorum.*"

Weaver brewed tea for the two women and they sat down. For a moment, they said nothing while they enjoyed the warm beverage on this unusually chilly spring day.

Shelia broke the silence. "Well, finish your story."

Weaver sipped her tea and dabbed the corner of her mouth with a paper napkin. "Well, as I said, Mary Benton and her advisors thought that if the children worked together, they could tackle large, systemic problems. Anyway, she called me and proposed a study to evaluate their capabilities. She said that her staff would take care of everything."

Weaver explained how Mary Benton wanted the children to stay at Carrington Farm, a retreat center operated by the Benton Trust. There, the children would engage in a series of decision-making exercises presented by the world's prominent scholars. Should the exercises show promise, the children would begin addressing real-life situations.

Benton insisted that Weaver be the on-site coordinator for the project as she worked with the children from the beginning. The project would begin the following September to allow time to complete all of the necessary arrangements.

"Shelia, this grant comes at just the right time!" Weaver showed her excitement. "The children are beginning to show significant progress in their chosen fields. Sara is able to scan texts in any language and almost immediately converse with a native speaker in the language. Chetana is rapidly becoming a renowned authority in bio-molecular studies and a regular lecturer at major research institutions. Ethan recently presented a professional paper outlining his mathematical investigation of the potential shape of two of the dimensions identified in string theory. They're so bright. I can't wait to work with them again."

❧

Several days after learning they would be together again, Sara initiated a holographic conference call with Chetana and Ethan.

As the images of her friends began to appear, Sara greeted them, "Hello. Wow, you really look good. You guys finally eliminated that annoying flicker. Everybody hates that flicker. They're going to love what you did."

Ethan nodded his agreement. "The solution was simple once Chetana described the molecular modulation that was causing the radiation feedback. She sure has a gift."

"You're so kind, Ethan," replied Chetana. "And we can be thankful for the hologram—this way we don't have to endure your perverted thoughts. The last time we communicated, I was about to kick..."

"Okay, Chetana, you've made your point," Sara interrupted. "Now, Ethan, what did you want to talk to us about? And don't go geek on me!"

Ethan looked at the holograms of the girls and the image of himself, satisfied that everything was working properly. "Sara, do you remember when we talked about hearing and seeing into another dimension?"

"Sure. Why do you ask?"

Avoiding Sara's question, Ethan continued. "Chetana, remember the first time we went to Johns Hopkins and you asked us to hold hands. That's when you told Sara and me about your gift."

Chetana's demeanor softened towards the young man. "Yes, I recall. It was the first time we looked into that pit you call a male brain."

Ethan ignored the comment. "I have been working on something. It requires the two of you. I don't think that it is wise to discuss it here—too many eyes watching what we do. I'll be in touch. Have to run."

As his image faded, Sara asked her friend, "What do you think he wants? Sometimes that giant brain of his scares me."

Chetana shook her head back and forth, but said nothing. She had an inkling of what he wanted from them—she worked with him on the problem of altering the structure of matter, not long ago.

Part IX

DIMENSIONS BEYOND

All Cannot Be Seen

Chapter 75

Location: Library Room, Carrington Mansion, Northern Virginia
Time: September 2034

Lieutenant Jenkins completed his call to the Bath County Sheriff's Office and walked up the limestone steps into Carrington Mansion conference center. The entry room, furnished in a Greek revival motif, once was the grand parlor for the mansion. On one side of the room were several dark walnut chairs with satin seats placed around a matching walnut table with a white marble top. Behind the table and chairs stood a fireplace with a decorative marble mantelpiece. A mirror set in a gold gilded frame hung above the mantel. Across the room from the fireplace stood a reception counter that matched the walnut furnishings in the room. Heavy draperies framed the oversized windows, their centers filled by pale sheer curtains to allow in light. Jenkins approached the woman standing behind the reception counter.

"Good afternoon. How may I assist you," the middle-aged desk clerk asked.

Jenkins acknowledged the greeting with a nod of his head and the tip of a hat he no longer wore. "Ma'am. Could you tell me where I might find Special Agent Cox?"

"Yes, sir. He and some of the clergy are in the library." The clerk pointed to her right. "Just follow the hallway. You can't miss it."

The dark oak floor creaked as Jenkins walked down the hall. Oil paintings of horses lit by small lamps guided his way to a set of double doors bearing a brass plate labeled *Library*. As he entered, he stepped back in time. This was Mr. Carrington's private library. Here he read, and on certain occasions, entertained his male friends with fine cigars and strong beverages. Floor-to-ceiling bookcases lined the walls. Each case, heavily laden with leather bound volumes that showed their age, their covers dry and cracked, their titles faded. An oblong table occupied the center of the room. Special Agent Cox and three men, dressed in religious garments that identified them as a rabbi, a priest, and a Muslim cleric, sat around one end of the table.

"Afternoon, gentlemen." Jenkins sat down at the far end of the table and tried not to show that he was more comfortable around felons than around men of the cloth. "I'd like to thank you for visiting with us. I'm Lieutenant Phil Jenkins of the Virginia Bureau of Criminal Investigation. I assume you've met Special Agent Cox with the Baltimore office of the FBI. We are investigating the disappearance of three children, here at Carrington. As this is an official investigation, Agent Cox and I will be making a video record of our discussion. Are there any questions?"

The three men looked at each other and shook their heads. "I guess not," said the rabbi.

"Well, then, let's begin." Jenkins faced the priest seated to his right. "For the record, we'll need each of your names and where you're from. Let's begin with you."

"If this is an official recording, then I shall use my correct title. I am, The Most Reverend Byron Chapman, Archbishop of Toronto, Canada."

In turn, the next man responded. "I am Rabbi Joshua Benveniste, of Temple Beth Shalom, Greensburg, Pennsylvania."

"And, I'm Mullah Yousef Shirazi, with the Islamic Center of Winston-Salem, North Carolina."

Each man spoke with a regional American accent, which surprised Jenkins. The archbishop sounded like he was from New England, although from Canada; the rabbi's voice was distinctively Brooklyn without a hint of Yiddish. The mullah's accent was a complete shock. He spoke with an accent common to South Carolina or Georgia. As he looked at the "three men of God," Jenkins smiled. *You can tell their religious affiliation by what they wear, but standing naked and talking, you'd never know which was which!*

The Anglican archbishop wore a purple rabat with a white clerical collar beneath a grey, herringbone sports coat. Black trousers completed his outfit. In the middle of the rabat rested a gold, pectoral cross. The rabbi, dressed in a black wool suit, wore a white shawl with blue stripes and fringes on each corner; the back of his head covered by a black skullcap. The mullah wore a white, collarless shirt, a blue vest and a dark gray robe of finely textured wool. Atop his head sat a white turban.

Not waiting for Jenkins to continue, Cox said, "I understand that you witnessed the disappearance of three children on Wednesday afternoon. Could you tell us what you saw and why you thought you should report it to the Sheriff's Office?"

The archbishop spoke first. "We arrived here around midday on Wednesday. After a short orientation session, around four-thirty I'd say, we were dismissed for the evening. Joshua, Yousef and I decided to take a stroll to stretch our legs. About halfway between the mansion and the cottage, Yousef directed our attention to the lake." He gestured towards the mullah with his open hand, and said, "I should let Yousef tell this part."

Mullah Shirazi bowed his head toward Archbishop Chapman. "Thank you, Archbishop. To be precise, it was five-sixteen, I checked my Stat-Com for the time to ensure that I could return for evening prayers. As we were walking, the evening sun cast sparkles off the surface of the pond—the one near the cottage. It caught my eye. I noticed three young people near the water's edge, a boy and two girls. Not far from them, say twenty-five feet or so, was a woman seated on a tartan blanket. I called my colleagues' attention to the loveliness of the view; a glistening pond with a backdrop of brilliantly colored trees, painted in reds and yellows. Surely the handy work of our Creator."

Rabbi Benveniste interrupted the mullah. "I saw a bench, not too far ahead of us. I suggested we sit and enjoy the view. We had just sat down when the children grasped hands—the boy in the middle of the two girls. It was about then it started to happen."

"What started to happen?" Cox asked.

The archbishop responded. "Well, we're not sure what happened. I can tell you what I saw. Yousef and Joshua said they saw the same. The three young people, holding hands, turned towards the woman and waved. She returned the wave. As she did, a silvery ball began forming over the pond, maybe fifteen feet from the youths. It wasn't that large at first, but as it moved towards them, it grew in size. I guess it was twenty feet across when it reached them."

"Yes, he is right," the rabbi confirmed. "It was wide enough to encompass all three at once." Having interrupted Archbishop Chapman, he continued with the account. "That's when it got—how do the young people say—weird. The ball, like thick fog, began to shroud them. I grew up near the coast; I've seen fog obscure everything around you in a minute. But this was different, as if the kids were becoming part of the fog!"

The young mullah sought to clarify what the rabbi said. "You've seen film and video portrayals of individuals fading away—the image getting more transparent—that's what happened. They virtually dissolved into the silver cloud. When you could no longer see them, the cloud began to shrink, growing smaller and smaller, until poof, it was gone."

Cox looked at Jenkins. On his colleague's face was the same sense of disbelief that he was experiencing. "You mean the young folks just disappeared before your eyes?"

Archbishop Chapman responded for his colleagues. "That's about it. I must say, it was peculiar. I've never seen anything like it. I recall looking back at the woman—the one seated on the tartan. As a hospital chaplain, I've seen my share of folks receive bad news. They get this odd look on their faces—can't describe it—but that's how the woman looked. About then, I think she called out, 'No! No! Don't, don't do it!' Once the cloud disappeared, she just stood there for a minute—spellbound I'd say—then ran towards the cottage. That's when Yousef started toward the cottage, followed by Joshua and me. Yousef got there before we did and confronted her."

Everyone looked to Mullah Shirazi, prompting him to speak. "I asked her what happened. Was there anything that we could do? She shook her head and went into the cottage without a word."

Jenkins gave the mullah a questioning look. "She didn't say anything to any of you? Nothing?"

"Nothing," the three clergymen replied almost in unison.

Jenkins shook his head, took out his notepad, and looked at his three witnesses. "And which of you called the Sheriff?"

Rabbi Benveniste responded. "I'm the one who called, but we all agreed that the authorities should be notified. After all, we saw three young people suddenly disappear into a strange fog. You don't see that every day!"

Archbishop Chapman and Mullah Shirazi nodded their heads, confirming the rabbi's statement.

"Okay, I understand," Jenkins said. "So here's the sixty-four dollar question. What do you think happened to the children? Could it have been just a prank? The fog could have hidden their disappearance. You know, like in a magic act."

The archbishop sat up and assumed the posture of a person whose creditability was suspect. He pulled back his shoulders and spoke in a firm voice. "We didn't think so at the time. We walked down to where the woman had been sitting. She left the blanket, so it was easy to find the spot. Then, we went to where the children stood at the edge of the pond. We could see trampled grass, but nothing else." The archbishop looked to the two other clergy then turned to Jenkins. "No, sir! I'm convinced that this was not a 'cheap prank' as you suggest."

Cox processed what he heard. "Could they have just slid into the water and hidden behind the bank? You said the three of you ran to the cottage. They may have slipped out of the water while you were not looking."

The clergymen shook their heads. Rabbi Benveniste answered for them.

"No, sir. I don't think so. While it's possible that they used the cover of the fog to slip into the water, we would have seen them leave the pond or there would have been some indication on the bank. Nowhere was the grass damp."

Mullah Shirazi quickly added, "We were at the cottage for only a couple of minutes before we returned to the pond. When we didn't see anything where the children had been, we walked most of the bank along the nearside. If the young people swam across the lake, a hundred feet or more, they would have been seen."

Jenkins showed his frustration through his sarcastic tone. "Okay. So, what do you gentlemen think happened? Where did the kids go?"

A moment passed as the clerics looked at each other and reflected on the Lieutenant's question. They nodded their heads to show their agreement.

The young mullah broke the silence. "I'm afraid you will not like our answer. We discussed this very thing at some length. Our conclusion rests on our common religious beliefs. We are—I believe you know—joined by a singular supreme being, be he called Allah, Yahweh, or God. And, there is evidence in our holy scriptures that guides us to our answer."

The mullah paused to seek support from his colleagues for what he was about to say. The rabbi and the archbishop nodded their encouragement for him to continue. "In faith, we believe that the three young people were accepted directly into the presence of our Supreme Being."

"Say what?" Jenkins forcefully conveyed his skepticism by partially rising from his chair before he gained his composure and sat back down. "I don't wish to be disrespectful gentlemen, but that sounds a lot like horse poop to a country boy like me."

Archbishop Chapman repositioned himself in his chair and made a conciliatory gesture with his hands. The Canadian cleric began in a polite voice, "Bear with us, please. We've since learned that each these children possessed special powers. Gifts from God? Who is to say? There's evidence throughout our scriptures and holy writings of mortal men being taken into heaven, or whatever you wish to call the special place in which our Creator resides. In the Islamic tradition, the Prophet Muhammad traveled through the sky from Arabia to the Al Aqsa mosque in Jerusalem in a single night. That same night, he ascended into heaven and spoke with God. In the Old Testament, the Second Book of Kings, the Prophet Elijah ascended into heaven in a chariot. I could go on with such examples, but I believe these are adequate. So, as incredible as it may seem, we believe that these were children of God, called to be with him."

Cox, seeing that Jenkins was in no mood to continue a discussion about supernatural and religious phenomenon, moved to conclude the meeting. "Gentlemen, thank you for coming this afternoon. I believe that we have heard enough. I understand that you will be leaving in the morning. Should we need additional information from you, we will contact you."

After the clerics departed, Jenkins turned to Cox. "Can you believe that horse hockey? I know that I may not be the sharpest knife in the kitchen drawer, and while I admit being raised in the church, all this is a bit farfetched. Children ascending into heaven—come on!"

"Yeah, I have to admit that it does sound a bit implausible. However, the evidence may be on their side. When the forensic team swept the edge of the lake, the morning we arrived, they found squat, zip, nada!" Reflecting a moment, he suggested, "Let's ask the 'good doctor' what she thinks happened. She never came straight out and told us what she thinks happened."

"Aah, whatever you say." Jenkins was tired and shook his head in resignation. "Let's see what Doctor Weaver has to say. Can't be any worse than what we just heard. Call her. Tell her we're coming. And by all means, please tell her to start that coffee. I, dang sure, could use some."

❧

As Cox and Jenkins walked back to the cottage, they paused along the way to study the area around the small lake. Cox wanted to evaluate what the clergymen said about the children not being able to leave the area without being seen.

"Well, Cox. What do you think?"

Cox did not answer as he concentrated on the problem. Troubled, he said, "Hell, Jenkins. I have to agree with those clergy. I can't see how those kids could have hidden in the water and then got out without someone seeing them. This is about where those clergymen were standing when the fog appeared. You can see the whole pond from here."

"Yeah. But, if they didn't hide in the water, where the hell did they go? Here's another thing you have to ask yourself. If someone didn't abduct them, what's their motive for creating this hoax? Are they just a bunch of smart ass kids who wanted to show off?"

"I don't know, Jenkins." Cox ran his finger back and forth across his lower lip as he thought. "I keep going back to what Weaver said about these kids. They were genius. Between the three of them, they could have created something to fool everybody. But on the other hand, I recall what she said about NSA keeping an eye on the boy to protect him. You heard all the stories Weaver told us about people trying to control the two girls, like those Indian fellows and that guy from Swedish intelligence. Maybe they just wanted to be left alone."

Jenkins was tired and irritated. His temper was wearing thin. "It's getting late. Let's finish up with Weaver. Maybe she can give us a motive for what happened."

Weaver, Jenkins, and Cox decided to sit on the patio behind the cottage. The evening sun cast long rays of light across the pasture and the pond below the cottage. For a moment, they sat quietly and drank the coffee Mitzi made.

Cox broke the silence. "Just before we left, you mentioned how a National Security Agency agent contacted Emily and Kevin Lake in San Francisco. Do you recall seeing anyone here that may have been watching the children?"

"No. No one was here. Ethan made sure of that. When we arrived, he encrypted all of our communication devices. He even created a device to block any surveillance device within five miles of the cottage. He said, 'they can watch where we go outside, but they can't hear what we say inside.' Mitzi smiled, as she remembered Ethan's words. "He said that NSA tracked him using ultra-high altitude hovercraft but he was working on something to block that as well. He was such a genius!"

Jenkins and Cox nodded to acknowledge that they understood what Weaver meant. They now understood more about who the children were and what they could do.

Assuming an official agency demeanor, Cox turned on his lapel camera and looked towards Mitzi. "Doctor Weaver. We spoke with the clergymen. They clearly put you at the scene of the incident and claim that you witnessed everything that occurred. From the first day we questioned you, you hinted that something unexplainable happened. For the record, tell us what you saw and what you think happened."

"Let's begin with what I saw. We were enjoying a picnic when the children decided to walk along the bank of the pond. They said they were going for a stroll. From where I was sitting I had a good view of the area, so I wasn't concerned." Weaver inhaled deeply as she relived the events of that day. She fought back a tear that formed in her eye. "When they reached the edge of the pond, I saw Ethan, Sara and Chetana grasp hands. They looked back at me and waved. Just then a mist formed over the water and moved toward them. As it approached where they stood, they started to melt away, to grow almost transparent. That's when it happened. They simply disappeared into the mist. Is that pretty close to what those priestly guys told you?"

Jenkins and Cox acknowledged Weaver's question with nods.

"Before I try to explain what I think happened, let me give you a little background about why I believe the way I do." Mitzi took the last swallow of coffee and set the cup on the ground next to her chair. "I'm a biologist, not a physicist. I know very little about quantum mechanics, string theory—any of that stuff—especially multidimensional space. Most of these theories require a comprehension of math that I don't have. But remember, Ethan excelled in math. I think he saw a way to open a door to another dimension. But, he couldn't go there by himself. He needed Sara and Chetana."

"What do you mean?" Jenkins appeared interested and wanted Weaver to be as clear as possible about what she said.

Mitzi Weaver was about to step off into the deep end of the pool and she knew it, but the time had come—the time to tell what she believed. "Okay. Here's what I think happened. I'll be brief. First, each child possessed distinct talents. Ethan had the highest IQ and was a math genius; but he also possessed another physical attribute that is important, his vision. He once described the flashes of light he saw as torn sheets of plastic wrap, glowing with electrical energy and moving very fast. Neither Sara nor Chetana could see these images but they had other talents. Sara received messages—heard voices—from somewhere and Chetana could sense matter at the molecular level." Weaver stopped, hesitant to say more.

"Okay. We know that," Jenkins said emphatically. "But what do you think happened?"

Mitzi did not answer for a moment but chose to look into the eyes of Cox and Jenkins. *Now is the time to tell them. Courage. Speak!* "Gentlemen. You may think I'm crazy, but I believe that they stepped into another dimension."

"Oh, no! Not you, too." Jenkins could not control his emotions. "You sound like those guys up at the mansion."

Mitzi defended her statement. "I know it sounds crazy—that somehow, there are more dimensions than our own—but the scientific community is now convinced that there are other dimensions. String theorists predicted ten or more dimensions must exist over fifty years ago—in the middle of the twentieth century, for Christ's sake."

"Now wait a minute." With skepticism in his voice, Jenkins tried to digest what Weaver said. "This Sara, the one who could speak so many languages, didn't you say she could converse with her voices? So you're suggesting that she spoke to these things and the boy saw them?" Incredulity marked every word he spoke. None of what Weaver said was believable to him.

"No. She never said she could speak to them, only that she could communicate with them."

"Yes, I recall that," Cox confirmed. "You said that it was like she received a whole message all at once, like an electronic billboard lighting up. There's nothing but black, then instantly, a whole message is displayed."

"Yes, that's right."

Jenkins started again, "And this Chetana, who could communicate with everything, what did she do?"

Mitzi corrected Jenkins. "Chetana didn't communicate like Sara did. She described her ability as 'knowing' how everything around her felt. I believe she could interact with the very basic structures that form all matter. Physicists have long known that all matter is composed of infinitesimally small, string-like structures. We're talking about one-dimensional structures, if you can imagine such a thing. These structures are ribbons of energy only a millionth of a billionth of a billionth of a billionth of a centimeter long. Unimaginable! Celia Foxe once tried to explain it to me. She said that if an atom was as big as our entire solar system, then a single string would only be the size of a telephone pole."

Jenkins could not contain himself. "How in the hell can anything that small communicate with a teenage girl?"

"Okay. Okay, let's take a minute here." Cox shook both of his hands in front of his chest—his palms facing Jenkins. When the redness in Jenkins' face subsided, he continued. "Let's assume that Chetana could interact with these strings, how did she contribute to the disappearance of the three of them?"

"Well, like I said, she could interact with everything at its most basic level—a single string of energy, if she wished. I'm certain that she altered their molecular structure to allow them to past into another dimension."

"Ooh, horse poop!" Jenkins blurted out, his annoyance evident. "That's going too far." Jenkins wiped his hand across his entire face and leaned toward Mitzi. "Lies and misstatements from suspects are the stock and trade of police work. I've heard almost everything in the past twenty years, but this is too much to handle."

"You asked me what I believed. I'm trying to tell you!" Mitzi paused to catch her breath. "I believe Chetana reduced them to their most basic elements—to their very essences. Strange as it sounds, I'm convinced that they traveled from this existence to another."

Jenkins stood, stared at Weaver as if looking into her soul. He removed his lapel camera without saying a word and walked into the cottage, followed by Weaver and Cox. Inside, he gathered his leather satchel and headed toward the front door of the cottage.

Neither Cox nor Weaver spoke as they watched Jenkins gather his things.

When Jenkins reached the door, he spoke without emotion. "Doctor Weaver, unless the FBI has cause to hold you on some federal charge, you are free to leave. I caution you not to interpret what I just said as an exoneration of your actions or of your involvement in this case." Turning to Cox, he added, "I'll be in touch."

Cox nodded his head several times but did not speak; there was nothing to say. When Jenkins departed, the FBI agent asked, "Do you really believe that the children stepped into another dimension? Are they forever lost in that dimension?"

Mitzi Weaver, who saw Ethan, Chetana, and Sara as her own children, tried to speak. Her emotions prevented her from doing so. After a moment, she gained her composure. "I guess we may never know what really happened. But somehow, I think we will. I'm reminded of something that I learned in Sunday school as a child. I think it went something like, 'if you have faith as small as a mustard seed, you can say to a mountain, move and, it will move.' Maybe, all we need is a little faith. Moreover, if we do have faith, I'm hopeful that one day we will see the children again. Ethan will probably say something like, 'See, we did it!' and smile that big smile of his."

Cox acknowledged what Mitzi said with a nod of his head and a small grin. Without speaking a word, he gathered his personal items and left. He would not forget this case, nor would he speak of it to anyone after he prepared his official report.

❦

Tired from her two-day ordeal, Mitzi Weaver chose to stay the night in the Caretaker's Cottage after Jenkins and Cox left. The drive back to Baltimore would be too much; besides, she must complete a difficult task. Although she called the parents when the children disappeared, she only said that the children left the grounds—in part, because she hoped that the children would return. This evening, she must call the parents again. Mitzi dreaded doing so, but the parents needed to hear what really happened, and they needed to hear it from her. There would be questions. She had to make them understand.

❦

Mitzi completed the last call just before midnight. Exhausted, she slept in the next morning. The new day brought a new perspective on things. Her ordeal with the two officers was over; life could return to normal. True, she would have to deal with the University Provost and his staff when she returned to the campus. Without question, there would be an inquiry, but all would soon blow over. Unfortunately, her expectation did not materialize.

When Weaver tried to return to her office, she was detained at the security desk. The young officer on duty notified his supervisor that she was present. The supervisor appeared and presented her with an envelope.

"Doctor Mitzi Weaver, the Provost has personally directed me to give you this letter. You are not to return to this facility nor to any other building on campus without his approval. If there is any personal item that you need from your office at this time, I will escort you there. You are not to take any materials, digital or printed, nor any electronic devices that are the property of the University."

Mitzi opened the envelope. The terse letter inside stated that she was officially on administrative leave until further notice and directed that she was not to return to the campus until advised to do so. Losing the children was a blow; losing the opportunity to find comfort in her work worsened her pain.

Epilogue

THEY ARE WITH US

Location: Mitzi Weaver's Residence, Baltimore, Maryland
Time: October 2034

Mitzi Weaver sat on the balcony of her townhouse overlooking the Port of Baltimore. On a small island in the middle of the harbor sat Fort McHenry, America's crucible of freedom. She felt comfortable in her home in the Little Italy section. She loved jogging through the neighborhood, taking in its special aromas. This morning she did not go out. The hurt in her heart was too great.

Cold wind from the harbor nipped at Mitzi's face and made the belt of her housecoat dance about. A cup of English breakfast tea provided some warmth for her hands but gave little relief from the depression that gripped her. As she drank the last swallow of tea, the security system chimed, alerting her that someone was at her front door. Hurrying inside, she opened the front door.

A young man wearing a metallic uniform dismounted his personal hovercraft. "Is this the residence of Doctor Mitzi Weaver?"

"Yes. I'm Doctor Weaver."

"I'm Jesse with Global Land Services. Got snail mail for you." He shoved an electronic tablet at Weaver. "Need verification. Just place your hand on the screen."

Weaver obliged. The tablet emitted a sharp bleeping noise confirming her identify.

"Thank ya ma'am." The young man reached into a pouch sown into his uniform. "Here's your letter. Don't see many of these things. Been delivering stuff for over six months—this is only the fourth one that I've delivered." As he turned toward his craft, he called back, "Hope that's good news."

Mitzi smiled to the courier, nodded her head in agreement, and stepped inside. *I need some good news. Who would send me a letter? No one sends letters these days. Hum, no return address. Can't be from the university; they put their name on everything.*

Weaver opened the envelope and removed the letter from inside. *Good quality paper. It's handwritten. Who'd write me? Ethan! Has to be. His mother made him practice cursive as a child—I remember him writing notes to Emily. When did he write this? There isn't a date.*

She sat down and smoothed the folds from the cream-colored paper. In a soft voice, Mitzi began to read the letter aloud.

Dear Doctor Weaver:

If you are reading this letter, something unexplainable has happened to Chetana, Sara and me. I hope that it has not caused you too much pain. We considered telling you of our plan but we knew that you would try to stop us. I feel compelled to handwrite you this note; what I have to say is for you and you alone. To send it electronically would subject it to the prying eyes that scan every word that flows through InstaData.

You know that I am not a religious person. It is easier for me to comprehend quantum theory than to tackle issues grounded in faith alone. While I don't embrace any particular religious teachings, I am certain that there is a creator—an omnipotent force—that shaped our universe. Each time that I consider the scope of our reality, from the infinitely small to the vastness of space, I know that some greater power is at work. I am convinced that such a power did not create our unique reality and stop. Surely, there are many universes like ours and many dimensions within each of them.

Chetana, Sara and I believe that we possess the ability to move beyond our three dimensional world into an adjacent reality. What lies ahead of us is not known. Like ancient explorers, we must risk sailing to the edge of the earth if we are to learn what lies beyond. We must summon the courage to go there!

I am not sure what we will find or if we will be able to return, but it is a chance that we must take. May this not be our last communication, for you are dear to the three of us!

Your friend and more...Ethan

Time froze for Mitzi Weaver. She read the short note a second time, and then again. The buzzing sound of the videophone startled her. She reached for the remote control and touched the receive key. A familiar face appeared on the screen.

"Hi. It's Shelia, but I guess you can see that. Can't get use to these things."

Shelia Rowan was a friend from the genetics lab. Mitzi had not spoken with anyone from the lab for two weeks, not since she was lead off the campus. It was good to hear her friend's voice.

"Shelia. So nice of you to call. How are you?"

"I'm fine. Are you okay?"

"Oh, about as good as could be expected under the circumstances."

Shelia apologized, "Forgive me for not calling sooner. Things are crazy around here without you."

"I'm sorry. Maybe I'll be able to return ..." Mitzi could not go on.

"Hey, don't you worry. Anyway, I thought you would like to know what happened yesterday. You'll never guess who dropped in."

"Who?"

"That Mrs. Benton. Did she call you?"

"No. Why?"

"Well, she came here looking for you. Said she was in Costa Rica when the children disappeared—on some eco-tour. Anyway, when she got back, there was a message from a sheriff over in Virginia. She said where in Virginia, but I don't remember. I guess it was where you and the kids stayed. Apparently, she's real tight with the sheriff—kept calling him Jonesy. Seems he gave her a copy of some investigation report."

Mitzi interrupted. "That would be the report Jenkins and Cox prepared. I can't imagine what they said about me."

"Not nice people, uh?" Shelia briefly paused then continued with her account. "Anyway, you'll never believe what Mrs. Benton wanted to tell you."

"I'm sure that she was disappointed. She has been so nice to me."

"She may be nice, but I'm not sure she's all together! She wanted you to know that she is arranging a *séance*! She's going to try to contact the kids. Can you believe it?"

Mitzi was speechless for a moment. "Shelia, are you joking?"

"Nope. That's what she said. You wait. She's going to call. Have you ever been to a real *séance*? Sounds fascinating!"

Mitzi could see her friend wave to someone. Before she could reply, Shelia spoke.

"Ooops! Gotta run. My graduate assistant is here. We'll talk later. Thought you'd like to know about Benton. Take care of yourself."

Mitzi was stunned. She did not know what to think about Shelia's message. The videophone screen turned to blue and then to black as it shut down. In the darkened room, she was alone with her thoughts. *It's been two weeks since the children left. I miss them so.*

She pulled her housecoat tightly about her and curled up in her favorite chair. Her world seemed so bleak. Suddenly, a flash of light caught her eye. *What's that?* Another flash appeared. And another. She strained to follow them about the room when she heard a soft, familiar voice echo within her head—it was Ethan.

"Are you there?"

She nodded and said aloud, "Yes! Yes, I'm here! Where are you?"

We are here with you. We are the light! Come to us.

Mitzi Weaver smiled and extended her hand toward the flashes of light. "Tell me how?" A fog began forming in the small living room like the one she saw over the pond. A new reality lay ahead—a reality with her children.

About the Author

Vic Rizzo, a Texan by birth and a New Mexican by choice, lives in the mountains outside of Albuquerque, with his wife and two Australian Shepherds.

With a doctorate in business, Rizzo worked as a hospital administrator, an international management consultant, and a collegiate administrator and faculty member before retiring in 1996 to pursue sculpting full time. As a successful sculptor, he has produced over two hundred pieces and received abundant recognition for his work.

Are You There? is his first novel and reveals his diverse interests in genetics, astrophysics, quantum theory, theology, the nature of the universe, and the psychology of growing up. It is the fruition of an interest in creative writing that began when writing video vignettes depicting leadership situations at work. A short story, "Why Does the Rooster Crow?" galvanized his interest in writing, and two poems, "A Broken Man" and "Twice Fallen" expressed feelings about the Vietnam War. He describes the two years spent writing *Are You There?* as a true learning experience.